Chasing Scandal

The Wolverton World, Volume 2

Leslie V. Knowles

Published by Leslie V. Knowles, 2021.

This is a work of fiction. Similarities to real people, places, or events are entirely coincidental.

CHASING SCANDAL

First edition. June 15, 2021.

Copyright © 2021 Leslie V. Knowles.

Written by Leslie V. Knowles.

For Dale McCann - Fellow writer, Forever friends

CHAPTER 1

Langstone, Surrey, England, 1810

It seemed to Julia Dorsey that she'd always been a coward, but every once in a while, like today, she remembered being bold and fearless. Today the breeze carried the scent of lavender that filled the garden, lifting her spirits and making her twirl and laugh as she had done when she was very small. She was too old for such nonsense, but no one could see her but the servants, and they would not carry tales. So she spun around and around, reveling in the sun, the scent, the silliness of it all.

The rattle of approaching carriage wheels made her come to an abrupt halt.

Who? No one but the occasional tradesman came to her modest two storied home. *Perhaps someone took the wrong road.*

She did a quick spin in the opposite direction of her twirl to counter her dizziness.

Balance restored, she tucked a loosened strand of hair behind her ear, pulled her bonnet into place and tied it properly as she rounded the side of the thatched cottage.

The carriage stopped in front of the door and she recognized her cousin's burley footman, Ned Smith. Though she'd not seen her cousin Renard since he'd given her this refuge, his footmen occasionally arrived with messages or requests that she shelter rescued ladies in need of safe haven. Her cottage was a logical stop on the way to London from Portsmouth where military ships returned from the Peninsula.

Ned exited the carriage carrying a slip of a girl of perhaps seven or eight years old. The child's blond hair clung to the wool of his coat and she wore but one shoe. Her delicate skin was pale as wax, her eyes glazed and unfocused. But worse, much worse, blood covered her once fine dress and dripped from the arm she clutched to her chest.

Bile rose in Julia's throat and her lungs locked. Though she'd been rescued from the French Terror years ago, time had not reduced her panic at the sight of blood, nor had it eased the pain of losing her family.

"Found her in a crashed coach," Ned told her. "Knew you'd take care of her."

Although his hulking presence usually made her feel vaguely uncomfortable when he was near her—there was simply too much of him, his words steadied her. "Take her to the yellow bedchamber."

She glanced toward the carriage to see who else might emerge. The child would not have been traveling alone. But the carriage was empty. Realization dawned and her heart stuttered, then swelled with pity. *The poor child.*

Julia strode into the hall, up the stairs to gather medical supplies, told her maid to fetch hot water, and steeled herself to control her panicked nerves. She was in England, not France, and the chaos of the Terror was long over. She could do this. The child needed care and a comforting hand just as she once had.

When she reached the guest room named for its butter yellow walls and jonquil curtains she sat on the edge of the bed and laid a gentle hand on the little girl's shoulder. "Where do you hurt, sweeting?"

"My head and arm—" The child's eyes filled with tears and her voice was little more than a whisper, "—but Mama is hurt worse." The tears spilled over and her lips quivered. "She's bleeding too... and she cried." She turned her head toward the doorway where Ned stood. "Will that man bring Mama, too? And baby Phillip?" Her worried eyes turned back to Julia. "He didn't cry."

Julia glanced at Ned, but his grim expression required no words.

Julia swallowed hard before answering. "Your mama was hurt too badly to come. Baby Phillip is with her." She gently probed the girl's slender arm. It wasn't broken, but a deep gash still oozed blood. Several lesser scrapes and darkening bruises marred her delicate skin, but only the gash required binding.

Her maid arrived with a porcelain bowl of warmed water. Julia dipped a square of cloth into the water then wrung the excess from it and willed her queasy stomach to settle. Still, her thoughts skittered around as she wiped the blood from pale skin. How to find words for what would cause far more pain than the gash in her arm, and a loss that would never completely heal?

The stark truth would hurt far more than sewing the tender flesh. Life—and death—didn't spare frightened children any more than it did adults. Delaying the moment wouldn't make it any less painful. If her childhood had taught her nothing else, it had taught her that. Julia took the girl's uninjured hand in hers. "What is your name, child?"

"Alice Goodwin."

Julia stroked the back of the child's hand. "I'm sorry, Alice, But she and baby Phillip, have gone to heaven."

The child said nothing for several seconds, and Julia had to blink away tears of sympathy. Alice turned wide eyes to Julia. "Will Papa come?"

"He didn't travel with you?"

Alice shook her head. "A man came when we were leaving and Papa said to go ahead and he would catch up, but he never did."

"I will send word to him so he knows you are safe." She put a gentle hand on the girl's uninjured arm. "Until then, you must be especially brave while I sew your cut together. Then you must rest so your arm will heal."

She turned to her maid. "Molly, we will need some willow bark tea flavored with warm milk to help Miss Alice sleep once I have finished tending her wound."

Molly bobbed a quick curtsey and left the room.

Julia's hands shook, so it took Julia several tries before she managed to thread the needle. She released a breath, inhaled, then slid the needle under the two sides of the gash and pulled the edges together. Alice made no more than a slight whimper though tears pooled and ran from the corners of her eyes during the ordeal. By the time Julia finished, and wrapped the stitched arm in clean linen bandages, exhaustion threatened to overcome her concentration and her stomach threatened to disgorge her supper.

Molly returned and Julia reached for the mug. "Drink this, my dear. It will help you sleep."

Alice took a sip, grimaced, but dutifully finished the contents. Julia's heart ached for her. The poor child. She knew just how bewildered and frightened young Alice must be. Julia pulled up the blankets and smoothed them over her temporary charge. "Molly will stay with you so you're not alone." Without thought, she bent and placed a light kiss on the child's cheek before leaving the room. "Now sleep."

"I'll be on my way," Ned said when they left the room. "I'll report this to His Lordship as soon as I get to London." He stopped halfway down the stairs. "He'll want to be the one to contact the girl's father."

Some of the tension knotting her stomach eased.

Renard will take care of it. He always knows what to do.

And she would not let Renard down, either. Her cousin knew he could depend on her to care for the child until he contacted Alice's father. She'd proven her worth when she'd cared for the young ladies in need of safe place to stay whenever he'd asked. She'd done her part to help those women begin better lives just as he had saved her when the rest of her family had been slaughtered in the frenzy of the French Terror. Despite that chaos, he'd brought her to England, become her guardian and anglicized her name. She was even more fortunate that he still provided her with a home and living expenses though she was three and twenty and should have married long ago. She quite literally owed him her life.

When they reached the ground floor Ned didn't linger, but climbed back into the carriage to continue to London where he would report the incident to the earl.

Cousin Renard's instructions arrived three days later. Her eyes widened as she scanned the message.

Julia,

Keep the child out of sight. The accident is suspected to be a kidnapping gone wrong. Do not contact the child's father lest those responsible discover where she is and renew their efforts. Beware of strangers. I shall send further instructions soon.

Renard

A ripple of alarm went through her. This was the first time she'd had a charge who might be in actual danger. Had the perpetrators heard the footman approach and fled without the girl? Julia's cottage was remote and the village small, so she would know if strangers came searching for the missing child. A thread of anxiety pulled her nerves tight. It paid to be wary.

TRISTAN SHEFFIELD REMOVED his hat and smoothed his hair while he stood in the receiving room of the Earl of Ravencliffe's London townhouse until the butler informed him that Tristan had arrived. Early morning light filled the room and a newly added painting on the far wall caught his attention. He strolled over inspect it. The landscape had the bucolic splendor admired by men raised in the country. He did not care for Ravencliffe's recent acquisition any more than he liked country living.

He didn't like broad open spaces with no convenient shadows in which to take refuge or from which to observe. The running water of flowing streams hid the sound of approaching footsteps and the fragrance of so many flowers made his nose itch and his eyes water. His reactions to scents made him feel vulnerable and he liked that even less.

He preferred London. It might be dangerous, it might be loud, and it often offended the nose with noxious odors, but the city had its own charm, and he knew his way around every part of it. Until he was ten, he'd not known there were places like the scene in the painting. Until he was ten, it wouldn't have mattered if he had.

"His Lordship will see you in the library."

Tristan turned and smiled at the earl's elderly butler. "Thank you, Billings, I'll see myself up." He handed the man his hat, then climbed the curved staircase. At the top he turned left, rapped on the door, and entered the extensive library. Tristan's immediate superior at the Foreign Office William Hartley, Earl of Ravencliffe, sat at the far end of the room. Sunlight lit his fair hair and glowed halo-like behind the far-from-angelic earl.

Tristan glanced around the room and verified they were alone before stating the obvious. "You have a new mission for me?"

"I do." The earl gestured to the low table between their chairs that held a silver coffee pot and a china cup and saucer. "Pour yourself a cup of coffee, Tristan, and I'll explain the situation."

Tristan crossed the thick blue and gold rug and took a seat in the wingback chair beside his host. Tristan's half-brother, Lucien, and Ravencliffe had been school friends long before Tristan started working for the crown, so his casual order for Tristan to pour his own refreshment didn't rankle. From anyone else, Tristan would have seen it as a deliberate slight to remind him of his inferior rank.

He reached for the pot and poured, then sat back and observed the bland expression in Ravencliffe's hazel brown eyes. "You look bored. It must be serious."

Ravencliffe's lips quirked. "You know me well."

He sat forward, elbows on knees, his expression now focused and intense. "For the last year we have noted an increase in the loss of supplies reaching the troops on the peninsula. At first we wrote it off as the normal problems of supplying troops, but the interceptions have occurred with a frequency we cannot ignore. Someone is selling information, and Richard writes that the shortages are affecting his men greatly."

Richard, William's twin brother, served on the Peninsula with Wellington. It came as no surprise to Tristan, then, that this mission included personal as well as political concerns.

"The Earl of Summerfield supervises the Quarter Master and controls the schedule and routes for the army's supplies, but his health has failed greatly this past year and word is that he has not much longer to live. I believe his need to delegate may have tempted someone to sell that information to the French." He stood and walked to the tall window that overlooked the street below. The sunlight revealed a jaw tight with tension, though he retained a relaxed pose.

Tristan had never been introduced to Summerfield, but the earl's dedication to the crown was well known. It would be a sad day for the royal family when he passed on.

After a minute, Ravencliffe turned away and came back to his chair. "Lord Goodwin recently took over the supervision of the Quarter Master from him, but I have received word that Goodwin lost his family in a fatal accident recently. I fear he might well be too consumed with grief to be any more in control than the earl."

Ravencliffe picked up a sealed letter and leather folio and handed them to Tristan.

"You are to take this letter of introduction and my condolences to Lord Goodwin with the offer to assist him in his duties so he might deal with his bereavement. His estate is located an hour's ride from Portsmouth proper, so you'll be able to examine the local chain of command for problems. The details are in the folio. Though you will keep me informed about your progress, I leave it to your discretion as to the frequency of those reports. I give you the same latitude in the manner in which you conduct your investigation."

Tristan took the folio. "Then I am at liberty to follow any leads without waiting for special permissions?"

"Investigate however you feel necessary, so long as you locate the turncoat."

Perversely the need to leave town to accomplish his mission, even one as potentially dangerous as catching a traitor, provided Tristan with a sense of relief. He would be absent during his half-sister's first season, and in a manner she could not question.

Nor would his half-brother Lucien, Duke of Wolverton, need to deal with the old family scandal. Scandalously acknowledged bastard brothers did not lend favor to ladies entering society among the ton, even for the sister to a duke. Anne generally took offense when confronted by the reality of his place in society. Though much younger than him, it had warmed his heart when she stood up for him in the past, but now she was making her debut in London society. He had attended her come-out ball without drawing too much attention to his presence, but had only danced with his sister's immediate circle before leaving. He didn't want to blight her season with the duress of defending him to those who considered him unworthy of notice, and if he remained in town, it was only a matter of time before someone's snub did just that.

He finished his coffee and rose. "I shall leave for Portsmouth at dawn."

CHAPTER 2

Tristan turned his horse over to Lord Goodwin's stable boy and approached the broad stairs to the house with trepidation. Much as he sympathized with the viscount's loss, he hoped the man's grief would not interfere with his investigation.

The estate sat back from a high promontory overlooking the inlet on which ships passed from Southampton dockyards to the wharves of Portsmouth. The sharp tang of the sea was less prominent here, though the dampness in the air reminded one that it blew over the sea to reach the land. Gulls soared overhead and called to one another as stridently as they did along the wharves.

A black wreath on the door confirmed Ravencliffe's report of the Viscount's recent bereavement, as did the extremely somber visage of the butler who answered his knock. Tristan presented his card and stepped across the threshold.

"Mr. Tristan Sheffield to see Lord Goodwin with condolences from the Earl of Ravencliffe."

"I shall see if he is in."

Tristan gazed around the entry hall noting that Lord Goodwin's taste in artwork ran to the perilous adventures of life at sea. Wild expanses of ocean and sky appealed to Tristan no more than the open pastures of country life. The confines of the few ships Tristan had boarded in the past had revealed a wealth of places from which to observe, but the limited escape routes made his neck prickle.

The butler returned and led him upstairs to a spacious drawing room decorated in the old style of gilt and brocade. On the wall over the mantle hung a large family portrait of a lovely blond woman and a sweet-faced girl of three or four years. They both looked vaguely familiar. The man who rose to greet him, however, bore little resemblance to the proud husband and father in the painting. Ravencliffe had indicated Goodwin's age to be in the mid-thirties, but his recent loss showed the stark ravages of grief until Tristan would have taken him to be at least ten years older than that.

"Ravencliffe heard of your misfortune and sent word requesting I offer his condolences personally."

"Thank you, Mr. Sheffield." Goodwin gestured toward the chair opposite the one he'd vacated. "Connors will send the maid with refreshments. Do you prefer coffee or tea... or perhaps some spirits?"

"Tea would be most welcome."

An uncomfortable silence loomed for a moment after the butler gave an acknowledging bow and left the room. Tristan searched his mind for some way to broach the real reason for his visit. Normally, he stuck up conversations with ease. He made droll observations or asked engaging questions. But how did one introduce the business of the crown into a house of mourning? He felt a bit like a bully about to kick a man whose hands and ankles were bound. He turned to look at the painting again.

"My mother died shortly after I turned nine," he surprised himself by saying. "It's terrible to lose someone you love."

Goodwin closed his eyes and his posture stiffened. When he reopened his eyes, he stared directly at Tristan. His brown eyes reflected an anguish that made Tristan flinch. "It is worse to know you could have prevented it."

"I understood it was an accident, my lord." Tristan's gut clenched. He understood guilt all too well. All the regrets in the world couldn't undo the results of a thoughtless act or restore his father back to life. It was a fact he lived with every day.

"Carriage accidents are unfortunately common," Tristan responded. "You cannot blame yourself. Had you been with your family you might well have suffered the same fate."

The maid entered and set a tray with tea and a plate of scones onto the low table between them. Goodwin studied him closely while she poured and presented their cups before leaving the room.

"I believe I remember meeting you a few years ago." Goodwin said when they were alone again. "Are you related to the Duke of Wolverton? You have the Caldwell look about you."

"He's my half-brother." Tristan acknowledged. He waited for the inevitable alteration in Goodwin's demeanor, but the change was not as he expected.

"I recall the connection," Goodwin said before taking a sip of his coffee. "I believe my daughter spilled her lemonade on you during a fete at Lady Ridley's."

Tristan remembered the family then. Lady Goodwin had been horrified and apologetic, though the fault had been Tristan's. When he'd replaced the child's lemonade and apologized for bumping into her, she'd given him a sunny smile of forgiveness then charmed him with childish prattle for the next quarter hour.

Goodwin cleared his throat but looked away before saying, "I believe you are familiar with the rougher side of life."

"I am."

He brought his gaze back to Tristan, a flicker of hope now burning in their depths. "You might well be the answer to prayer."

Tristan stilled. He was many things, but no one had ever considered him an answer to their prayers.

Goodwin stood and walked over to look up at the portrait. "Not long after I took over for Lord Summerfield I received a note offering a large bribe if I provided information about the cargos scheduled for the Peninsula. I ignored it."

His hands clenched at his sides. "A second note threatened to harm my family if I did not respond. I still refused, but decided to remove my family to London where they would be surrounded by extended family and friends."

His throat worked and he rubbed the back of his neck. "My wife had recently given birth to my heir and had chosen not to take part in the season in order to spend time with him." He glanced to where Tristan attended his every word. "She is," he faltered, "*was*–a most devoted mother who declined the services of a wet nurse. My wife's murder," His mouth firmed into a grim line. "And I'm sure it *was* murder, is the result of my refusal to pass along information regarding supply lines and dispersals. It's my fault they died."

Tristan understood the guilt and anguish of that kind of loss, and the anger that life could be so cruel. He'd experienced similar pain, the same regrets. Time did not erase the emotional scars created by stubborn pride.

Goodwin resumed his pacing. "When a messenger arrived from Portsmouth informing me of a problem, I sent my wife and children ahead along with two footmen and the postern riders. I planned to catch up with them on horseback by nightfall."

He stopped, returned to his seat and sat heavily. The grief filled his expression once more and he said, "I found the crashed carriage and my wife and son." He broke off and took several deep breaths, again fighting to control his emotions. "Even the footmen and outriders. But not Alice. I thought perhaps she'd been thrown from the carriage or wandered away. I searched everywhere. I even had workers lever the carriage upright in case–" His gaze again turned to the portrait. "She wasn't there."

Tristan supplied the obvious. "Someone took her, and now they're using her to force your hand."

"The latest ultimatum came with a package containing one of Alice's shoes as proof that they hold her. They'll sell her to a child brothel unless I forward the information they demand." He shuddered and his voice turned harsh. "She is only seven years old."

Tristan looked at the painting of the child who had charmed him that day, remembered another child... one with ginger hair and wide brown eyes..., and set his jaw.

"If I don't comply by the end of the month, they will sell her. Yet, they claim that so long as I cooperate she will be kept safe." He shook his head and his fists clenched. "I cannot trust such fiends to keep their word." His eyes narrowed. "You should know I will do all in my power to save my child, even if it means I hang as a traitor for doing so."

Tristan recognized the defiant resolve and knew the man was no traitor. He also knew that the threat was real. Girls of all ages served men in the brothels of London. That ginger-haired child, Maisie Hobbs, had been sold by her own father for a case of gin at the tender age of six. Her three sisters had been sold at similar ages. Maisie now ran her own house and her sisters were dead.

"I'm being watched, Sheffield." Goodwin gestured. "If I search for Alice they'll act and she'll be lost. My butler has been with the family for many years and can be trusted, but it's clear that someone is keeping the blackmailers informed of my every action." He raised his eyebrow and his lips twisted into an ironic smile that did not lighten the intensity of his gaze. "They'll know I received a visit from the Foreign Office."

He leaned forward in his chair, his body rigid and his gaze intense. "I have no right to ask this of you, but I beg you to act for me." He reached out to clamp his hand on Tristan's arm. "Find my daughter."

Tristan didn't need Goodwin's plea for help. As soon as he'd understood the child had been abducted he'd known what he would do. Goodwin's tight grasp only underscored Tristan's resolve to uncover the devils who would destroy an innocent child in order to commit treason.

Goodwin kept his intense gaze on Tristan. "Find her before I act against my own principles and the crown. But if all goes awry and they make good their threat, take her from that place." His eyes reddened, filled, then spilled over. "Hide her and keep her safe." His posture collapsed and he pounded his fist on his knee. "She is an innocent pawn in an evil game."

"Not only will I find your daughter," he promised. "I'll find whoever is behind this and see that he pays the price for his actions. It is he, not you, who will be punished."

Goodwin closed his eyes, then met Tristan's gaze again. "Thank you. Once I know she is out of danger I will resign my duties and recommend the post, in future, be assigned to a single man of no family."

"Where did the attack happen?" Tristan asked. "I'd like to look at the scene directly to determine how to trace them. More importantly," he added, "who do you suspect might be driven to act so despicably?

CHAPTER 3

Julia fought the queasy fluttering that assailed her middle when her carriage neared the outskirts of Portsmouth and she caught the first whiff of the mudflats at low tide. She despised the fact that after all these years she still had difficulty with the crowds along busy streets. Her mind knew the noisy bustle was not a murderous mob, but her child-heart still raced and her palms felt clammy inside her gloves.

She was all the more aware of her demons since Alice had come under her charge. The child's sweet nature made a welcome break in Julia's normal routine, but her presence had triggered the return of nightmares Julia had believed laid to rest. Jumbled and filled with screams, they always left her with aching loss and loneliness. She might be a grown woman, but a part of her would always be the five-year-old orphan, Juliette d'Orsey.

Julia took a deep breath, forcing herself to ignore the panic the odor of tar sent through her. The brine-sharp decay along the docks always filled her with apprehension and an unreasoning need to flee. Scolding herself for her foolishness, she descended to the street in front of the cobbler shop and waited for her maid to join her. She rarely came to Portsmouth, but Alice needed shoes and Julia needed fabric to make her additional clothes. Though she and her maid had managed to cut down two of Julia's old dresses, they were not appropriate to a child's needs.

Alice said she often traveled with her father to Portsmouth, so Julia dared not bring her to town if the child was in danger of kidnapping. Consequently, Julia had traced Alice's foot on the paper she carried in her reticule and Alice remained at the cottage in the care of the cook. The shoes, Julia had decided to explain if the cobbler asked, were for a neighbor's daughter who had heard she planned to travel to Portsmouth.

TRISTAN STEPPED OUTSIDE the tavern on Broad Street and took a deep breath, relishing the sharp brine scent. He no longer minded the odors of fish and sweat that went along with life along the edge of the sea. In fact, he was disconcerted to discover how quickly he'd adapted to the rough life so familiar to his childhood. The ease with which his carefully cultured speech had returned to coarse accents and slang disturbed him more. He'd fought many a battle over the taunts of upper-class bullies before mastering the refined conversation of his half-brother's world.

The wind churned white caps on the gray-green of the sea and low dark clouds threatened rain. When he reached the street, a fresh breeze from the east picked up and nearly pulled his cap from his head. He turned his head quickly down to prevent the hat from flying across the dock before making his way through the busy crowd of dockworkers, sailors, and merchants who filled the narrow streets.

Overhead, gulls swooped up and down, stealing bits of fish and screeching their success as they flew away. One bold bird flew by, snatching a scrap of bread from the hand of a small, rail thin boy of around five years old. The child protested loudly, then began to cry. No one appeared to notice either the incident or the crying child in the crush of busy pedestrians. Tristan recognized the boney frame of a street child and knew that scrap was most likely his only food for the day.

He also knew that any coins the child received would immediately be turned over to his family, be they blood relatives or a gang of other street children connected by survival. Stepping up to a nearby cart he bought a fresh bun and an apple. "Here, boy," he said as he approached the child. "Eat this before you share the wealth."

The child's eyes rounded when Tristan put the bun in one grubby hand, the apple in the other, then put a tuppence into the brim of the boy's cap. In a flash, the boy darted off to an alley and out of sight. Tristan hoped he managed to eat something before his family found him and demanded their portion. He'd have given the child a shilling, but that much wealth would have put him in danger instead of favor on the streets.

He traced his way past several taverns until he reached the more refined shops. Not surprisingly, he saw a few men he knew, though the rough clothing he wore and his unshaven face made him virtually invisible to the gentlemen who did not expect to find Wolverton's scandalous relation outside London.

He had turned to face a window when one such acquaintance passed him, and was about to resume his way along the street when a woman's sultry voice caught his attention. It drifted through the doorway and stroked his imagination.

"Thank you for your time, Mr. Tanner." Undeniably feminine, and pitched lower than most, the low timbre made him think of midnight exchanges and tumbled sheets. Distracted and intrigued, he waited to see who belonged to that siren's voice.

The practical lady's boot that came into sight a moment later did not fit his fantasy image of dainty satin slippers and gauzy negligees, nor did the dun brown woolen skirts of the travel dress above it.

Her face, when it came into view, was neither homely nor beautiful. She looked down to watch where she stepped so he could not yet see the color of her eyes, but she had a straight nose of average length and her chin was neither round nor pointed. Her lips had a soft plumpness that kept them from being too thin, yet fell short of the lush fullness he preferred. In short, it was a disappointingly average face.

A simple hat, of the same brown and as plainly practical as her dress, allowed only a glimpse of tightly bound dark hair. Tristan felt strangely let down. This ordinary woman would never be associated with midnight rumpled sheets. He glanced toward the doorway. Perhaps the voice belonged to a different woman who remained inside the shop.

The woman in brown turned her head to speak back into the shop. "Thank you, again, Mr. Tanner. I shall expect the shoes within the week."

The low tenor of her voice caressed his imagination once more. How could such a seductive sound come from such a prim and plain female?

"Aye, Miss Dorsey," the cobbler replied. "I'm glad we could be of service to you and your neighbor's child. If you decide you'd like the black half-boots for yourself, send word and we'll deliver them as well."

The woman turned, nearly collided with Tristan, and looked up. Large, luminous green eyes surrounded by thick black lashes sent his body into rigid alert. So much for the average features he'd considered a mismatch to an unforgettable voice. Eyes like that could make a man forget to watch his back... and a voice like that could seduce a man to sell his very soul.

"I beg pardon, Miss." Tristan gave her an appreciative grin before stepping back. "I was too busy watching where you were going."

Her eyes widened before her hand flew to her throat in a defensive gesture, but she quickly recovered, though her skin blanched.

"Excuse me," she murmured before stepping around him and quickly entering the draper's shop next door.

Damn. Even her murmur raised his instincts. For several seconds he stared at the shop's door, bemused, aroused, and caught off guard. Nature had an ironic sense of humor.

An hour later, Tristan entered his miniscule room on the top floor of the Mariner's Inn. Thanks to the cobbler, he now knew the woman, Miss Julia Dorsey, was a spinster whose wealthy cousin allowed her to keep her own home in a cottage near Langstone. With that information, the mismatch of plain clothing and bewitching voice and eyes became clear. Her "*wealthy cousin*" was no doubt her protector who kept his mistress well out of sight of his wife.

That speculation explained her solitary cottage, but what now intrigued him was the fact that in the four or five years she had lived in the area, she had never made a purchase for any of her neighbors. Nor did the cobbler think she interacted with the local townsfolk a great deal.

She was known as "Miss" rather than "Mrs." which indicated no children in residence with her, though the order had been for a small girl's walking shoes. Sturdy, but of the softest leather. Not the kind purchased for farm children.

He had questioned the various shopkeepers along the main avenue about such unusual purchases before he'd heard that seductive voice, but he might have missed the vital connection had the woman herself not intrigued him.

He needed to locate the cottage and see if Miss Dorsey truly lived alone, or if a small blond girl of seven years currently resided there. The woman's story could be true, but his gut told him he'd found the kidnapped child. It wouldn't take long to satisfy his suspicions. What's more, if he was right, he would also know who sold secrets to the French.

Tristan had assumed the kidnappers were men, yet he knew women could be just as devious. Despite the common view, he had long ago recognized that the women who survived and thrived in Seven Dials knew how to use their wits as well as their bodies to do so. Some of the most vicious brothels in London were run by women. This woman was younger than one would expect and didn't have the look of a procuress. *Ah, but that voice.* Her voice alone promised hidden depths.

THE COBBLER REFUSED his monetary offer for directions, protesting that he could not in good conscience send a stranger to a single lady's home without her permission. Henry Porter, a former dockworker with a peg leg turned cobbler's helper, however, had no such qualms. Three days later, Porter allowed him to tag along when he delivered the completed shoes.

Tristan halted his horse and dismounted behind a line of birch tree trees while Porter continued along the dirt road. Across a long, open field, tucked under the shade of a giant oak, he spied the cottage. He worked his way around until he could observe both the front and back of the two storied, thatch-covered home of Miss Julia Dorsey.

A lark trilled overhead as he tied the reins to a low branch and the tall grasses at the edge of the trees sounded like whispers in the soft breeze. The sharp smell of freshly scythed grass and the mixed perfume from tangles of wildflowers filled the air. He fought the urge to sneeze.

The back of the cottage flanked a kitchen garden, a narrow track, and a paddock where a chestnut gelding grazed. Beyond that stood a small stable, barely large enough for the horse and a gig. The broad open space around the cottage made it impossible to approach without being seen.

Tristan watched as Porter dismounted at the back of the cottage and knocked at the servants' door. A woman, whose plump figure and flour-dusted apron identified her as the cook, opened the door, and accepted the package. She then stepped out of sight, returned, and pressed a coin into his hand. They chatted for a moment. Finally, Porter said something that made the cook laugh before she shut the door.

A movement at a window on the second floor caught his attention, and he had a quick glimpse of a child's face and blond hair before a woman in the shadows pulled her away.

CHAPTER 4

Porter mounted his horse and rode off in the direction of Portsmouth. Tristan continued to watch. After a while, a man of lean build and late middle years emerged from the woods behind the paddock carrying two buckets of water that he poured into a trough at the side of the paddock. The horse ambled over and nosed the man affectionately before taking a drink. No one else appeared to be employed outside.

The near silence of his surroundings made Tristan edgy. He knew and paid no attention to flies or rats foraging on street refuse in the city, but the drone of distant bees and the rustle of field mice made him too aware of the difference between the country and the city. The silence made him aware of odd things like the beat of his heart and the pace of his breathing. It made him aware of his thoughts, as though his mind were separate from his body—as though the world was a dream he observed but in which he did not actually exist. He took a deep breath and pressed his hand against the rough tree bark to regain his sense of reality.

His brother, Lucien, often said he found the natural silence calming, but for Tristan, the overwhelming silence always felt smothering. He needed noise, action, and challenge to feel a part of the world around him. With a bit of luck and planning he would be gone from this bucolic nightmare and back to London soon.

Perhaps a quarter of an hour later, the child came through the kitchen door and skipped across the yard to the stable. Tristan frowned when he saw the long linen bandage on her arm, but other than that, she appeared to be in good health and spirits. The Dorsey woman followed at a sedate pace that made it clear she did not fear the child escaping. Equally clear, the child did not fear her captor. Perhaps she truly was the neighbor's child and not Alice Goodwin.

For that matter, if the Dorsey woman was some lord's mistress, the child might be hers. Often, the children from former lovers were kept out of the way of a woman's current protector. The child might live with a relative, visiting only occasionally.

He looked around, searching for a way to get closer so he could verify the girl's identity. If she wasn't Alice, he needed to refocus his search quickly and return to the port city or the capital to trace other leads. His fascination with a woman's voice had no place in the fate of an innocent child. Yet something in his gut told him he could not ignore the possibility he was right, either.

The older man emerged from the stable as the two of them approached and the child halted abruptly until he said something to her that made her grin before she dashed around him and inside. He and the woman exchanged a few murmured words before he headed across the yard and into the cottage.

With the man's location accounted for, Tristan made his way through the trees and around to the area behind the stable. From there he'd be able to assess the true identity of the girl and her relationship to the Dorsey woman.

When he reached the back of the building, Tristan eased close to the wall and dropped into a crouch to press his ear against the wood. The mewing of kittens and girlish giggles followed by a breathless, "Oh, Miss Dorsey, they are all so sweet!" told him why the child had gone directly to the stable.

"When I go home, do you think I could have one? Papa won't mind."

"They are far too young to leave their mother yet, Alice, and I don't know how long you are to stay with me. We shall have to see when the time comes."

The Dorsey woman's voice touched that inner chord with Tristan again. Warm, caressing and pitched a bit lower than most, it soothed at the same time as it aroused his instincts. He could picture her smiling as she spoke. Odd how the woman's voice could heat his body at the same time as her words could chill his heart. Miss Julia Dorsey did, indeed, harbor the kidnapped Alice.

Just because she claimed not to know how long the child was to be at the cottage didn't mean she wasn't a part of the blackmail scheme, but it opened the door for doubt. *Who was he kidding?* Of course she was involved. Alice's length of stay depended on Goodwin's compliance with the woman's demands. Lying was a survival skill courtesans developed early. Kept mistress, procuress, or unwitting accomplice, the woman held a child who'd become the pawn in a treasonous plot.

Another giggle sounded before Alice said, "The orange one is the color of marmalade. I would call him Toast."

Light womanly laughter floated on the air and Tristan gritted his teeth, frustrated by his body's response when he knew better than to be fooled by seductive laughter and eyes the color of moss after the rain.

"An excellent choice. You should name them all, though I'm not sure we'll be able to distinguish between the two tabbies."

"Oh, that's all right. Cats never answer to their names, anyway."

Both of them laughed then, and Tristan eased away from the stable. His question answered, he needed to plan how to take the child back before Goodwin was compelled to disclose information. Nearly three weeks had already passed and the deadline was just a week away. The man had lost too much already to be forced into treason in order to save his only remaining family. Tristan needed to take the child somewhere equally obscure and out of the way. It had been pure luck that he'd discovered her whereabouts, and he didn't trust luck. It turned bad far too easily.

JULIA JERKED AWAKE, her heart pounding as she tried to drag breath back into her lungs. Her skin prickled, her throat burned and her eyes watered with panicked tears. The shadow of her nightmare faded, but as always, it left her with a slight headache that she knew would linger well into the next day.

She'd not had the nightmare for years, but since Alice's arrival, Julia had fought her way through the night terrors at least half a dozen nights. She always woke knowing that something lurked in the shadows ready to crush her.

She recognized that Alice's danger had released her own childhood fears. The girl reminded Julia of herself, of the *Juliette* before revolution and death had turned her into a shadow being who preferred solitude to the claustrophobia of strangers. Before she had become a coward.

Resigned, she rose and donned slippers and her wrapper then lit a candle. She would not be able to go back to sleep tonight. Nor would she be able to focus on a book.

Crossing the hall, she checked on Alice. Moonlight filtered through the glass and cast windowpane shadows across the bed. Alice lay curled on her side, deeply asleep.

Downstairs, in the sitting room, the fire had been tamped down for the night, but Julia knew how to coax it back into life. She had learned many practical skills since coming to the cottage. She soon sat in her favorite chair, filling in a section of tapestry by the combined light of the fire and table lamp. The familiar pattern of thread and cloth helped soothe her jangled nerves. As her pulse settled and her fingers worked the steady rhythm of laying threads onto cloth, Julia wondered what life would have been like had she conquered her wariness of crowds and been able to finish the season Renard had planned for her.

Alice made her fiercely aware of how much she wished she had been able to make a match and have children of her own. At church each Sunday, the only times she ventured into society, she had watched young girls mature, marry, and bring their babies to be christened in a cycle of family that she envied. She adored the toothless smiles of the babies and forgave the defiant cries of restless toddlers who wanted to run up the aisles of the chapel instead of being restrained by harried mothers and nursemaids. Her own children, if she'd married, would now be the age she'd been when her family had been torn from her.

And what of her husband? *Those imaginary children would require a father.* That thought made her prick her finger, and she dropped the needle to suck the drop of blood that welled. She pulled a muslin square from her workbasket and pressed it against the small hurt to stop the bleeding. She had adored her father. She had loved to see her parents together, laughing, teasing, and surrounding her with love.

She remembered warmth and safety and joy before revolution had torn it from her. To experience that again, to fill up the empty center of her being with family, had been her dearest hope.

Yet, most men made her nervous. The occasions when she ventured into Portsmouth, where far more men filled the streets than women, she often had to control her breathing. She worked hard to appear calm and serene, but in fact, leaving Portsmouth often felt like the aftermath of her nightmares.

Look at how she'd reacted to the man outside the cobbler's shop. He'd not touched her, but she'd felt as though he had. His clear, startling crystal blue eyes had darkened in interest when their gazes locked. Then he'd grinned in a way that made her heart race before she bolted for the draper shop as though all the hounds of hell nipped at her heels.

Little had changed since her governess had broached the subject of marriage when she turned seventeen. The woman, an impoverished widow herself, had not explained much, only that a woman's role in life was to marry and submit to her husband in order to give him an heir. Something about the word *submit* had exploded an avalanche of emotions she'd not been able to explain nor even question.

She set aside the cloth she'd pressed against the pinprick and resumed sewing. Julia sometimes had other dreams. Dreams from which she awoke with yearning. Dreams in which she did not submit, but shared. She didn't think she would fear a man who shared. A vision of crystal blue eyes formed at the back of her mind and *she wished...*

CHAPTER 5

Tristan strode down the wharf, portmanteau in hand, as he mentally checked off the list in his head: walking shoes, two dresses, shift, stockings, petticoat, cloak, bonnet, comb and nightrail. Alice would be adequately clothed until he could expose the mastermind and return her to her father. Once he notified Ravencliffe and arranged for someone to relieve him of her care, he would bring the Dorsey woman and her cohorts to justice. He doubted she worked alone. Satisfied he'd not forgotten anything, he crossed the street to return to the inn.

Passing the mercantile, he spotted a wooden doll in the window and stopped. He remembered how his half-sisters had squealed with joy when presented with dolls on special occasions. Tristan also remembered how little Maisie Hobbs had stared at them whenever she spied dolls in shop displays. Cloth dolls, wooden dolls, dolls with fine porcelain faces, they all fascinated her. She'd loved the rag and stick baby he'd made her before her father sent her to join her sisters. *Alice isn't much older.* He entered the shop.

An hour later, he had loaded the portmanteau and his own necessities into the back of Goodwin's low phaeton, drove out of Portsmouth and turned onto the road to Langstone. Goodwin and he had agreed that Tristan should take the Viscount's vehicle. Riding horseback made for a quicker search, but he'd need a carriage to travel with the child once he found her. A task Tristan vowed he would accomplish despite the odds against him. And he had. Satisfaction made him smile with grim intent. Now he had to steal her back.

The salt tang of the sea air diminished as he traveled further away from the docks, though sea birds still swooped and glided overhead, their cries strident over the marshlands. That was another thing he disliked about open spaces. Sounds carried for long distances, a fact that made it difficult to pinpoint the location of its source. Not impossible, but difficult.

At Langstone, Tristan drove into the tavern yard. Several carriages filled the grounds and a sand-colored mongrel wandered about investigating scents and occasionally finding someone's leftover crumbs. Inside, the place was small, but clean, and filled with the aroma of hearty stew and English ale.

He ordered a meal and arranged for an extra basket of provisions so he wouldn't need to stop once he'd secured the child. When he finished his meal, he sent a report to Ravencliffe confirming that he'd located the girl and would take her to Hartford Manor. Few knew that his father had willed him the property in nearby Surrey, but Tristan had sometimes used it for a safe house on previous assignments. He drove out to wait in the woods by the cottage until dark and all had gone to bed.

Anticipation furled along his spine. He'd learned to pick locks early in life so getting into the house wouldn't be difficult, but abducting the child without rousing the household was the challenge. He studied the light spilling from the windows, noting when they shifted to the upper floors, then waited for them to be extinguished and the house to settle for the night.

He had considered taking the Dorsey woman for questioning at the same time as he took the child, but ruled that out in favor of quick action and travel. Alice's safety came first. Until he knew if Miss Dorsey had a partner, he needed to avoid delay. He had no doubt that he would be able to trace the woman if she fled. Ordinary as her appearance was at first glance, no man would forget those eyes or that distinctive voice.

As he waited in the darkness, Tristan appreciated the cloud cover that obscured the full moon. Though moonlight made driving a carriage at night easier, it also raised the chance of revealing his clandestine movements. He'd attached a miner's lantern low to the front of the phaeton to light his way once they were out of sight of the cottage.

Time passed slowly and the air took on a dampness as the hour grew later. The temperature dropped, and the crickets and other creatures of the night gradually ceased their constant rhythms. He'd learned that they only went quiet when an intruder entered their territory or wet weather threatened. Rain complicated things. He hoped the roads remained dry until he was well away with the child.

While he waited, he remembered how the little girl's chatter had charmed him that day when young Alice spilt her lemonade. He'd envied her open innocence and the fact that she'd never gone to bed hungry or shivered with cold when weather changed for the worse. He'd had no reason to believe she ever might face that possibility.

Yet her father's position left her particularly vulnerable to the predators who existed at all levels of society. The children of the streets learned early to beware of strangers who showed undue interest in them. Alice showed no wariness of her captor and must have accepted whatever story she'd been told to explain her time at the cottage. Once he removed Alice from danger, he would have to teach her how to stay safe.

Two full hours after the last window went dark he walked the horse and carriage to the back door of the cottage. The lock offered no resistance to his tools and Tristan eased open the door. He lit another miner's candle and adjusted the cover to permit only the narrowest and lowest beam to light his way. As he'd surmised, the lamp revealed a short hall with cloaks hanging from pegs on one wall and the entry to the kitchen on the other. The faint aroma of roasted chicken from the evening meal lingered in the air.

He waited a moment, listening for the house sounds that assured him all were asleep. So far as he'd observed, the only servants were a maid, the cook, and the man of all work he'd seen by the stable. Still, as he moved past the kitchen, he checked to see if a scullery maid or pot boy slept by the fire. No one.

He climbed the back stair to the upper floor, careful to place his steps close by the wall to avoid creaking boards. At the landing, he paused again. To the right, nearest the stair, was the room where he'd seen the child through the window. He caught the scent of cut roses when he pushed the door open. A quick inspection showed it to be a sitting room with pale walls, wing-backed chairs and a settee covered with several pillows. Not what he pictured for the lair of someone threatening to sell a child into perversion.

Along the corridor on the left were two doors opposite each other. Which one? The room on the right would have a view of the front of the property and, by its placement, would be larger than the room on the left. Doubtless, the master quarters.

The left one, then. He again stayed close to the walls as he crossed the landing and made his way to the door beyond the sitting room.

He turned the handle and slowly opened the door to the smaller room. Now that he was inside the cottage, stealth and calm leashed the impatience that drove his need to rescue and escape without alerting anyone. He took two slow breaths to settle his pulse, and surveyed the room. A lighter patch of darkness revealed the location of a window. Tristan crept closer until the pale lantern beam caught the shape of the bed on the far wall. He set the lantern on the table beside the bed and hoped Alice slept as deeply as had his sisters had when they were her age. He needed to get her down the stairs and as far away as possible without waking her. She might well cry out before he could assure her he meant her no harm.

Leaning down, Tristan slipped his arm under the pillow, supporting her head and shoulders. With his other arm wrapped around her torso and the bed quilt, he lifted the sleeping child from the bed and tucked her around his body. She turned her head to fit against his chest, and his pulse kicked, but she did not wake. Another deep breath. He lifted his foot to the edge of the bed and used his knee to support her while he adjusted the blanket to keep her warm.

Careful not to jostle her, Tristan snuffed out the light, then settled Alice into a firm hold and carried her to the door. Now that he knew the layout of the cottage, he didn't need its faint beam to guide him. Subtle shades of dark on dark guided him to the landing and staircase. He used the stairwell wall for an anchor as he counted the twenty-eight steps down to the back hall. He adjusted his hold and managed to open the door, slip through it and shut it again with only the snick of the doorframe when it closed.

The carriage horse turned his head when Tristan approached. He didn't need a skittish horse and jangling traces to disturb the child or household, so he reassured the beast with a low voiced, "Easy, boy." The gelding's nostrils flared to catch Tristan's scent, but he didn't shy away.

Tristan moved past the horse, and a quick step on the wheel hub launched him into the seat. Alice stirred, making a soft questioning sound before he soothed her back to sleep. Satisfied she had not truly woken, he placed her onto the seat. It was deep enough to hold her slender form without having to resort to the cording he'd brought to secure her while they moved. If she woke, he didn't want her to think she was a prisoner. The quilt held her firmly and she gave a soft sigh before snuggling deeper into its folds.

Tristan waited until they were about a quarter of a mile from the house before he lit the phaeton's lamp and set the horse's pace to a brisk trot along the road to Surrey. During the hours he'd waited to act, the dampness in the air had increased to a mist. The thick clouds still threatened, and Tristan hoped the weather held until they reached the manor.

An hour later, the mist became a steady rain.

Damn.

"JULIETTE! S'ECHAPPER! Juliette—!" Her sister Beatrice's voice screamed at her, spearing her with terror. She tried to move, but her arms were trapped. She fought to free herself, struggling, crying, screaming for her sister!

"Beatrice!"

Julia woke as she always did at that moment.

She sat up, tears rolling down her cheeks. She never knew if her scream was real or part of the nightmare. Real or not, her heart pounded and her hands shook as she wiped away the dampness. She fought to distance herself from the vivid grip of her dream. She drew her knees up and wrapped her arms around them as though that would hold the shards of her emotions together. Shuddering, she buried her face in her arms and concentrated on taking slow, deep breaths.

Some nights the dreams took longer to fade. Tonight they lingered and she fought to remain motionless for several minutes. It took a while for her to stop panting. Her heartbeat gradually slowed. Her hands still betrayed a slight unsteadiness when she lit her bedside lamp, but she finally felt ready to let the simple discipline of needle and thread soothe her nerves.

Before going to the sitting room, she stepped across the hall to check on Alice. A faint whiff of leather teased her nose as she did. John, her manservant, must have stopped to talk to Alice before retiring to his room in the attic.

She reached for the knob, but realized the door stood open. Cold apprehension gripped her. A new, waking nightmare enfolded her when she saw the stripped, empty bed.

"Alice?"

Had Alice had a bad dream, too? She might have sought refuge in the wardrobe as Julia had when she was small. She checked, but all was undisturbed. *Perhaps the sitting room?* Julia quickly searched that room, then downstairs and the rest of the small cottage to no avail.

She loves cuddling the kittens.

Turning, she hurried back to her room and pulled on clothing and boots, then yanked her cloak from the peg before she hurried out the kitchen door to the stable. As soon as she lifted the lantern to light her way, she saw the recent footprints and wheel ridges across the bare dirt. Fresh horse droppings nearby left no doubt a carriage had remained in the yard long enough for someone to take Alice.

Anger and fear for the child sent her stalking to the stable to saddle her horse. *They won't get away with stealing her.* She grabbed the halter from the wall and moved the mounting stool outside the paddock gate. No one was going to threaten sweet Alice.

Within minutes, she guided her chestnut horse out of the stall to the mounting block. Heavy, damp mist chilled her face as she rode into the yard holding the lantern high in order to see the direction of the tracks. The light wavered with the movement of the horse and she quickly realized that the lantern only confused her search more so she snuffed it out. Passing a fence post, she hung it there before directing the chestnut toward the dirt road that led to Langstone.

Much as she wanted to race down the road, she dared not urge the horse faster than a steady trot without moonlight to guide her. She didn't know how much of a lead the kidnappers had, but she hoped she could catch up to them before they left the dirt road. It would be far harder to discover their direction once they reached gravel. Were they taking Alice back to Portsmouth or were they bound for London? Her heart pounded and her stomach roiled.

When the rain started soon after, she prayed that whoever had taken Alice would be slowed by the quickly forming mud. The resinous scent of wet foliage combined with the damp earth as the horse trotted over the wheel tracks she could only hope had been left by the escaping carriage. She brushed her hand over her face, slicking away the gathering wet that chilled her skin.

As she struggled along in the darkness, she sorted through ways to get Alice away from the kidnapper. She had no weapon – nor did she know how to use one. The shiver that passed through her had little to do with the cold and far more with the realization that she had no idea how to save Alice. Yet she couldn't leave the child in the hands of the people who had killed her mother and baby brother.

Julia's thoughts circled around in the dark. Perhaps she could lure Alice away much as the kidnappers had done. Even the depraved needed to sleep, didn't they? If all else failed, she would contact Renard who would know what to do. He had rescued so many women and girls from desperate situations.

She rode on.

The horse's pace gradually slowed as the once solid road thickened into wet clay that clung to hooves and made a trot dangerous. The rain fell steadily, soaking the wool of her cloak and trickling down the back of her neck. She had been reduced to a slogging walk when she heard a man's voice cursing in a manner most unbecoming of a gentleman.

CHAPTER 6

Though her hands shook with trepidation and the increasing cold, Julia quickly turned her horse aside and guided him behind a thicket of trees where she slid out of the saddle. Her boots squelched when they sank into the two-inch-thick mud. Struggling to keep her balance, she pulled her feet free of the muck so she could tie the horse's reins on a nearby branch. The heavy soil clung to the hem of her cloak, weighing her down as she cautiously crept toward the grunts and curses ahead.

The further from the road edge she went, the more the blanket of leaves thickened and created a spongy layer that cushioned her movements. Her pulse quickened as she tread slowly and carefully, testing each step she took. It wouldn't do to wrench an ankle out of carelessness. She took a steadying breath and inhaled the earthy mulch aromas of mushrooms, crushed leaves and emerging new growth.

Her eyes had become accustomed to the pitch black as she'd traveled and now could see black on black nuances with occasional forms of gray. She imagined she could distinguish a green cast to the leaves and a brown cast to the gray tree trunks she passed.

So intent was she on locating the source of the rude language, Julia almost missed seeing an improvised shelter at the right edge of the trees. She moved closer and recognized the quilt rigged over a tree branch as the one taken from Alice's bed. Underneath, wrapped in a man's coat and sitting above the mud and leaves on a portmanteau, Alice leaned against the trunk of the tree.

Julia changed direction and slipped under the quilt, holding her finger to her lips when she touched Alice's shoulder. Startled, Alice jerked around then lunged to hug Julia. "Oh, Miss Dorsey! You've come after all. Mr. Sheffield said you were asleep and he didn't have time to wake you." She pulled back, a wide grin of delight visible despite the dimness of the night. "Papa sent him for me."

"That man is lying. He isn't from your papa." Julia whispered. "Your papa wouldn't steal you away in the middle of the night. He wouldn't take you without telling me."

"But Mr. Sheffield is one of Papa's friends. I know because I spilled my lemonade on him at a party once."

That stopped Julia for a moment. *Mr. Sheffield?* The child knew her abductor? Dear heavens, what kind of a man turned on his friends in such a way? *How despicable!* A wash of angry heat flashed through her at such callus betrayal.

Another male burst of irate frustration filled of the darkness to the right and Julia knew she must get Alice away from such a man as quickly as she could. Much as she wanted to know what the man looked like so she could confirm his identity when he was finally brought to justice, she didn't dare linger.

"Is the carriage mired in the mud?" she asked Alice.

"Yes." Alice nodded her head and giggled. "He put me here until he can pull it out and told me not to worry if he used naughty words."

"Well, he most certainly is doing that." Julia muttered. If she acted quickly, perhaps they could escape before he managed to free the carriage and return for Alice. He obviously had not thought it necessary to restrain the child nor did he suspect that the abduction had yet been discovered.

"Mr. Sheffield was wrong, Alice." Julia told her. "He should not have taken you away. Your papa would not be happy if you became ill sitting under a quilt in the rain. We will go back to the cottage where you will be warm and dry."

"But I want to go home," Alice protested. "I miss Papa." Even in the dark, Julia could see her distress.

"You will go home," Julia promised. "But it could take hours for Mr. Sheffield to free the carriage. First we must get you warm and dry." She stood and held out her hand. "Come. We need to get you safe."

Alice listened to the continued grunts and curses from the road ahead, then stood and took Julia's hand. "We should tell him we're going back."

"He will know when he sees you are gone."

Oh, yes, Julia thought. *He will know.* And come back to the cottage. When he did, his methods would be more forceful. She would have to make alternate plans of her own. But first, they needed to get away from the despicable Mr. Sheffield.

TRISTAN STOOD BACK and surveyed his latest attempt to pull the carriage from the nearly axel deep sludge that trapped the wheels. The steady rain had forced him to maintain a slower pace than he'd preferred, and that slower pace had pressed the wheel deeper into the thickening clay.

When they'd halted, trapped, Tristan had been forced wake Alice to move her under the shelter of the trees. He'd quickly set her confusion at ease when he told her his name and reminded her of their first meeting. When he told Alice that her father had sent him to keep her safe, she had assured him Miss Dorsey was doing that.

He had countered that if the Dorsey woman were doing her job right, Tristan would not have succeeded in carrying her off. It was a test, he'd explained, and Miss Dorsey had failed in her job.

Alice had defended her friend though she accepted his logic. When he had rigged the quilt shelter over her, Alice had told him that testing Miss Dorsey while she slept wasn't fair.

After settling Alice in the shelter of a tree thicket near the road he had turned up the lamp affixed to the front of the phaeton and tackled coaxing the horse forward while trying to prevent the wheels from sinking deeper. The more he coaxed, the deeper the wheels ground into the soggy clay. The deeper the wheels dug, the more rainwater seeped into the new runnels, creating more pungent muck. He hated mud. Dirt brushed off, clay clung... and reeked of decay.

Finally, in the last half hour or more he'd gathered leaves, branches and sparse grasses to place in front of and behind the wheels to provide traction. Wet, cold, stinking of slime and impatient, he prayed the tangle of vegetation would finally allow him to pull the carriage out of the dip in the road that had ended their progress.

He slogged back to the horse and pulled on its harness, all the while praising him as he strained again. The leather pulled taut and the wheels creaked in protest. The branch under the front left wheel cracked and rocked forward. He pulled again. His muscles burned and sweat combined with the rain to run down his face. The phaeton lurched again and he nearly lost his balance in the sudden release when the carriage broke free. Moving back to the wheel he quickly layered more grass to prevent the wheels from being trapped again before he could load Alice back in and be on their way once more.

He took a moment to catch his breath but straightened and cocked his head in the direction of the girl's shelter. *Voices?* More than Alice talking or singing to herself. The child's treble carried through the air despite the masking patter of the rain, but it was the lower pitched, quieter hint of answer that caught his attention. He didn't need to hear the voice clearly to know to whom it belonged.

Crouching low, he silently made his way to the thicket. When he reached the shelter, he found the quilt and portmanteau, but no Alice. A branch cracked to his right and he quickly followed. He caught up to them as the Dorsey woman helped Alice onto the chestnut horse he'd seen at the cottage.

He leapt forward, pinning the woman's arms and pulling her away from the horse. "Oh, no, you don't."

Alice cried out as did the woman who struggled wildly, kicking out and catching him on the shin. Alice shifted on the saddle as though she would come to the woman's assistance but Tristan called to her. "Alice, stay where you are," he ordered. "I'll not hurt her."

"But it's Miss Dorsey!"

"I know who she is," he grunted. "What I want to know is why she came after you."

"She woke up," the child declared. "I told you she took care of me. She passed the test after all."

The woman tried to free her arms by suddenly going slack and sinking down, but he recognized the maneuver the instant she shifted and he tightened his grip. His arms now clamped around her breasts and the male in him responded to the plump firmness. He made himself reposition his grip around her ribcage. She tried to kick him again but he lifted and turned her at the same instant. Her foot caught nothing but air. He clamped tighter.

"Stop fighting. I don't want to hurt you." He spoke low into her ear. "You are upsetting Alice and annoying me."

She struggled a moment more but he held her firmly, determined that she would realize the futility of fighting him. Finally, she stopped trying to break free. Her body remained rigid and stiff, but she no longer bucked, kicked, or wriggled her shoulders. They both panted from their exertions.

"Very well," she said. "Please remove your hands from my person."

"That's better," he approved. "However, I believe I prefer to keep you under control."

He moved the woman closer to the horse before shifting his hold so that he held her with one arm while he gathered the reins and led them back to the mired carriage. The narrowness of her waist didn't escape his attention. Nor did the soft pressure of her breasts and hip. She might be a traitor, but she was also a woman whose physical attributes couldn't be denied.

At the phaeton, he swung the woman up and into the carriage with the warning, "Do not try to escape, Miss Dorsey. You will come with Alice and me and we'll resolve matters once we arrive at our destination."

"I do not trust kidnappers, sir. I do not trust you."

"You have no choice." He pulled a length of cording from under the seat and quickly bound her wrists together and anchored them to the side of the seat.

When Alice saw what he'd done, she protested. "But Mr. Sheffield, she passed the test. Why did you do that?"

"We will sort this out, Alice, but first I must make sure Miss Dorsey does not attempt to run away."

"But – !"

He reached down and lifted her to sit beside Miss Dorsey. He gently tapped her nose with his forefinger and captured her gaze. "It is necessary. Do not untie her. I need to get your things."

Moments later, he urged the horses forward one more time and started for Surrey at last. Beside him, huddled under the damp quilt and the carriage's hood, both his passengers rode in silence and the atmosphere pulsated with their disapproval. Or perhaps the chill was his body reacting to the effect of wet linen and night air.

It wasn't the first time in his life he'd been miserably cold and exposed to rain in the night, but it had been fifteen years since it had been a regular experience. He didn't like it any better now. He adjusted the reins to increase their pace and mocked his pampered self. *You are getting soft, Gutter Rat.*

The rain ceased just before dawn. At some time in the night, he realized that the sense of silence beside him had altered and that both child and woman slept. His eyes burned and his face and hands were stiff with cold. When he passed over the narrow bridge beside a familiar ancient oak, he released a thankful breath. Almost there.

Gravel defined the road at the far side of the bridge. The clomp of hooves as they crossed the bridge, followed by the rattle of the wheels, woke his passengers. He felt them stir and shift, the movement no longer random.

The carriage reached the top of a rise, and Hartford Manor, the house he'd inherited from his father, came into view. Few would think it suited an upstart raised in the lesser environs of London.

More great oaks surrounded the grounds and early morning light gave the warm stone facade a soft cream color. He had always liked the house. Though the place was grander than he would ever need, the house was small when compared to the other homes his father had owned. But it was his. Had it not been in the country, he might have spent more time here.

In a rather sleepy voice, Alice asked, "Where are we?"

"Yes, Mr. Sheffield," Miss Dorsey asked, her low voice caressed his senses despite her ironic tone. "Where are we?"

He turned to face them, taking in the flush of sleep that still warmed their skin. On Alice, it raised the instinct to protect the innocent. On Miss Dorsey, it raised entirely different instincts that had nothing to do with innocence. Her eyes dilated slightly when she looked at him and he knew she reacted to him as well. Too bad she was a traitor.

"We are at our destination, at last." He sent them a sardonic smile. "For reasons that should be obvious, that is all you need to know at present."

He turned back, clucked at the horse and they descended the rise. At the front of the house, Tristan climbed down and faced his passengers again. "The house has no live-in staff and is maintained by infrequent custodial visits administered by solicitors. We shall be required to fend for ourselves."

He lifted Alice down and set the portmanteau beside her. When he released the woman's hands from the side of the seat, he didn't loosen the bonds around her wrists though he assisted her to stand as well. Once on the graveled drive, he picked up Alice's things and took Miss Dorsey's elbow to guide her up the stairs to the door. "We shall not be disturbed."

He stopped when Alice stood firmly in front of him, her arms folded.

"When are you going to untie Miss Dorsey?" she demanded.

"That depends on Miss Dorsey."

...And if she was as guilty as he thought.

CHAPTER 7

Inside, the walls and ceilings reflected the manor's more recent age, with none of the gilding or intricate plasterwork of the past century, which further suited Tristan's preferences. Their footsteps echoed in the empty space. Cloth covers protected the receiving room furniture, and the paintings that had once graced the walls had long ago been put into storage. Still, the entry hall had only the slightest hint of dust and the freshness of the air inside told Tristan the overseer had visited recently.

He led his two irritated guests to the upper floor. "Alice, this will be your room for the duration of our stay." He opened the door to a moderate-sized oblong room papered in light green. Pale morning light slanted through the window onto a green and gray patterned rug, a graceful oak bedstead and a matching vanity. He placed the leather case on the bed. "There are dry clothes in the case," he told her as he stepped back into the hallway. "Please remain here until I return," he added before shutting the door.

The Dorsey woman had remained silent after that question when they awoke, but now she turned her gaze on him and he recognized the fury and loathing it contained. "How could you betray the trust of a child?"

"Alice is in no danger from me," he retorted before guiding her into the room across the hall from Alice. "You, on the other hand, will face far more danger if you do not answer my questions."

He pulled her into his room, locking the door behind them. He let go of her arm and went to the writing desk to move its chair to face his fireside wingback chair. "Take a seat, Miss Dorsey," he ordered.

When she did, he redid the ties and secured her wrists to the chair's arms. Her dress still clung damply to her form, emphasizing cold-tautened nipples, and though her jaw clamped tightly, she could not control her shivers. The instant he finished restraining her wrists, he strode to the bed and pulled up the quilt folded at its foot and arranged it around her like a cocoon.

"What are you doing?"

"Making sure you do not die of lung fever during interrogation."

Having made sure she could not escape, he went back downstairs to move the carriage to the stable, see to the horses and retrieve the provisions and his own valise. Lack of staff guaranteed privacy, but it also made more work. By the time he returned to the house, his exhaustion weighed on him like the great sacks of grain he'd hauled while working the docks undercover.

Tristan selected an apple from the provisions basket and brought it upstairs to Alice. He found her curled up in the center of the bed, sound asleep. He set the apple on the vanity and returned to his room.

Once there, Tristan went directly to the wardrobe and put the contents of the valise on the shelf with the few items of clothing he kept there for unplanned visits. Selecting a shirt and trousers from the collection, he turned his head to tell the woman in the chair, "If you are of a modest mind, Miss Dorsey, you might wish to close your eyes for a few moments." Her eyes widened when he pulled off his shirt to expose his chest. The incessant rain had washed away the gritty mud from his clothing during the long night, but the clammy linen irritated and chaffed. "I have had enough discomfort for the time being."

Brilliant rose washed her cheeks and she quickly averted her face. *Interesting.* In his experience, kept women did not blush at the sight of a man's naked chest.

He wiped himself dry with a towel he took from a drawer at the wardrobe's base, then pulled the clean shirt over his head. In deference to his foster mother's attempts to civilize the feral child he'd been, Tristan made sure the tail of his shirt covered his anatomy before he removed his pantaloons.

"Your modesty will no longer be tested," Tristan told her minutes later as he bent to light a fire at the hearth. True, he was in his stocking feet, but otherwise he now wore the clean, dry clothing of a respectable country gentleman. He moved his boots beside the hearth to dry. His eyelids still felt coated with sand and he would kill for a glass of brandy, but first he needed to question the paradoxical woman tied to his desk chair.

He settled into the wingback chair beside the hearth and crossed his legs before asking, "What is your real name and with whom are you working?"

"My name is Julia Dorsey. I do not work for anyone." Now that she did not defend the child, Tristan picked up a note of anxiety. "I am a *lady*."

Such sincerity. If he had not interrogated lying women in the past, he might have believed her. "Forgive the insinuation," Tristan mocked. "I did not say *for*, I said *with*."

He leaned back and folded his hands. "You have held Alice for nearly three weeks, which means you are part of the scheme to force Lord Goodwin to betray England to the French. So again, with whom are you working?"

"You are mistaken, sir." Her green eyes narrowed and frustration tinged her voice. "My cousin's footman was on an errand from London when he discovered an overturned carriage and brought Alice to me. Her mother and baby brother were dead, but she was alive and bleeding. My cottage was nearby so he brought her to me. I know nothing of schemes."

"An excellent story." Tristan approved with an ironic tone. "Had you not threatened Lord Goodwin, I might believe you."

"If Lord Goodwin is being threatened, it is not by me. You, on the other hand, betray the trust of a child by claiming to be sent by her father." She glared at him, her mouth downturned. "You stole her from my home in the middle of the night and brought us to a location you will not name."

She leaned forward to make her point and the quilt slipped to her waist. The warmth had softened the tips of her breasts, but the cloth still clung to her curves and jolted him with awareness. She had obviously rushed after him without donning stays.

"Cousin Renard warned me he suspected the accident was a kidnapping attempt before he contacted Lord Goodwin to inform him that Alice was safe with me." She stopped and raised her eyebrow as she told him, "I know my cousin, but I do not know you. So I might ask you the same question. Who are *you*, and why would you betray your friend?"

"Lord Goodwin was told that Alice is being held prisoner and will be sold to a brothel if he does not pass on military secrets."

Her face drained of all color and her eyes blazed with revulsion.

"You are lying. If that is what he believes, you obviously intercepted my cousin's message and forwarded your own."

"More likely, *you* are lying.' Tristan said bluntly. That sent an angry red flush across her features. *She played the part of the injured innocent well.* Was her reaction guilt or indignation that he had not fallen for her story?

He offered an alternate theory. "Or your cousin is lying."

"Cousin Renard is a man of honor. He would never do something so heinous," she declared with conviction. "He risked his own life trying to get my family out of France during the Terror. The rabble murdered my parents and siblings, but he managed to rescue me. If not for him I would be dead."

Tristan sharpened his gaze. *The Terror?* Now he knew she lied. She couldn't be more than twenty. Too young to remember that bloodbath. Nearly eighteen years had passed since then.

"That story, too, is a lie. You couldn't remember those events even if you were there."

"I was only five years old, but the horror of that day is burned into my memory," she retorted. Her voice trembled with emotion and her eyes flashed defiance. "The French rabble killed my family and Napoleon is no better than the mob who stole my birthright. Why would I do anything to help that cause? Why would I lie about such a thing?"

"To gain sympathy from a gullible interrogator?" He sent her a sardonic smile. "To protect your partner in crime?"

She slumped back against the chair, but held his gaze. "It is clear I am wasting my breath. You will not believe anything I have to say, nor do I believe you. We are at an impasse."

Turning the tables of accusation was a common tactic used to cast doubt in the interrogator's mind. He often used it himself. But something in his gut wanted to believe her. Tristan seldom denied his gut instincts, and his gut instincts told him the woman truly believed her story. However, that didn't mean her story was the truth. Nor did it mean it was not lust instead of his gut that wanted to accept her claim.

"I think you may believe what you say," he finally acknowledged. "But if you aren't a willing participant in this treasonous scheme, you have been made a pawn in it. Despite what you have been told, I am an agent of the crown and Lord Goodwin sent me to rescue his daughter."

She sat up at that. "If that is true, why did you not approach me in the daylight as an honorable man?"

"I doubted the kidnappers, *you*, would release her simply because I asked." He gave her a droll grin. "Even if I said *please*."

"I am not a kidnapper."

"I still do not know that," he countered. "However, I shall notify my superior of your claim and he will verify your history. In the meantime, you will remain here, with Alice and me." He stood and readjusted the quilt to cover her. "You will be so good as to give me your cousin Renard's full name and I shall allow you to change into dry clothing."

Now that he suspected Miss Dorsey might be an innocent in the deadly game someone played, Tristan knew his conscience would plague him if he didn't ease her discomfort.

"If you are truly with the Foreign Office, you should have asked me that first." Those green eyes suddenly gleamed with smug amusement. "Renard is what my French grandmother called him. You would know him as Thomas Foxley, the Earl of Summerfield."

The Earl of Summerfield? Besides being Lord Goodwin's predecessor, the earl was one of the staunchest patriots of the kingdom. The man had served the Foreign Office for nearly thirty years. During that time, he had not married, nor did Tristan remember hearing if he had any other close relatives. Certainly, no one he knew had ever mentioned a cousin.

She had to be lying again. But tossing out a name that well known would be folly if not true. Had Goodwin told Summerfield of the threats? If so, why had Goodwin not said so?

Summerfield had stepped aside because he was ill with consumption, too ill to have been a part of Alice's rescue if the Dorsey woman's story was to be believed. *He would have connections, though*. Had his sources suspected the threat of danger to Goodwin's family, directed to intercept, only to have his men arrive too late to prevent the "accident?"

Once Ravencliffe sent someone to guard the child and free him to pursue his original mission, he would search out those connections.

Family ties made men vulnerable. Was that why Summerfield never married? Was that why no one knew of a young female cousin?

What the devil was going on?

CHAPTER 8

Julia enjoyed a moment of satisfaction at the shocked recognition that twitched across Mr. Sheffield's cheekbones and slackened his jaw before her irritation returned. Cousin Renard, who had insisted she call him by his family nickname since she was a child, was above reproach. The Earls of Summerfield had been faithful supporters of the Kingdom for more than five generations, even defying the commonwealth and Cromwell. She did not know exactly what Renard had done for the government before his health began to fail, but she knew he wielded a great deal of power and had the respect of the ton. If Mr. Sheffield was who he said he was, her cousin's word should make him release her.

When she'd viewed him in the morning light, she realized he was the man she'd seen in Portsmouth. The one who'd flirted with her before she taken sanctuary in the drapers shop. Was that how he'd found her?

"Will you untie me now?" she asked. "I am hardly a threat. You are far larger and stronger than I."

He did not answer, but she watched him weigh her words against his suspicions and accusations. The longer he studied her, the more uncomfortable she became. She squirmed. The wooden seat was not made for comfort. His eyes narrowed. Abruptly, he left the room.

She shifted in the seat again. Where had he gone?

He returned minutes later, a collection of lady's clothing in his arms. He set them on the bed, then came to untie her wrists. When he'd finished, he looked at her, crystal blue eyes clear, direct, and commanding. A shiver that had nothing to do with her wet clothes flashed from her belly down to her toes and up to her fingertips.

"Do not think to escape. If you try, I will hunt you down long before you succeed in reaching another estate or the main road. Alice is now my responsibility and you remain my prisoner until I receive confirmation from my superiors."

He stood and backed away from the chair to allow her to rise. "You are of similar height to my foster mother if slighter, so the clothes on the bed should suffice until your own are dry."

She let the quilt drop from her shoulders and the cooler air immediately chilled her damp clothes. When she crossed the room and picked up the jonquil-yellow day gown, he told her, "It is some years out of fashion, but, we will not be entertaining, so I doubt it matters."

The dress might not be of the latest fashion, but it was lovely. Pale green embroidered leaves accented the neckline and hem and a matching band of green ribbon anchored the finely pleated skirts below the bodice. A slow warmth crept up her neck and heated her cheeks when she noted that he had also brought the full array of undergarments. She shivered, though the room was losing its chill as the fireplace did its job.

She did not quite meet his eyes as she thanked him. "If you will tell me where I might change –"

"You will change here," he said bluntly. "You will not be left alone until I receive confirmation that your story is true."

"If you will wait outside the door, then –"

"That would leave you alone." He stepped over and behind her. When she felt him tugging on the strings at the back of her dress, she gasped and tried to move away.

"Don't be alarmed. I'm merely acting the Abigail for you." He tugged her back. Her bodice slackened and she quickly caught the cloth before it could fall away and expose her to his gaze. Her face burned with mortification. She had not bothered with stays in her rush to save Alice. Her shift was old, worn, and thin. She closed her eyes and fought to keep her breathing even.

That he had begun undressing her in so efficient a fashion shocked her as did the strange shafts of awareness that tightened her belly and bosom. Her breath shortened, catching whenever his knuckles brushed bare skin. He didn't linger at his task, nor did he take further liberties, but she felt his every touch with acute embarrassment. *And longing*? Was she *that* kind of woman?

As soon as he finished, he stepped away and walked over to the door before taking an arm-folded stance in front of it. His eyes glinted with an intensity she recognized. Inexperienced as she was, she saw that he had been as affected by his actions as had she. A tiny flame of pride lit inside her at the sense of power the knowledge gave her.

When he said, "There is a chamber pot beneath the bed should you need relief," the burst of pride withered.

"Surely you do not expect me to use a chamber pot in your presence," she protested.

"Nature makes its own demands, Miss Dorsey. I am sorry that the current situation does so as well."

He would not leave her alone? Then she would grit her teeth and deal with the abominable circumstances as though such exposure made no difference to her. She didn't blush in front of her maid, she would not blush in front of Mr. Sheffield.

She bent and pulled the ceramic necessity from under the bed and, using the bed as a shield, quickly finished. Returning porcelain bowl under the bed, she stood and turned her back on the man by the door. Defiantly, she allowed the dress to fall to the floor. When she lifted the hem of her shift. she took a quick breath for courage and jerked it up and over her head.

Turning to take the dry shift from the pile of clothes on the bed, she peered through her lashes at the man by the door. Relief – and disappointment? – washed over her when she saw he'd focused his eyes at the floor, though he maintained his guardian posture in front of the door. Now that she knew he did not watch her, she managed to pull on a dry shift and—*thanks be*—*stays*, and dress in short order. When she was effectively covered again, she bowed to the necessity of aid and said, "If you would be so kind as to act as Abigail once more, Mr. Sheffield, I am ready."

WHEN HIS PRISONER HAD turned away from him to shed her outer clothes, Tristan set his jaw and lowered his eyes. Loosening the woman's clothing had left his body throbbing with desire and his brain empty of any thought but of how much he wanted to lick and nibble the soft skin at the base of her neck. The tendrils of hair that had slipped loose in the wet struggle on the road were rain fresh and had taken on a slight wave as they dried.

He listened to the changes in her breathing as she removed each garment. The dress made only the slightest rustle as it slithered to the floor. There was a moment of silence, then the sound of her short inhale told him the instant she removed her shift. He didn't need to raise his eyes to know she stood beside the bed clad only in stockings.

He listened to the soft creak of the bed as she sat to remove those stockings. He could picture the fine cotton rolling from thigh to knee to ankle and finally falling free of delicate toes. He suffered through that vivid image twice until the bed creak told him she now stood sorting through his foster mother's castoffs. *Naked.*

That image stiffened his member and threatened to overwhelm him with the clarity of his imagination. He nearly abandoned honor in order to see if his vision came anywhere near the reality, but he willed himself not to give in. Whatever she was – a lying and guilty part of a conspiracy or an innocent woman giving sanctuary to an endangered child – he would allow her the dignity of dressing unobserved.

When she announced that she was ready for him to finish doing up her ties, he lifted his gaze and swallowed hard. The dress made her skin glow with the warmth of a summer peach and the neckline dipped to reveal the rounded tops of her breasts. She held the bodice in place as modestly as she could, but it mattered not. She had a bosom worthy of choir song.

He cleared his throat and reached for the ties, forcing himself to ignore the flush that rose on her skin when his fingers brushed her narrow waist. It didn't help that the flutter of her pulse told him she was as aware of him as he was of her. If he were to remain sane, he would have to recruit Alice to do the service in future.

Tristan gave a final tug on the laces and secured them with a double bowknot. A wave of exhaustion rolled over him despite the urges that kept his body aroused. Miss Dorsey and Alice had slept along the way, but he hadn't. Grimly, he acknowledged what he needed to do next.

He turned away to pick up the fine wool shawl that still lay on the bed and wrapped it around her shoulders. "I am sorry this is necessary," he told her." He led her back to the chair where he tied her wrists again. "But I need sleep and I cannot leave you free to roam about."

THOUGH JULIA INSTINCTIVELY protested against being restrained again, she said nothing. Her heart still pounded from the unsettling experience of his touch. He had not taken liberties. His touch had been as impersonal as that of her maid, yet she had been acutely aware of his breath on the back of her neck, the slight brush of fingertips and knuckles as he adjusted the laces of her borrowed gown.

Close as he'd been, she'd breathed in the mix of leather, fresh linen, rain and... male. Such intimacy left her shaken by more than the unexpected desire to lean back against him in a silent plea to be held. That need battled with the shadow of something she could not name but that frightened her.

He didn't linger when her wrists were secure. He picked up the discarded quilt from the floor, walked to the bed and lay down without saying another word. He rolled himself in the quilt facing away from her. His shoulders relaxed within minutes, and she knew he slept.

What to do now?

The dry clothing made her confinement more comfortable, but the seat was hard. He'd locked the door from the inside when he'd returned with the clothing and tucked the key in the pocket of his pantaloons. With nothing to do but wait for her captor to wake, Julia sorted through her options.

She would not leave Alice with him, no matter that he claimed to be an agent of the crown. Just as he would not believe who she was without proof, neither could she accept his claims on his word alone. She did not doubt his threat to hunt her down if she tried to escape, though, and to travel unknown roads without escort would be as dangerous as taking her chances here.

Alice didn't fear him. In fact, Julia had observed that he saw to the child's needs with attention and kindness even when he'd ordered her to obey his commands. His eyes, though. Their piercing, clear blue clarity seemed to know her every thought and Julia worried he would see her fascination with him.

She must have dozed off, for she woke when she felt hands loosen her bonds. Mid-day light slanted into the room telling her several hours had passed. He must have felt the sudden tension in her arms because he stopped what he was doing and looked into her face.

"I imagine you are ready for something to eat." He finished untying her and helped her stand. "There should be some edibles in the root cellar in addition to the remaining bread and cheese I brought with us."

"Where is Alice?"

"Waiting most impatiently for us to join her in the hall. She is not happy with the way you have been treated."

"Neither am I," Julia responded tartly.

That startled a laugh from him. "No, I don't suppose you are."

He grinned, and the grim man who'd run roughshod over her for the last twenty-four hours or more turned into a charming rake that sent her pulse racing.

He opened the door and Alice launched herself at Julia, hugging her fiercely. "You are all right!"

"I told you so, Alice," Mr. Sheffield said. He put his hands over his heart and struck a wounded pose. "I am hurt you did not believe me."

Alice let go of Julia and spun around, her fists on her hips and her chin jutted out. "You tied her up!" she declared. "I am most angry with you."

He knelt to face her, his teasing replaced with gentle persuasion. "I had to restrain Miss Dorsey so we could be on our way safely and quickly. I am sure you know that people often must do things that they do not wish to do. I promised your father to protect you. To keep my word, I will do whatever it takes."

Alice studied him for several seconds, and Julia had to admire the way he had made his point. At last Alice relaxed her arms and told him, "I shall forgive you, Mr. Sheffield."

She reached for Julia's hand and looked up at her. "Let's go downstairs. Mr. Sheffield said there is apple juice in the kitchen."

CHAPTER 9

Tristan's exhaustion had eased, though his doubts remained as he followed them down the stairs. He'd slept for two hours, enough time to alleviate the grittiness from his eyelids and the fog of exhaustion from his brain. Experience had taught him to be aware of a kind of internal clock when he slept. He smiled grimly. That instinct had prevented his being caught by watchmen when he sheltered in abandoned buildings or overlooked alley corners as a child. The skill still served him well in his work for the crown.

He'd also learned to plan ahead. Following his meeting with Goodwin, he had alerted his superior to the situation, adding that he'd bring the child here if he found her, and arranging for a courier watch the house until he succeeded. He'd write another report this evening for the courier to deliver, and ask Ravencliffe to verify the Dorsey woman's story.

He would also request someone be sent to take over the child's security because it wouldn't be safe for Alice to return home until the perpetrators were in custody. Once free of her care, and clear about Miss Dorsey's status, he'd renew his investigation and expose the traitors who threatened both child and England.

For now, they would find something to eat, then he'd take them into the drawing room and remove the covers from the furniture so they'd have a neutral location to spend their time until matters were sorted. He was impatient to track down the footman who'd delivered Alice to the Dorsey cottage. He needed to know how soon the man had come upon the scene. It couldn't have been too long after the crash if the child was still bleeding. He didn't like cooling his heels, but like it or not, they'd be secluded here for at least a week.

He stepped into the large, well laid out kitchen. In its center stood a sturdy oak worktable surrounded by stools. Alice sat perched on one. Miss Dorsey stood beside it.

At one time the room had been stocked with every provision and tool a cook and her staff could desire. Now, used only occasionally by Tristan, it held only the barest basics. The Dorsey woman frowned when he locked the kitchen door to the outside.

Tristan handed her a crock with apple cider and showed her where to find the crockery and cooking vessels. While she poured some cider for Alice, he descended the stairs to the cellar to look for some root vegetables. As he'd expected, the selection was meager but enough to stave off hunger for a day or two if necessary. Ravencliffe would arrange for fresh provisions within days. For now, though, they could eat.

He ducked behind a stack of empty barrels, baskets and burlap sacks and through the underground passage located there. The passage led to a smoke house built at a short distance from the house for safety, and served Tristan as a convenient location for sending and receiving confidential missives. The simple expedience of opening the air vent at the back wall told any passing courier that he was in residence.

Having set his signal, he returned to the cellar and gathered a basket of potatoes, carrots and onions.

When Tristan entered the kitchen again, he set to work scraping and cutting the vegetables, dropping them into the pot while Miss Dorsey brewed tea and sliced the remaining bread and cheese from the inn. It struck him as an incongruous domestic scene. Captor, prisoner, and rescued preparing a meal as though all were normal and cozy. Oddly, it felt comforting. Such scenes did not take place in the home of a duke, and it had been many years since he and his mother had shared such mundane chores.

When he finished he said, "Miss Dorsey, if you would come with me, I need to collect a few more things from the carriage." She raised her head and he saw the startled wariness in her eyes. "Alice can stay here and finish her cider. We'll only be a few minutes."

"Of course, Mr. Sheffield." Her lips pressed together tightly as though to prevent her from saying more, but she followed him as he unlocked the door and crossed the kitchen yard.

A small courtyard of paving stones had been laid along the back of the house to prevent workers from tracking mud inside. Beyond the paved space, a kitchen garden lay fallow with only a few volunteers remaining from the fall harvest and winter snow. His tenants had not yet begun the spring planting.

"Did you wish to speak with me?" Miss Dorsey asked as she followed him to the stable.

"I told you I intend to keep you with me at all times until I receive confirmation of who you are," Tristan told her. "I see no reason to alarm Alice by keeping you bound and locked away, but you will not leave the house without me, nor will I leave the house without you."

"Do you intend to tie me to the chair every time you need to sleep?"

He stopped at the stable door and turned back, his expression suddenly grim. "No," he assured her. "You will sleep in the bed... with me."

Her face drained of color and her eyes blazed, dark and horrified. He shared her dismay, if for another reason. The idea of sharing his bed with this woman without touching her made his whole body ache.

"You will be bound but unmolested," he assured her, "Neither will I let you out of my control."

"I prefer the chair." Her color rushed back flame red and as heated as the fury in her expression. "It is enough that I am alone in a house with a man who is not my husband," she sputtered. "I cannot –"

"Your virtue is not in danger." His body protested that vow, but he would not abuse the circumstance. "If you are concerned for your reputation, no one other than my superior will know you are here. So long as no one knows of the situation, your reputation will remain as intact as your virtue."

He sent her a sardonic look. "In society, so long as the *appearance* of virtue is maintained, virtue exists. I am sorry, but it is the only solution. I cannot chance that you are not who you say you are or that you might find a way to contact your cohorts."

"I will sleep in the chair," she maintained stubbornly.

"So you say." Come nightfall she would find he, too, could be stubborn. And he was in charge of this matter.

They entered the stable and Tristan quickly saw to the horses' needs, then stepped around to the back of the phaeton and opened the boot. Reaching in, he removed a long wooden box. They returned to the kitchen in silence.

Tristan placed the wooden box on the table in front of Alice and nodded to indicate she should open it. When she did, she gave a little squeal of delight. "Oh! Mr. Sheffield, thank you!"

She reached in and pulled out the wooden doll he'd seen in the Portsmouth shop window. Dressed in the latest fashion, the doll wore a dress of rose pink trimmed in braided white ribbon, a dyed-to-match straw bonnet, and smart black leather half boots. Her face and limbs had been painted a delicate peaches and cream complexion with rose pink lips and blue eyes. Her blond wig swept into a coil at the back with short curls clustered over each ear.

"Look, Miss Dorsey," Alice said as she moved the jointed arms and legs, "She moves like a real person." She arranged the doll in a variety of poses, obviously fascinated with the doll's novel structure. After a few moments she stopped, tucked the doll into the crook of her arm and slipped down from her stool. She came to stand in front of Tristan, a broad smile on her face and her eyes sparkling with delight. "Thank you, Mr. Sheffield. I shall treasure her forever."

"You are most welcome." A warm tide of pleasure made Tristan clear his throat before he asked, "What will you name her?"

"Harriet." A brief shadow washed over her expression. "It was Mama's second favorite name after Alice."

Tristan cleared his throat again and suggested, "It will be some time before our soup is ready. I propose that we retire to the drawing room so you and Harriet may become better acquainted."

Tristan finished writing his report to Ravencliffe while Miss Dorsey was commandeered to take part in an imaginary tea party with Alice and Harriet. Between Alice's childish play and his earlier precaution of locking all the doors to prevent escape, he excused himself to check on their soup. The aroma of cooking vegetables filled the kitchen, and a quick lift of the lid verified it was not in danger of scorching. Satisfied soup was well on its way to being ready, he shifted the pot so it would stay hot but not boil away.

Before leaving the kitchen, he slipped into the root cellar and down the tunnel to the smokehouse. Tristan quickly opened the smoke vent and placed the report in the messenger bag that hung from the wall. His missive to Ravencliffe before leaving Portsmouth had included Miss Dorsey's name, so perhaps Ravencliffe would recognize the connection with Summerfield, if it truly existed. The sooner Tristan could resolve the situation and return to the investigation, the happier he would be.

After their supper, Tristan produced the other items he'd bought in Portsmouth with an eye to ease of transport as much as for entertainment. When he handed Alice the bag of spillikins he invited Miss Dorsey to join them in a game.

When her turn came, she frowned in concentration as she tried to move a narrow stick from the pile without disturbing the rest of the stack. Each time she freed a stick, she laughed in delight, and Tristan's pulse leapt at the sound. He didn't want to believe she was a willing partner in treason, but he couldn't be sure. And until he knew for sure, he couldn't let down his guard just because her laugh made his senses smolder and she had a voice that seduced a man's soul.

An hour or so later, Alice yawned in the middle of a move, causing her hand to slip and lose the final point. Miss Dorsey suggested it was time for the child to go to bed.

Tristan cleared away the game, then locked the doors, put out the lamps and climbed the stairs after them. During their game, Miss Dorsey had relaxed and her low-pitched voice seduced without effort. He was a fool and an imbecile to share his bed with her for no other reason than to assure that she did not escape in the night.

His lip lifted in wry amusement. He should tie her to the chair as she demanded. It would certainly make sleep easier for him. He could sleep anywhere and should probably take the armchair by the fire himself, but he had learned at the age of ten that he preferred featherbeds and coverlets. Yet, having a woman as alluring as Miss Dorsey lying next to him did not bode well for a restful night. Sleep lost in pleasure did not leave a man as tired as sleep lost from frustrated arousal.

He waited outside Alice's door until Miss Dorsey exited the room with a quiet, "Sleep well, my dear."

He gestured for her to cross the hall to his room. "Do you play chess? If you are not ready to retire we might spend an hour or two testing our skills."

He opened the door and she hesitated a moment before entering the room. He sympathized with her plight, though he had no intention of letting it sway him. She had no reason to believe he would not accost her in the night, any more than he had that she would not attempt to escape. She was embarrassed and nervous despite her stiff-postured bravado—or one damned fine actress. He locked the door and pocketed the key, then lit the lamp before he moved to add kindling to the fire.

Miss Dorsey had seated herself in the desk chair again.

He chuckled.

She rested her wrists on the wooden arms and sent him a challenging glare. Miss Dorsey knew how to make her point, though it was a futile one.

"You had only to say you did not wish to play," he said with a grin. "We could go back downstairs and retrieve your book if you prefer." He gestured to the short stack of books on the desk. "Or you may avail yourself of one of those while I choose another." He reached for her hand, drew her out of the hard backed chair, and led her to the one by the fireplace. "Either way, you may enjoy the comfort of a hearth chair instead of the less pleasant wooden one."

She raised a defiant gaze to his but said nothing before she seated herself in the chair. He was almost tempted to let her have her way just to avoid the discomfort of sharing the bed with her.

But he wouldn't.

CHAPTER 10

Julia wanted to resist when Mr. Sheffield took her hand, but the amused glint in his expression told her he understood her message. The hour was not late, though it was full dark. Perhaps a game of chess would ease the tension that had leapt between them when he locked them inside the room together.

Other than his insistence that she not move freely, his behavior toward her and Alice didn't fit her expectations of a kidnapper. When he smiled, the amusement warmed his eyes and stole her breath. How could she react so disturbingly to a man she didn't trust?

The few times their hands had brushed during the spillikins game she'd felt a wash of anticipation flow through her. They were large, long fingered hands, with slightly calloused fingertips that made her skin tingle when he'd loosened her clothing earlier. Yet he demonstrated a steady delicacy of skill and the keen ability to see beyond the obvious moves to those that would gain him the most points.

He had teased her and Alice the whole time and, as often as not, their laughter cost them points. Alice didn't seem to mind. If fact, disturbing the stick pile made her laugh harder.

He brought Alice a doll.

Blast and bother, his concern for Alice almost made Julia forgive his outrageous threat to tie her to the bed next to him for the night. She licked her lips, her mouth suddenly dry. *Almost.*

After such a teasing, lighthearted evening he could not mean to follow through. He'd chuckled when he'd seen her take the seat he'd bound her to that morning. So many of his mannerisms were those of a gentleman. He had given the appearance of serious intent at the time, but perhaps that had been for effect.

Convinced that he had not meant to do more than gain her cooperation, she sat in the hearth chair and turned the board around so the white pieces were in front of her. "I choose white."

He grinned at her not-so-subtle attempt to control the play by making the first move. "As you wish."

It didn't surprise her that he played well and with precision. What did surprise her was his approval when she made strong counter moves. When he made the inevitable move to checkmate he said, "You play an excellent defensive game, Miss Dorsey. You would be wise, though, to adapt some offensive moves. Permit me to demonstrate."

He walked her through the game as they had played it, but offered strategies that controlled an opponent's choices. Julia enjoyed the lesson, quickly understanding the slight change in approach he exhibited. They began a new game, and she made moves she would have overlooked before in defense of her pieces, but now saw the advantage of occasionally sacrificing a pawn or bishop to gain an advantage one or two moves later. In the end, she surprised them both by declaring, "Check-mate!"

"Very well played, Miss Dorsey. Perhaps we can enjoy another match tomorrow night." He stood and returned the game pieces and board to the drawer, then rolled the table to the side of his chair again. "But it has been a particularly long day."

The ease of the past two hours evaporated in an instant. Julia strove to remain calm, but her lungs didn't seem to be able to function normally. Her trepidation flooded back. What if he truly meant to force her to share the bed? Had his behavior over the last hours been calculated to make her more receptive to his scandalous threat? She concentrated on taking even breaths as she rose and moved stiffly to the wooden chair again.

Before she could take the seat, however, he blocked her by the simple expedient of stepping between her and the chair. "I fear, Miss Dorsey, that you have forgotten our earlier discussion. I assure you once more, that I have no designs on your virtue, but neither can I permit you to sit in a wooden chair all night."

"If that is the case," Julia grasped at the explanation he offered, "The hearth chair is more comfortable and would suffice."

"It will not." He led her to the bed and handed her the cotton night-rail he'd included in his earlier offerings. "You will rest better in proper night clothes." He stepped behind her and, to her consternation, untied her dress and stays again. Though he did not linger in his work, his knuckles brushed against her skin and sent quivers of intimacy racing along her nerves. No man had ever touched her bare back before. His determined and efficient actions left her speechless with indignation and alarm.

As soon as he finished and let her go, she rounded on him, searching for words scathing enough to express her refusal to be treated so dismissively.

Before she could, he said, "I suggest you change your clothes while I prepare a territorial boundary that may appease your sensibilities somewhat." With that, he walked to the wardrobe, where he pulled out the lower drawer and removed another quilt. He turned his back on her and began forming the quilt into a long, bulky roll. "If you do not change your clothes," he added over his shoulder, "I shall complete the job for you."

Julia trembled, frustrated and furious. She matched his determination, but not his physical strength. She wanted to lash out at him but knew it would not change matters, nor did she doubt he would strip her with the same matter-of-fact efficiency he had shown in loosening her clothes in the first place. Deciding to bow to dignity over further humiliation, she pulled the nightgown over her head and quickly undressed using the voluminous cotton as a privacy curtain.

When her head emerged from the neck opening and her outer clothing landed on the floor about her feet, she saw he had set the rolled quilt down the center of the bed. She also saw the laughter that lit his eyes when he faced her. "Excellent. You show practicality as well as good sense."

"You give me no choice."

Blessedly, he ignored her by sitting on the far side of the bed to remove his boots while she unrolled her stockings and removed her shoes. When she finished, though, she felt as if her exposed toes brought blatant attention to her nakedness beneath the single layer of cloth. She had not felt so vulnerable since leaving France as a child. *She was such a coward.*

She picked her clothes up from the floor to set them across the contested chair and knew she could not put off the moment of defeat any longer. *Best get it over with.* She walked determinedly to the bed, but before she pulled back the covers he handed her a hairbrush. "You might wish to braid your hair for the night."

She suddenly realized how disheveled her hair must be. She had been so distracted by the events into which she and Alice had been thrown that such matters had not crossed her mind. The hastily formed chignon from the night before had slipped low and several strands had escaped and been tucked behind her ears throughout the evening. Yet it seemed a final intimacy to let down her hair in front of this man who had humiliated her modesty.

Be practical and sensible. If she did not brush and braid her hair, it would be a hopeless snarl by morning. Her modesty might have been crushed, but she still retained her dignity. She turned away and pulled the remaining pins from her hair. Working as quickly as possible, she efficiently formed a single thick braid before turning back. He held out a length of ribbon. She gritted her teeth in frustration as she bound the ribbon around the end of the braid.

She sat on the edge of the bed, but before she could lie down, he stepped to her side and looped the leather ties around her wrists once more. "Again, I am sorry I must take these measures, Miss Dorsey, but I cannot take chances you are not who you seem." He pulled the bonds tight enough that she could not wriggle her hands free, but with enough ease that they did not chafe.

To her shock, he then knelt and looped a second set of bonds around her ankles. When his hands brushed the bare skin of her calves, embarrassment bloomed hot and sent a bright flush from her ankles to her burning cheeks. When he finished, he abruptly stood, bent and lifted her further onto the bed so that she lay between its edge in front and the rolled quilt behind. He adjusted the hem of the gown so she was decently covered, then pulled the blankets over her, tucking her in as though she were a child.

He'd said nothing after his apology, but his mouth had a grim twist to it by the time he tucked the blankets around her. She almost believed he regretted his actions, but as she lay trussed and under the covers in the bed, she dismissed the thought. She would not look to see what Mr. Sheffield did but closed her eyes tightly and willed herself not to care.

She scrunched them tighter when she felt the bed sag behind her moments after he blew out the candle. The blankets shifted, but the sheeting pulled tighter as he lay down.

TRISTAN ROLLED AWAY from the woman whose alluring voice, intriguing eyes, and elusive female scent had tormented him for hours. When he'd knelt to tie the restraints around her slender ankles he'd felt the tremors that belied the artificial calm she tried to portray. It had taken all his restraint to confine his touch to those ankles and not explore the extent of her response to his touch. The flush that bloomed while he worked nearly undid his resolve but, no matter his personal inclinations, it was his duty to take all possible precautions. He found it ironic that it was his sense of honor that made him behave in such an ungentlemanly manner.

The evening had revealed a woman of warmth, humor and intelligence whom he wished was as free of treachery as she claimed to be. Her outrage and denial he discounted as the role of offended innocence. However, he doubted any-one could fake the subtle nuances of innocence that she'd displayed so consistently since he'd prevented her from re-claiming Alice on the road. Which made the coming night all the more torture.

If he absolutely believed she worked with criminals he would not feel so despicable about forcing her to share his room and bed. Certainly, if there was an actress of Miss Dorsey's age who still led a pure life he'd never met or heard of one. An experienced woman of the world knew how to show dismay and indignation at his order, but he'd noted those moments when she thought herself unobserved in which little gestures gave away bravado-buried fears.

He hoped Ravencliffe's response arrived soon so that this farce could be resolved. If her story proved true, he could as-sign her a room—and bed—of her own. Or, better yet, he could take her and Alice to London and place them under Ravencliffe's protection. Remote and unnoticed as his prop-erty was, he worried that his correspondence with Raven-cliffe might alert Alice's abductors to her location. He pre-ferred to investigate his original assignment relieved of concern for Alice's safety, and without the disturbing proximity of the woman sharing his bed.

He lay on the top sheet to put another layer of distance between himself and Miss Dorsey, but he feared it made little difference to either of them. Even with the rolled quilt between them, he could feel the woman's rigid posture.

"You may relax and sleep, now." His amusement when he spoke didn't hide the gruffness his of awareness. "I have lain atop the sheet and am reasonably clothed in shirt and trousers,

She drew in a sharp breath.

He chuckled. "I prefer my bed sport to be voluntary and unfettered."

She made an outraged hiss.

Still, he knew she lay in the dark, stiff and alert. It was not until he'd forced his breathing to even out so she thought he slept, that she finally dozed. It was far longer before he did.

Dawn was little more than a promise when Tristan came awake with the sense that something had disturbed him. Another carry-over from his childhood was that he did not wake gradually but in a single moment. That instinct, too, had saved him from disaster more times than he'd ever bothered to count.

The sound came again. A muffled whimper escaped shortened breaths.

He rolled over and saw Julia Dorsey huddled into a trembling ball. He reached out and gently touched her shoulder and she cried out in terror, struggling even more against bindings that restricted her attempts to break away.

Jerking away from him nearly sent her over the edge of the bed to the floor. He grabbed her shoulders and pulled her back, half covering her with his body in an attempt to hold her still.

"Miss Dorsey—*Julia*—wake up! His weight on her sent her into a greater kicking frenzy and she let out a scream that made him clap his hand over her mouth before she woke Alice.

"Julia! Hush! All is well. You are dreaming."

All sound suddenly ceased beneath his hand when her eyes opened and she focused on Tristan's repeated assurances. Her heart beat frantically beneath his where he anchored her to the mattress and her breath rasped in his ear. Tears glistened in her eyes and, when she blinked, they made a damp track along her temple to disappear into her hair. Something deep, dark and raw wavered in that moment before consciousness fully surfaced and buried her vulnerability behind a protective shield.

Her shift into wakefulness refocused his attention to the warm softness he held down. A faint scent of cedar and jasmine floated up from the gown making him all the more aware of the tempting softness of her breasts. He clutched an exceedingly slender waist.

The tension in her muscles altered from frenzied defense to frozen affront. "You said you would not accost me, Mr. Sheffield."

Her caustic words assured him she was awake and no longer in danger of falling over the edge. His body assured him it was morning and a desirable woman lay beneath him.

He rolled away and out of his side of the bed before his body's reaction sent her into panic again.

"You were in danger of casting yourself from the bed and injuring yourself. It was necessary."

Behind him, she let out a jagged breath.

He recognized the sound. The demons of night always managed to tear away a bit of soul when they succumbed to daylight. The terrors of childhood never quite left one, though the cause was often long forgotten. Were her nightmares residue from the uprising in France or did they have another cause?

Desperate to get away from the disturbing woman, he grabbed his boots but did not stop to put them on until he reached the kitchen. The brisk morning chill didn't reduce the heat racing through him from that brief and disorientating awakening. Holding Miss Julia Dorsey down with his body had solidified his mental image of the woman he'd deemed angularly thin. Petite, fragile – his lips twisted. Not fragile in spirit – *delicate of form*. In short, exactly the form to go with large green eyes and a sultry voice that had haunted him since Portsmouth.

He used the servant's privy outside, then kindled a fire in the stove and put the kettle on before mounting the stairs again. Before re-entering the room, he smoothed his wrinkled shirt, adjusted his trousers and clamped a rein on his heightened response to the woman who had disturbed his sleep in more ways than one.

CHAPTER 11

Disoriented by the nightmare she never quite remembered for all its impact on her sleep, she'd struggled, unable to escape her restraints, and sharp panic had burned though her every nerve ending. Mindless in her terror, she'd fought to be free, the echoes of her sister's screamed warning more real and terrible than ever before. Distant as the memories were, they tangled with the overwhelming need to fight her way out from under a man's broad chest and get free of his restraining arms.

She'd opened her eyes when Mr. Sheffield's voice pulled her from the grip of her nightmare and been mortified to know he'd witnessed her cowardly fears. The blue gaze that met hers had been filled with pity as though he could see into her soul. For an instant she'd felt a kinship, then embarrassment had flooded her consciousness, and she'd dragged her dignity into place and reminded him to keep his distance.

When he finally escorted her from the room into the hall, she skirted him carefully. Her nerves still jumped and the throbbing headache that followed disturbed nights had her holding the banister tightly as she the descended the stairs. Neither of them spoke of the morning incident, but she doubted that situation would continue long. He studied her too closely to leave his questions unanswered.

Alice joined them in the kitchen, and she set out bowls while Julia prepared tea and porridge. She chattered throughout the meal, telling Mr. Sheffield about the kittens at Julia's cottage and the embroidered sampler she had begun there.

When Alice told him how cook made a batch of sweet biscuits just for her, Julia realized with a jolt that her small staff would wonder at her disappearance. Yet she could do nothing to remedy the situation. She was a prisoner in an unknown location with no way to escape. Nor could she leave Alice behind even if she found a way to do so.

Mr. Sheffield responded to Alice's prattle, but Julia knew it was a matter of time before he asked her to explain to him what she couldn't explain to herself.

When they finished eating, Alice asked, "May we go to the river you said was nearby?"

"We shall go as soon as I have filled the fish larder with water," he told her. The small stone walled holding pool near the kitchen door would require several buckets to fill, but would also allow him to keep fish fresh for several days. "Hopefully we'll catch a fish or two for our supper. There is a bucket at the bottom of the cellar stair. Will you fetch it while I clear it of leaves?"

She disappeared down the stairs, and he remarked, "I had almost forgotten the way little girls talk without pause. Now that my sisters are older, they do occasionally lapse into silence."

Julia smiled, but her eyes stung with a sudden memory. "I remember my brother once clapped his hands over his ears and asked Papa to make me stop."

Her memories of life in France were like vignettes. A whiff of lavender always enveloped her with the warmth of her mother's hugs. Cloves reminded her of the slightly rough texture of her father's jaw when he nuzzled her neck to make her laugh. She remembered few specifics before that terrible day when the shouting crowds destroyed her family, but the emotions—the love, and trust, and joy—of that time sometimes eased and sometimes sharply magnified her sense of loss.

IT WAS LATE AFTERNOON when Tristan deposited three perch into the larder before cleaning three more for their supper. Alice had soon lost interest in holding the fishing pole and turned it over to Tristan while she explored the riverbank and Miss Dorsey showed her how to weave a daisy chain.

"My Papa once brought home a fish as big as me," Alice told Tristan as they feasted on pan-seared fish. "He said that there are even larger fish in the sea – some as large as boats." She looked from Tristan to Miss Dorsey, "Though I think mostly he was teasing. He likes to tease Mama and me." She stopped, looked down, and fell silent, using her fork to shift a piece of potato around on her plate.

A flash of sympathy squeezed Tristan's heart but he had no words that could change what had happened.

"I was just a bit younger than you when I sailed to England and saw fish larger than Mr. Sheffield." Miss Dorsey commented before the silence lingered too long. Her words made Alice look up again, and curiosity replaced the misery in her expression. "They were quite unlike any fish I've ever seen in a river."

Alice speared the piece of potato and took a bite, chewed thoughtfully, then asked, "What did it look like?"

"There were three of them, all a dark gray color, with long narrow snouts," she mused. "I remember Beatrice and I were quite worried when we first saw them because they were so big, but the men of the ship said they brought good luck to mariners." She smiled at Alice. "We soon realized they followed the ship in a most playful manner, leaping from the water as though dancing a frolic."

Tristan turned his gaze sharply to her face. *Beatrice?* Miss Dorsey had told him only she survived the slaughter, so who was Beatrice?

"Have you seen such creatures, Mr. Sheffield?" Alice shifted her attention to him and Tristan knew his questions would have to wait until later. But Miss Dorsey would answer them as soon as the child was in bed.

"No. I have not ventured across the sea," he answered. "However, I have caught fish larger than perch. The salmon in Scotland grow quite large." Remembering an incident at the Wolverton country estate, he chuckled. "Though perch hold a fond place in my heart since the year I refer to as *The Brothers' War*."

"The brothers' war?" Clearly intrigued, Alice gave him her undivided attention. Tristan noticed that Miss Dorsey had also straightened in her seat and faced him with a curious expression.

"As boys, my brother and I were particularly competitive. I found him to be pompous and insufferably superior, and he considered me to be vastly inferior and disgustingly rude. I wanted to knock him down a peg, so I tormented him unmercifully and he retaliated in kind. Our father was unaware of most of our conflicts because we knew he wanted us to get along and were careful to engage in our challenges when he wasn't around.

One day, after he told me I stank of the gutter, I sneaked a bucket of perch into his room and hid them behind the wardrobe, inside the drawers, under the bed and in his favorite pair of boots. He found the fish in the boots the next day, but it was another week before anyone thought to search for more." Tristan shook his head at the memory. "After Father took a switch to me for giving the maids extra work, he made me sleep in that room until the stink faded."

That made Alice giggle and Miss Dorsey chuckle.

"*Did* your brother retaliate?"

"Yes, he did. A small tin box that I valued disappeared some weeks later. Of course, he denied taking it." Tristan realized too late that the story had led him down a path he'd not intended to take. The tin box had contained a folded drawing of his mother and a lock of her hair. It had been the only thing he'd brought with him to the Wolverton household. It lay snug in a drawer in his room even now.

Curiosity sparkled in Alice's eyes and Tristan concluded, "Suffice it to say, I didn't believe him." He glanced at Miss

Dorsey. "After some *persuasion*," He paused a wry grin spread across his face. "he returned the box."

With that, he stood and gathered their plates. He would be wise to avoid stories about his childhood. Though he and his brother had resolved their differences, so many of his memories centered on his rebellion against the people who saw him as inferior because of his low beginnings. That brief quiet moment following Alice's mention of her mother made it clear the child knew how different her life would once she was finally allowed to go home.

Tristan waited, curiosity barely suppressed, until Alice was in bed for the night and Miss Dorsey had taken a seat in front of the chessboard before asking, "Who is Beatrice?"

She raised her head sharply, clearly surprised at his tone. "My sister."

"I thought you were the only survivor."

"I am." She met his gaze and he saw again that well of sorrow that had surfaced in the aftermath of her morning nightmare. "She died almost as soon as we arrived in England."

"How did she die?"

JULIA FLINCHED. HOW did Beatrice die? Julia's memories of the time tended to scramble whenever that question rose in her own mind. She made herself swallow the flair of panic that rose like bile and made her throat ache.

When Cousin Renard had led them down the gangplank from the ship, she'd been terrified of the crowds of people bustling about in the growing dark. He'd found a lean-to shelter beside a narrow alley and told them to wait there while he arranged for a carriage to take them to his townhouse. She and Beatrice had believed themselves safe, but before he had returned, two foul smelling, bearded sailors had discovered them. Then all had been confusion and dizziness and shock.

"We were waiting for Cousin Renard who'd gone to get a carriage. I must have dozed, because the next thing I remember was Beatrice shouting frantically, yelling for me to run, then a sharp pain when I hit my head." *Or had someone hit her? Someone else had shouted—her cousin? The words made no sense, and darkness had overwhelmed her. The next thing she remembered was the scent of damp wool and the sensation of being carried.*

"I remember nothing else until Cousin Renard put me in the carriage then left to search for Beatrice."

Julia had waited for them to return, terrified of everyone who walked past the carriage and into the nearby tavern. The lively music and squeals of laughter from inside made her head throb and the ringing in her ears worsen. She huddled in the dark, too frightened to cry, chilled and shaking despite the woolen lap robe Renard had wrapped around her.

After an endless wait, Renard had climbed into the carriage and tapped the roof with his walking stick. Only then had he turned and told her Beatrice was dead. It had felt like Paris all over again. Maman, Papa, her brothers... now Beatrice. All dead.

She took a deep breath, the horror of the moment still vivid and gut wrenching, though so long ago. "I don't know exactly what happened to her, Mr. Sheffield, but I know she tried to protect me and died for her effort." Her voice shook.

She met his gaze with defiance and declared, "That's all that matters."

Cousin Renard had never spoken of Beatrice, or any of her family, again once he'd made that terrible pronouncement. It was as though her other life had never been. She took her cue from him and never spoke of her childhood. She'd banished all memories of that time... Except for the nightmares. She never knew what would set them off, only that the dreams left her with a quivering stomach and throbbing headaches.

After so many years of avoiding all thought of that time, her heart released something tight and raw and forbidden. Images flooded through her in a kaleidoscope of memories. No single moment, but a burst of love and joy, and loss and sadness, all at once. It was as though she'd taken back a scrap of her life. Beatrice was gone. Maman and Papa were gone. As were her brothers. But they had once lived. They had once been happy.

Mr. Sheffield studied her for several seconds, then said, "I may not know if you are truly Summerfield's cousin, but I do believe you suffered the loss of someone you loved deeply. I am sorry for your pain."

Julia saw compassion in his eyes and relaxed the tight clasp of her hands in her lap. She didn't know what to make of the man. He could flay one alive with a harsh look yet soothe as quickly with a smile or gentle word. He'd gone to considerable effort to prevent Alice from realizing he still held Julia prisoner and he appeared sincere when he apologized for what he deemed necessary actions.

She realized she trusted him, and believed he really did act on the behalf of both the crown and Lord Goodwin. But would he ever trust her?

CHAPTER 12

Julia slept better than she had since undertaking Alice's care. She drifted awake, relaxed and at peace, ready to begin a new day. She shifted, and opened her eyes in shock when she realized her wrists and ankles were not bound as they'd been when she went to sleep. Her stomach lurched, and she lay still as she absorbed the fact that he'd touched her while she slept. Yesterday she'd decided she trusted him, but this tested that trust. What's more, did this mean he trusted her?

She didn't need to look over her shoulder to know Mr. Sheffield was not beside her on the bed. She sat up, then rose to check the door. The handle turned easily and a brief glance into the hall showed the Alice's door was open. Voices drifted up the stairwell and confirmed that Mr. Sheffield and Alice were in the kitchen. She closed the door and dressed as best she could without anyone to assist her with the back lacings. Satisfied that she was decently covered, she descended the stairs.

When Julia entered the kitchen, she halted in amazement. A basket of eggs sat on the large worktable along with a jug of milk, two loaves of bread and a round of cheese. A haunch of ham showed signs of being sliced and the aroma of ham filled the air. She lifted her unbound hands and nodded toward the bounty of fresh foods. "Does this mean you've heard from your superior?"

Tristan looked up from where he stoked the stove's fire. "I arranged for him to send provisions after I confirmed where Alice was. When I have definitive answers I shall tell you." He turned a slab of ham. "As to the other," He glanced toward Alice who was playing with her doll and paid no attention, "The doors on the ground floor are secured, so you may move through the house at will."

So, in other words, nothing had changed.

"I look forward to that moment," she said sweetly.

She poured milk into a mug and handed it to Alice. "What is your superior's name?"

"King George the Third."

Julia clamped her mouth tightly, determined not to respond to his insolent answer. Instead, she began breaking the eggs into a bowl for their breakfast.

A small sound warned her before his breath tickled her ear, raising gooseflesh and making her jump. He leaned close and whispered, "Ravencliffe. The Foreign Office."

She stepped away quickly, then turned to see him grin.

"Your ears turn red when you are angry, did you know?" he teased.

Julia stared at him, not sure if she should slap him for the familiarity or cover her ears in mortification. "I do not believe anyone has made me angry enough to do so in the past, Mr. Sheffield. You have proven yourself to be unique in my experience."

"Why, thank you, Miss Dorsey," he said with a sweeping bow and a wink at Alice, who watched with wide-eyed interest. "Everyone should be unique in some way... and being the first in your experience would be a true honor."

Julia felt the heat spread from her ears to the rest of her body, and her eyes suddenly stung with shocked dismay. She had come to think of him as a gentleman she could trust. His innuendo was lost on the child, but not on her. Unable to face him, she turned back to the eggs.

Silence stretched as she worked.

"I apologize, Miss Dorsey," he said at last. "I should not have teased you in that way. My comment was beneath both of us. I pray your forgiveness."

Manners demanded she respond in kind, and Alice would not understand the boundaries his remark had crossed. "Of course, Mr. Sheffield. I am sure you did not intend disrespect."

Liar.

TRISTAN WATCHED MISS Dorsey's stiff back as she whipped the bowl of eggs and called himself every type of fool. She wasn't the type of female to be entertained by suggestive teasing. She'd been irritated at his flippant comeback when she asked who his supervisor was. Then, when he'd whispered Ravencliffe's name, she'd held her own, but he'd taken it a step too far.

Damn and blast! The hurt he'd seen in her expression before she flushed and turned away had been like a blow to the gut. He hadn't meant to treat her with disrespect. He needed to make it up to her.

Breakfast was a bit more subdued than the day before, but Alice appeared not to notice as both he and Miss Dorsey strove to respond to her chatter. When Alice told him about the embroidery sampler she had completed under Miss Dorsey's guidance he remembered that there might well be floss threads and hoops in the rooms his foster mother had used when she visited some years back. As soon as they finished breakfast, he led them to her sitting room.

The cupboard was locked and he did not know the location of the key. Undeterred, he asked Miss Dorsey for a hairpin. Working deftly, he used the pin to unlock the cupboard where there were, indeed, hoops, threads, handkerchief squares and needles.

"I thought you needed a key to open a lock," Alice said as he worked.

"Normally, you do, and should," Tristan agreed. "But it's useful to know how to release a lock when the key is not available."

"You speak from experience?" Miss Sheffield's voice held a note of condemnation and Tristan knew she'd not yet forgiven him his rude behavior.

"Yes, I do." He reformed the pin and handed it back to her. "As a child I escaped several risky situations by picking locks." He turned to Alice. "Would you like to learn?"

"Oh, yes!" Alice said. "I should like it very much."

"Mr. Sheffield! You should not teach a child to pick locks! It is not –"

"Would you like to learn, too?"

She stopped and stared at him in surprise.

He kept his expression neutral. "You never know when some arrogant troublemaker may decide to lock you into a room against your will."

He took great pleasure in watching her disapproval shift into reluctant amusement. "I believe I would, Mr. Sheffield."

Alice worried her lip while she worked, then grinned when she succeeded in opening the cupboard door after just a few tries. Miss Dorsey caught on just as quickly. For the next hour they learned to shape and manipulate hairpins to lock and unlock the cupboard. When they succeeded in mastering the cupboard door, they moved on to picking the bedroom door lock. By the end of the morning, Miss Dorsey had lost her stiff distance and he felt she might have forgiven him his bad behavior.

After a meal of bread and cheese, they walked to the riverbank again. Alice made a game of hiding behind trees and jumping out at them. Tristan soon reversed the game, and before long, Alice begged to know how he managed to hide so effectively though he was so much larger than she.

"Oh, ho," he laughed. "Time for troublemaker lesson number two – hiding in plain sight." They might be safe for the moment, but once Ravencliffe contacted Lord Summerfield, others might well discover their whereabouts. Better safe than sorry. He glanced over and told Miss Dorsey, "Of course, I know how to spot people using these tricks, so remember that I shall not be fooled. However, when one's opponent does not expect to encounter such skills, they are quite effective."

Alice quickly learned to freeze in place and how to fade into shadows, but she tended to giggle and give herself away.

Miss Dorsey proved to be better at blending in to the surroundings than he would have liked. If she did try to use his lessons to escape, he would have the devil's own time to find her. Though he would. He only hoped she did not test her skills – or his.

HE AWOKE THE FOURTH day some time before dawn to find Miss Dorsey curled up against him, her head nestled on his chest. Her arm lay across his chest and her torso pressed intimately against his side. At some point the rolled quilt had flattened and she'd instinctively turned to him for warmth. An instinct that his body responded to with enthusiasm.

He carefully tried to ease her from his side, but her eyes opened, widened, and she rolled away with a gasp. "I—beg your pardon, Mr. Sheffield," she whispered.

He turned onto his side and drew his knees up to disguise his condition until he could control it. "Under the circumstances, I think you might as well call me Tristan," he said with a droll smile.

She kept her back to him, curled into a ball with only the tender flesh of her nape visible. "I believe it might be best if we maintain formality, Mr. Sheffield."

"We are hardly living a formal life at the moment," he countered. "It is time we accepted that. I shall call you Julia and you will call me Tristan."

Later, while Julia measured oat grains for their breakfast, Tristan made another trip to the smokehouse in hopes that

Ravencliffe would have sent word she was who she claimed to be.

To his great relief, the vent was open and the messenger bag hung from its peg. Tristan set the lamp on a stool and quickly pulled out the message inside. Scanning the contents, he heaved a sigh of thanks. Summerfield did have a French émigré cousin whom he'd rescued as a child.

He read further and frowned.

> *... I have this information from my mother. She remembers her as a young woman whose Season ended after the Barclay Ball some five years ago. Mother remembers that the girl became hysterical and created a scene when the crowd in the room overwhelmed her. Gossip said Summerfield sent her back to his country estate. She never returned to the city.*

A hysterical scene? That did not fit his impression of the woman in the kitchen. Determined? Yes. Passionate in protecting the child? Yes. Hysterical? Never. Then he remembered the frantic thrashing when he'd wakened her from her nightmare and paused. Perhaps.

> *I have sent to Summerfield for a description to be sure the woman you have in custody is the same person, though I have no reason to believe otherwise. Until the matter is fully settled, you are to keep them where they are. I shall inform you if matters change.*
>
> *Respectfully yours, etc.*

Ravencliffe

What to do, now? Did he continue to watch the woman's every move until the description removed all doubt? Her basic story had been verified, and his gut told him she was as innocent as she claimed. But was that enough? Tristan folded the message and returned it to the bag.

"Does your superior confirm the truth?"

Tristan spun around to see Julia in the doorway of the tunnel. The dim light revealed the irritated set of her mouth and that she stood with her arms crossed, her stance determined. He might well regret his lessons in stealth. He should have heard her before she reached the doorway.

"The oats are boiling, I take it."

She did not answer, but merely stared, unblinking, at him.

He picked up the lantern and crossed to the doorway. "He confirms Summerfield has a cousin who fled France. He has yet to receive a description to verify that you are she."

She had begun to relax her posture but stiffened again when he added the part about her description.

"He did not question my cousin?"

"He has sent word to Summerfield, but it was Ravencliffe's mother who remembered a female cousin."

Julia blanched. He noted that a vein in her temple pulsed frantically though she remained otherwise unmoving for a moment. Finally, she took a breath and deep rose washed away her pallor. "I suppose it was futile to hope that time had erased the events of the Barclay ball from anyone's memory."

So it was true. Tristan had no further doubts that she was indeed Summerfield's cousin. "I take it things did not go as you wished?"

"No. But then, you know that, don't you?"

"Ravencliffe's note gave few details, only that the crowded ballroom gave you great distress."

That startled a short bitter laugh from her. "I suppose you could say that." She shifted her gaze to the wall behind him. "A young woman making her debut does not push her way through the other guests screaming at top voice that she needs air. Nor does she collapse into a sobbing heap on the balcony when she finally breaks free of the ballroom doors." She returned her gaze to his. "I suppose I should have known such a spectacular and cowardly display would take more than five years to fade from social memory."

"Do crowds still frighten you?"

"I find them difficult," she admitted. "Though I hope I would not panic as before. The ballroom was over-crowded and it was as though I had no control over where I moved. The musicians played a frolic and the dancers surged in my direction. It was like the great crowd that swarmed around my family before Beatrice pulled me out of sight of the beasts who slaughtered the rest of my family."

She blinked and took hold of her emotions. "It was long ago. I prefer not to dwell on the past." She shifted her stance and faced him. "Must I endure another night in your bed — or might I be allowed my modesty and privacy at last?" Her face flamed when she spoke of *modesty* and he knew she was painfully aware that it was she, and not he, who had crossed the quilted barrier that morning.

"You will not attempt to leave or take Alice from my protection?"

"You still doubt my motives?"

"My orders are to keep you here until further notice."

"At least let me notify my household and let them know I am well and will return. They will be frantic."

"Out of the question. Someone might trace the messenger and put Alice at risk."

She bit her lip and looked away, then back again. Her stance finally easing, she promised, "I shall not leave Alice. Nor shall I spirit her away in the middle of the night."

Tristan nodded. "Then I believe we will both be relieved to establish different sleeping arrangements. I suggest you take the chamber next to Alice."

He stepped around her and returned to the kitchen. The change of bedchambers relieved his guilt, but the agreement left a hint of disappointment behind.

CHAPTER 13

For the first time since encountering Julia Dorsey on the road to Surrey, Tristan awoke refreshed. He scratched an itch on his bare chest, grateful that he'd not had to spend another night fully clothed. He sat up and swung his feet to the floor. Ravencliffe's note had raised his hopes that he would no longer need to act as Julia's jailor.

How did Julia sleep? Had she been plagued by nightmare again? He sincerely hoped not. Until yesterday, he'd been unsure of her claims of innocence, but he'd known her night terrors were real.

No hardened traitor blushed so easily.

He smiled.

She hated those blushes for revealing her vulnerability. And she was vulnerable. She presented a calm, practical and unflinching presence no matter that her crimson cheeks betrayed her inner conflicts. Anger, frustration, embarrassment, or awareness—every emotion brought color to her complexion. He thought it rather endearing. *Endearing?* Good God, where had that word come from?

Endearing implied affection. She intrigued him, she aroused him, but they were little more than strangers. Affection did not rise to the wary companionship they had shared in a single week's time. *Amusing*. That was it. Her blushes amused him with their naiveté.

As soon as Ravencliffe confirmed her identification, he would suggest that Julia go to her cousin's townhouse in London if she was still concerned about her abrupt disappearance. People would think nothing of her paying him a familial visit, especially if he was as ill as he'd heard.

He wished he could send them both to London and make them Ravencliffe's problem, but he couldn't be sure Alice would be any safer there. Until the culprits were exposed and in custody, Goodwin was still at risk for blackmail. So Tristan would have to harness his impatience until Ravencliffe sent a replacement for their protection. Perhaps Julia would remain with Alice. He paused in the act of pouring water into the washbasin. The thought pleased him more than he liked to admit.

He finished dressing and went downstairs where he was startled to find Julia already in the kitchen, slicing bread. Her chamber door had been closed and he'd not checked her room. It disturbed him that he'd not heard her passage in the hall.

"Good morning, Mr. Sheffield. Did you sleep well?"

"Quite well, and you?"

"Remarkably well." She kept her attention focused on her task, but he caught the slight acerbic bite in her words. "One rests so much better when not bound hand and foot."

"True." He knelt and loaded several pieces of wood into the firebox. "Just as one rests so much better when not obliged to share one's bed with an encroaching enemy." He didn't need to look behind him to know he'd irritated her. "I am sure we are both thankful such measures are no longer necessary."

Now if only Ravencliffe would free him to locate the blackmailer. Only Ravencliffe knew Tristan was not alone at the house. Not even the courier who watched for chimney smoke and message signals. Unless the traitor was part of Summerfield's staff and learned of their location when he responded to Ravencliffe's inquiry, they were safer here than in London. The deadline set for Goodwin to disclose the shipping dates and supply routes was at hand. Until Tristan succeeded in discovering the traitor, Alice remained in danger, and time was running out.

He arranged several thin wooden shavings then used a flint to kindle a fire before rising and putting the kettle on the hob. He took two cups from the shelf and set them onto the table. When she looked up, he said, "Now that I am no longer obliged to treat you as a prisoner, I shall not require you to accompany me to the river this morning. I propose to replenish the fish larder while you and Alice remain at the house. Isolated as it is, I prefer you both to remain out of sight as much as possible." He gave her a wry grin. "And fish bite better without a child tossing pebbles into the water."

Their gazes met. Her lips twitched. "I suspect you are right."

Before arriving at the riverbank an hour later, Tristan surveyed the perimeter of his property to reassure himself they remained unobserved. Hartford Manor was isolated, but not impossible to find if one knew who to ask. He shifted his position and admitted he'd left the house against his better judgment, for until he knew who had attacked Goodwin's family he must remain vigilant.

He finally settled at the riverbank a quarter of a mile beyond the spot where he'd fished the first day. Now that he didn't have to worry about Alice falling into the deeper water, he could fish from the deep pool his father had shown him the only time they'd come to Hartford Manor alone together.

That same day had been the only time his father ever spoke to him about his mother and he'd finally come to believe his father might truly have married his mother if he'd known of her situation, despite the scandal it would have caused. After all, the duke had ignored similar scandal to make Tristan part of his legitimate family. But, of course, His Grace hadn't married her, and nothing could change that fact.

Tristan cast his hook into the river and sat on an exposed boulder. With no other distractions, his thoughts returned to the delicately slender woman whose sultry voice and green eyes kept him half aroused night and day. He'd missed their game of chess the night before. He'd also missed knowing she slept beside him, though her absence was the reason he'd finally managed a decent night's sleep. He needed the distance to ease the disturbing effect she had on his concentration. He hoped Ravencliffe would not insist they remain together much longer.

Sunlight filtered through the early morning cloud cover as a slight breeze whispered through the trees and made the tall grasses sway and rustle. Tristan absorbed what most people called the silence of the country. It was not silent. True, the rattle of carriages or the shouts of venders did not fill the air here. Sounds did not bounce back against the walls of buildings, nor did the air vibrate from the constant motion of life.

He had to admit he'd enjoyed the fresh air and soft breezes when Alice had made daisy chains and he fished for their dinner the first day. He'd been charmed by Alice's giggles when she tried to hide among the shrubs and trees along the riverbank. What would it have been like to spend his childhood running free in open fields instead of dodging bullies in the mean streets of London's rookeries?

That question disturbed Tristan's city sensibilities while the never-ending flow of the river caused his eyelids to droop. Thankfully, each tug on his fishing line broke the spell and kept him aware of where he was and of how much time had passed since he'd cast his line into the water. Isolated they might be, but he did not feel comfortable leaving his charges unguarded for long.

After he filled the bucket with his catch, he gathered his pole, picked up the bucket and headed back to the house. The grassy bank sloped up to a stand of trees and he stepped into the light at the same time as he heard a branch snap. Then a burst of pain exploded across the back of his head and everything went black.

"NOW STITCH ALONG THIS edge here," Julia instructed Alice.

They sat in the downstairs parlor by the window piecing together scraps of cloth to form the folds of a doll's nightrail.

After having her hair brushed and braided, Alice had decided that Harriet needed sleep clothes in addition to the walking dress she already wore. By using four handkerchiefs, Julia had fashioned pieces for gown and sleeves that she now showed Alice how to sew together.

She had picked up two more pieces to match together when a movement outside the window caught Julia's attention. A carriage and four approached the house down the gravel drive. Alarm sent her pulse racing. Tristan had made it clear no one but his superior and the courier who supplied provisions and correspondence knew anyone was here. So who was this? Should she hide with Alice and let whomever it was think the house abandoned? Should they slip out the back and warn Tristan of the strangers?

Julia rose, thinking to shepherd Alice into the kitchen, when she noticed that the outriders looked familiar. As the visitors drew closer, she recognized her cousin's burly head footman, Ned Smith, and Tom, Renard's less bulky and slightly shorter second footman. Though she didn't recognize the coachman who drove the carriage, she let out the breath she hadn't realized she held. Cousin Renard had come for her.

When Julia opened the door, she saw that the men expected to be met with resistance. Both Ned and Tom held pistols at the ready.

"You may put those away, Ned. All is well."

She peered around him. "Does Renard need help to come inside? He shouldn't strain himself." Her cousin suffered from consumption and his letters of recent months had indicated that his condition had worsened until he'd been forced to cease his work with the Foreign Office. He had visited her only once in the past five years, so she had assumed he was too ill to travel.

"He couldn't come himself. He sent us to fetch you. Where is the fellow who stole the child from you?" Ned spoke in a low voice, again making Julia wonder if they expected Tristan to attack.

"Down at the river fishing for our dinner," she told him. "You need not whisper. We're not prisoners." *At least, not any more.*

The two men looked at each other, and Julia noted that they seemed to communicate some message silently. Tom tipped his cap and retreated from the doorway. It was clear they'd assumed Tristan was the threat her cousin warned her about when he'd written her that the carriage accident had been a kidnapping gone wrong.

"Mr. Sheffield misunderstood the situation when he stole her away. He's a friend of Lord Goodwin, who sent him to keep Alice safe." Julia stepped back to allow Ned to enter, then turned to lead him into the parlor. "He didn't know that you rescued Alice from the crash site, but believed she'd been carried away by kidnappers. He even suspected me until he learned who I was."

Ned's lip curled and he studied her in a way that made the hair on the back of her neck rise. "Treated you with a bit of disrespect, did he?"

There was no way she would reveal details of her time here to her cousin's footman. She had never quite liked him, finding him to be coarse and insolent, though he was absolutely loyal to her cousin. "Mr. Sheffield is an honorable man and has treated me as a lady at all times." *At least, most of the time... he had, after all, averted his eyes and apologized for binding her hands and ankles each night.*

"Well, you're to come with us now." Ned stepped into the parlor and motioned to Alice. 'Come along, child. Time to go."

Alice looked up from her sewing. "Where?"

"London. Now, come along with me." He reached out to take her hand, but she quickly put it behind herself and scooted away from him.

"Mr. Sheffield said I am to stay here until my Papa says I may come home."

Julia followed Ned into the room. "Ned works for my cousin, Lord Summerfield, Alice. He was one of the men who found you that day. Do you not remember?"

Alice studied the tall man but Julia thought it unlikely that she remembered much beyond the shock of her injured arm and her fears for her mother and baby brother. She turned her gaze to Julia and asked, "Does Mr. Sheffield know?"

"Tom will take care of him," Ned said before Julia could reply. "We must be on the road immediately. Now come." This time he caught her hand and tugged her forward.

"Wait," Julia protested. "Let me gather her clothes—"

"His lordship said not to bother with anything but you and the girl." He caught her arm with his other hand and propelled them both to the door. "There be lap robes in the carriage if you get chilled."

Alice turned, and tried to pull her hand from Ned's. "I want Harriet!" She protested.

"I said come, girl," Ned tugged her harder and shoved Julia forward.

"Ned, don't be in such a hurry. Let her bring her doll," Julia tried to draw her arm away, but he held fast. The set of Ned's jaw alarmed her and she stopped resisting. In a matter of heartbeats, she and Alice were bundled into the carriage.

Confused by Ned's blunt manner and his rush to be gone, Julia wondered if her cousin knew something Tristan didn't. She remembered her early assumption that Tristan had betrayed his friend and was guilty of the scheme. Yet within a few days she'd come to accept his explanations though she had only his word that he'd fulfilled his friend's request. Had she accepted his explanations too easily? Was he guilty after all?

Cousin Renard will explain when we arrive.

Tom came around the corner of the house and Alice called, "Does Mr. Sheffield know we are leaving?"

"I found 'im." Tom said as he climbed up to sit beside the coachman. "All's clear."

Ned shut the carriage door firmly, then mounted his bay gelding. The carriage lurched and wheeled them away from the manor. They were off for London.

CHAPTER 14

Awareness returned in the guise of throbbing pain at the base of Tristan's skull. When he moved his head, the agony expanded through his temples and into his forehead. The pulsing waves threatened to overwhelm him, he struggled not to lose his breakfast. For a moment, he lay still and breathed in the scent of crushed grass and damp earth. Grit pressed into his cheek. The riverbank. He'd been about to return to the house with fish.

Moving with great care, he managed to roll to his side and sit up. Only then did he try to open his eyes. The hazy sunlight sent another stab of pain ricocheting around his brain. It did not surprise him to discover that he could not focus properly. He closed his eyes again and swallowed hard, still fighting nausea.

Taking a deep breath, he pushed himself onto his feet, then stood swaying until he found his balance and sorted his scrambled thoughts. *Betrayal. Julia has Alice. Danger.*

He reached up to touch the back of his head, sending another wave of pain through his brain. He encountered sticky, drying blood where he'd been struck. He winced as much from the mortification of betrayal by a woman he'd been foolish enough to trust as from the raw wound. Julia must have followed him and stuck him down. The moment he'd

115

been foolish enough to leave her alone, the damned woman betrayed his misplaced trust and undoubtedly escaped with the child. She kept her word not to carry Alice off into the night, then acted by day instead.

He called himself every kind of fool for ignoring his first assumptions about her. Experience had warned him not to trust his gut or that instinct driven part of him lower down. He'd shown her ways to avoid being noticed. He should have remembered how plain and mousey he'd thought her in Portsmouth. He taught her nothing she did not already know.

He stumbled, caught his balance again, and staggered back to the house. How long had he been unconscious? He tried to assess the shadows. Longer, but not much longer. Julia must have packed and taken Alice as soon as she had rendered him unconscious. With every determined step his thoughts sharpened until he was able to ignore the pounding agony in his head.

The front door hung open. Anger shifted to unease. Julia would not leave the door open. It made their escape *untidy*. She might be many things, but she was not careless. She needed control and order.

In the parlor, he found the doll, Harriet, lying on the set-tee along with scraps of cloth and sewing supplies. Alice had been engaged in making clothing for her doll, but had not been allowed to take it with her. That, too, did not fit. No matter what threats Goodwin had received, Julia had treated the child kindly. She would have permitted the child to take the doll no matter how quickly she made her escape.

A pattern of dirt on the carpet caught his attention. A man's dirty footprint. *Someone else was involved.* That explained the open door, and his aching head, but did not answer the question of Julia's role. Was the man her partner, her paramour, or her captor?

No one but Ravencliffe and their courier knew the situation, *unless* someone had intercepted Ravencliffe's inquiry to Summerfield or—incredible as it might seem—could the Earl of Summerfield himself have orchestrated an abduction of the girl after Ravencliffe contacted him?

But why would the earl do such a thing? To protect her? She was safer away from prying eyes. The earl was one of the most respected and acknowledged patriots of the realm. No, it couldn't be him. *Summerfield is fatally ill.* If not Summerfield, then someone on his staff must be working for the French. Any other scenario defied logic.

The earl must have delegated much of his correspondence to his secretary or some other such staff member, and wouldn't know of the plot, his cousin's involvement, or of the vile threat to the child. What of someone else in his household? Whoever that someone was, he must have seen the earl's letter, discovered Alice's location, and taken her into his control.

The deadline for Goodwin to provide the supply dates and routes was at hand—and they had both Alice and Julia. The throbbing at his skull pounded a steady cadence. Find-them, find-them, find-them...

RENARD'S MEN SET A rapid pace and, inside the carriage, Julia and Alice braced themselves against the jostling motion. Alice had gone quiet, her face pale and her eyes scrunched tight, Julia's heart went out to her. *Poor child.* The rough ride so soon after her traumatic experience must terrify her. Julia put an arm around her shoulders and hugged her to her side.

"The coachman is an excellent driver," she assured Alice. "We shall arrive safely."

Alice opened her eyes. "Where are we going?"

"To London, as Ned said," Julia told her. "Cousin Renard has a townhouse there and you will be safe until your Papa can come for you."

Renard spent all his time in London since he disliked the family estate where she had lived until her failed Season, and before she moved to the cottage. He rarely visited her when she was growing up, preferring to be in the city, which he called the lifeblood of England. Remembering the crowded, noisy streets, Julia wished he'd sent them to the estate instead. She had her own traumatic memories.

Renard had been greatly embarrassed and disgruntled at Julia's disastrous come out. Only days earlier he had informed her that intended for her to act as his social hostess once she was of age. But her infamous breakdown had ruined his plans.

Little as she had seen him before her Season, she saw him less frequently after her ballroom scene. Instead, he had corresponded through quarterly letters that arrived with her allowance and the occasional woman in need. She'd seen him only once in five years.

Alice gazed at her, her eyes reflecting her concern. "Will Mr. Sheffield come, too?"

"I don't know, though I doubt it." Julia admitted. She stroked Alice's hair to comfort her. "He knows my cousin will look after us. His job is done."

"I don't like Ned," Alice declared. "I like Mr. Sheffield better. I want to stay with him."

Julia could not blame the child. Tristan had taken great pains to keep Alice entertained and charmed. Ned was blunt and coarse and cared for no one but her cousin. She admired her cousin if not his employee, but Renard was not a demonstrative man and, though they would be safe, they would not be entertained. Considering her frustration and embarrassment during her confinement in Surrey, she would never have imagined it, but she thought she preferred staying with Tristan too.

They did not stop except to change horses and arrived in the outskirts of London as the last of the twilight faded into dark. When Ned opened the door to the carriage Julia immediately reacted to the foul sewer odor that filled the compartment. Though the noise outside the carriage had increased as they entered the city, the recent tenor of sound held a note Julia remembered too well. The docks.

"This is not Renard's townhouse," Julia protested. "Why have you brought us here?"

"You're not to stay at the townhouse," Ned announced. "You'll be stayin' here 'til Lord Summerfield sends for you or sends you away." He grinned and reached to pull her forward. "His lordship were displeased to learn you'd let the child be taken."

His grasp tightened and he pulled her out of the carriage with a sudden yank. Julia nearly lost her footing on the step, but managed to avoid crashing into Ned, though she thought that had been his intent. She pulled her arm from his grasp and sent him a warning look. "Renard has been disappointed in me before, but he will not tolerate disrespect."

She inspected the neighborhood and fought down sudden trepidation. She had no funds of her own, and the area was too dangerous for her and Alice to make their way to the townhouse on foot. If Ned did not allow her to redirect the coach to Renard's residence, she had no choice but to stay where Ned delivered them.

The narrow street lay between tenements and taverns. The building on the corner had the look of a brothel. Raucous music, drunken laughter, and arguments already filled the evening air. Had Renard been so angry that he would banish them here?

No. A gentleman would never—*her cousin* would never do such a thing. The kidnappers had threatened Alice with life in a brothel. Perhaps Renard wanted her to understand the conditions Alice faced if Julia failed her again. *That was it.*

"You may take us to Renard now," Julia told Ned. "He has made his point. I understand."

"I don't think you do understand." Ned smirked. "You are to stay here." He turned back to the carriage door. "Get out here, girl. Ride's over."

Truth hit her like an icy bath of water. Ned truly meant to leave them here.

When Alice didn't move, Ned lurched up and grabbed her. Alice cried out in alarm and Julia leapt forward. "What are you doing? Don't hurt her!"

He stepped back down, Alice's struggling body clutched tight against him. "Tain't nothin' hurt but her feelin's," he said. "Come along, both of you. Room's on the third floor."

"This can't be right," Julia protested again, truly frightened, now. "Take us to Renard right now, Ned. I must speak with him."

Ned smirked. Holding the wriggling Alice he glanced at his partner, "She don't get it, Tom. Looks like we got to convince her."

Tom dismounted. To her absolute shock, he lowered his shoulder and tossed her over it before she realized his intent. The sudden move knocked the breath from her lungs and sent blood rushing to her head. His arms clamped around her legs and he boosted her hips until she could do nothing but hang down his back.

She struggled, panic thrumming in her heart, but Tom held her tightly. She tried to kick free, but he'd locked his arms around her legs at thigh and calf. She tried to bite him but movement made it impossible to get a grip on his flesh. Julia swung an arm free and pounded Tom's shoulder, to no avail. He wasn't as large as Ned, but he was larger than her and had wiry strength.

He had entered the building and climbed the narrow, creaking stairwell. Inside the building, the sewer smells of the docks joined those of rancid food, unwashed bodies, and mold.

Terrified, Julia pounded his back again. "Put me down!" she demanded. "Put me down, I say!"

"Shut yer gob." Ned said. "You're to stay here 'til 'is Lordship says otherwise."

"If you bother to tell him," Tom muttered as he shifted Julia higher on his shoulder.

She twisted to catch a glimpse of Ned who followed behind carrying Alice, his hand over her mouth. Huge frightened blue eyes peered over his hand and Julia knew that Ned was responsible for the scheme to blackmail Alice's father. No matter what Ned said, Renard would not treat her this way, nor was he a traitor. He was ill and her cousin had been betrayed by the men he'd employed and trusted for years.

They reached the first landing and Julia noticed of the sounds that echoed through the halls. Babies cried, children squabbled and adults argued. As Tom started up the third flight of stairs, she heard a door open.

"Help!" she cried. "Help us! We are being kidnapped!"

The door slammed shut

Despair flooded her, drowning what little courage she had. Those who lived near the docks either perpetrated unsavory actions or hid from them. No other doors opened until they reached the third floor and Tom entered a cramped, cold room.

He strode through to a second, smaller room where he bent and dropped Julia from his shoulder onto a thin straw-filled pallet on the floor. The pallet did little to alleviate the painful thud of her head and back when she landed. She immediately scrambled upright, her wary gaze taking in the Spartan furnishings.

A cheap narrow table sat against the wall flanked by two hardback chairs. No rugs warmed the floorboards, and no curtains covered the lone window set high on the wall opposite the door to the front room. Instead of a wardrobe, a half a dozen pegs protruded from the wall beside the door. A chamber pot had been set in the corner, but no screen provided privacy to the room's occupants.

Ned shut the door and set Alice down on one of the chairs with the warning, "You keep quiet or I'll stuff a rag in yer mouth."

Julia scrambled to her feet. "Renard cannot know of your actions. He would never approve of this."

Ned and Tom exchanged a look then both burst out laughing. "I told you she never had a clue," Ned told him. "Stupid bitch thought she was helpin' poor unfortunates like her." He said the last words with a sarcastic falsetto.

"What do you mean?" Julia recognized the mockery, and his words had a sinister truth at their core.

Ned faced her with a nasty grin. "Why, that his Lordship would approve of this and a great deal more. Stupid woman, your cousin has been selling women and secrets for years."

CHAPTER 15

Tristan checked Alice and Julia's rooms before he went to his own. As he feared, their few personal items remained behind. Someone had directed their hasty retreat and Julia had not bothered with their things. He, on the other hand, needed to be prepared for whatever he found whenever he tracked them down. It would do him no good to rush into a situation that he couldn't control and he must gather his wits before he chased after them.

In his room, he sloshed water into a basin and washed the blood from the base of his skull, then he pulled out the bag he'd unpacked days before and filled it with the necessities for another trip across country. Portsmouth had plenty of brothels, but since Goodwin's family was known in town, he thought London the more likely destination. At least this time Tristan was heading into territory he knew well.

His head ached and his vision had not fully cleared, but if he hurried, he might be able to catch them before they disappeared into the warren of alleys known as Seven Dials, or worse, the docks. Grimly, he added a change of clothes for both Julia and Alice. If he didn't find them quickly, he would need to provide them with clothes. Brothel owners often stripped their victims so they could not escape.

He stopped long enough to write a note to Ravencliffe reporting his ambush and new suspicions. He would arrive in London before the courier picked up the message, but Tristan did not plan to stop at the Foreign Office until he had rescued the child a second time. *And Julia?* His head pounded and his gut tightened when he thought of her. That would depend on what he found.

His blurred vision and aching head protested any attempt to urge his horse at a canter, let alone a gallop, which meant he traveled only a little faster than a coach. As he rode, the temperature dropped and the threat of rain grew until it was soggy reality. Though not a downpour, the steady fall only made focusing on the road ahead an exercise in concentration that made his head ache even more.

Unfortunately, the pace didn't prevent his thoughts from dancing around Julia's role in the situation. The woman plagued him. Her actions and reactions appeared natural and honest, yet he couldn't be sure he'd not been deceived. Cousin or not, it might have been easy for her to take advantage of the earl's illness. She had spent time in London—long enough to know his staff, though not to complete her Season. Again, was she complicit or coerced in this scheme?

If she was complicit, he'd been a blind fool to trust her.

During his childhood, he'd witnessed many a procuress enticing the innocent into ruin through deceptively kind words and apparent assistance. Those naive young women who accepted aid were forced to work off their debts for food and lodging in the streets and brothels all over London. Few lived long.

Yet he could not bring himself to accept that Julia aided the traitors who threatened Lord Goodwin in order to sell secrets to the French. A procuress would not have blushed at standing bare naked in a public house, but Julia clearly blushed at the slightest provocation. A reaction he realized frustrated her and made her blush all the more.

Who was behind this? Would Julia face the same fate as Alice once she discovered the truth? How long before they were sold to the highest bidder? That thought made him kick his horse into a faster pace. He would not allow either of them to be so despicably used. He didn't have much time, but at least virgin sales did not take place until word circulated to those who would pay well for the chance to deflower an innocent.

He reached the city proper but the crowds of vehicles and late night darkness made it impossible to trace their progress through simple observation. Still hoping to locate them, he directed his horse into Seven Dials and to his childhood friend's establishment. Maisie took only women who had already entered the life, but she knew all too well who preyed on children and the naive. Through her, he would find out when and where any auction would take place.

As he made his way through the narrow streets, he breathed in the rank odors that hung like a fog of desperation in the air. The lingering whiff of burnt onions mingled with the sour smell of unwashed bodies, and poverty gave proof that some things did not change. In the darkening streets he did not need the sparse lantern light to guide him. He needed only to follow his nose. The familiar smells clung like grime to his memories of life before his father removed him to the pleasure of baths, clean clothes, plentiful food, and hope.

"Here, gov, you lookin' for a bit o'fun?"

Tristan glanced at the flaxen-haired girl in the bright red silk dress who spoke. He took in the softly rounded blossoming body, freckled cheeks, painted lips, and decided she couldn't be much older than Rowena, his thirteen-year-old half-sister. Too aware of the blunt facts of life to be shocked at her youth—child prostitution was, after all, what he was here to save Alice from—he pulled a coin from his coat pocket. "Not today, luv, but here's a shilling for your supper. Tell your protector I was well satisfied."

The girl caught the coin deftly, then looked up, her eyes revealing wary gratitude. "You know Davie?"

"No, just his type." With that, he tipped his hat and continued down the street.

Maisie's place was well lit and music spilled into the air whenever the door opened to let in a customer. The painted exterior of the three-story building, set between a gambling hell to the left and a dilapidated rooming house on the right, spoke of Maisie's determination to make the best of a life for which she'd had no choice.

Moments later Maisie, herself, enfolded him in a hug of greeting.

"Tristan! Lord love a duck! What brings you here? I know you've never needed to pay for female attention."

"It's good to see you, too." Tristan hugged her back and gave her a quick peck on the cheek before stepping back. "You look well."

Maisie's copper-red hair and hazel eyes gave her a singular beauty marred only by the long, slightly puckered scar that ran from her left eye to the corner of her mouth. The scar pulled the corner of her mouth into a perpetual half smile that she claimed shifted business dealings in her favor. Competitors never quite knew if she was serious in their dealings, but the fact that she had survived her knife-wielding assailant made others wary.

Maisie studied him. "You've been traveling hard," she said as she took his hand and led him to her rooms at the back of the house. "I'll pour you a brandy and you can tell me why you really came."

As soon as he explained the situation, Maisie called two of her own house guards to go around the city and listen for word of any new arrivals. Tristan stood to go with them, but a dizzy spell caused him to stagger back into the chair when he rose. Maisie declared he looked like a drowned rat who needed food and rest and insisted he let her men investigate for him.

Two hours later, the men returned, and Tristan left Maisie's house with the assurance that Alice was not yet at any of the child brothels in the city. Nor had a woman fitting Julia's description appeared with a child in tow. He now knew the names and locations of the establishments that traded in children, and Maisie had promised to send him word if any house announced a special event.

The mist still fell, but it served to clear the city fog and made his progress to his rooms in St. James Street easier. Once there, he sent an update on the situation to Ravencliffe before allowing himself a few hours of sleep. Come daylight he would expand his queries throughout the city and pray he found them. The city had far too many places to hide.

JULIA GAPED AT NED, unable to take in his shocking announcement. *Renard sold women and secrets? Impossible!* "I don't believe you," she told him.

"Don't matter what you believe, m'dear," Ned told her. "It don't change the truth." He jerked his head toward Julia and instructed Tom, "Tie her up while I take care of this 'un." He pulled a pair of cord lengths from his coat pocket and tied Alice's hands together. Alice made no sound, but her small body trembled and her gaze darted between the two men in obvious fear.

Julia gaped at Ned in horror, then realized Tom meant to follow Ned's instructions. She quickly dodged when he attempted to grab her. Desperate, she lunged to the side and rushed to the door, but Tom caught her before she could turn the handle.

"Oh, no, ye' don't." He grunted when Julia elbowed him in the stomach, but hung on to her arm, then secured the other one. He evaded her attempt to kick him and shoved her against the wall, pinning her so she was pressed into the corner and unable to do more damage.

Tom leaned in, forcing Julia deeper into the corner until she could hardly breathe, let alone fight him for her freedom. The more she struggled, the harder Tom pressed her into the wall. The sensation made her heartbeat race frantically, and she struggled against both Tom and panic.

The memory of Beatrice's voice crying out surfaced as it did in her nightmares but free of the fog of sleep. Then, too, someone had held her down so tightly she'd been unable to breathe. She realized Renard had been there, though she'd long buried that detail.

Beatrice hadn't simply disappeared. She had been taken kicking, and screaming warnings that had only confused five-year-old Julia. Those restricting arms had been clad in dark superfine wool and released whiffs of clove and citrus as they clamped against her. *Renard's favorite pomander.* With that realization came the memory of Renard's voice ordering Beatrice to be taken away, and she knew Ned hadn't lied.

Dear God in heaven—No! Trust, affection and gratitude shriveled into a cold ball of betrayal that threatened to choke her. *I will not allow him to take Alice, too.*

She swung her head back hoping to catch Tom off guard, but he only grunted and leaned in even closer.

Hot breath touched her ear. Tom whispered, "Don't fight this, m'girl, you can't win and you'll only hurt y'self more." He secured her wrists behind her. "That should keep ye."

"Why, Tom?" she asked him as he tightened the cording. Kicking him with trussed arms only meant she could not defend herself if he retaliated. "Why would you go along with this?"

"His lordship saved me from the hangman before takin' me on, and he pays me well." Tom said. He gave a final tug on her bonds and spun her around to shove her onto the other chair. "That'll hold ye."

Ned had secured Alice to the other chair with a rope around her middle, her hands tied in front but her feet anchored together against one of the chair legs. She sat with rigid posture, her eyes wide with apprehension.

"Don't worry, Miss Dorsey," she told Julia. "Mr. Sheffield will come." She shot an angry glance at Tom when he laughed.

"Not likely with a broken head," Tom said bluntly.

Julia's breath caught. "You killed him?"

"Last time I saw him he wasn't moving."

Alice slumped and fell silent.

Julia wished she had kicked Tom when she had the chance.

"Now," Ned told her, "Tom will guard you while I report to his lordship." He grinned. "Then we'll see if he plans for you to join little Alice, here, in paying the price for failing to meet his expectations. You're a bit longer in the tooth than your sister was, but a virgin's still valuable merchandise."

Julia ceased breathing and her stomach lurched. Beatrice didn't die? She hated the desperate note in her voice but she had to ask, "What did you do with her?"

He laughed and exchanged grins with Tom. He brushed the back of one finger along her cheek, and she fought not to flinch. "I took her to Aphrodite's Academy." He dropped his hand back to his side and turned away. "As to where she is now—only the devil knows. She's probably keepin' him company. I just collected my money."

Nausea threatened and Julia closed her eyes, willing the sickness to abate. *Beatrice.* Oh, dear, *Beatrice.*

Julia latched onto Ned's dismissive words. If she didn't die that night, she could still be alive. More questions whirled around her mind like the pools that sometimes formed in the oceans during storms. Had Beatrice escaped? Had she remained in the brothel? Despite the odds, had she survived? Fear and hope swirled madly, until she was left with just one cohesive thought. *Could she find her?*

She opened her eyes when she heard Ned and Tom cross the room and pass through the door to the front room. Julia caught a glimpse of a threadbare settee before the door swung shut followed by the scrape of a key turning in the lock.

Alice spoke, bringing her back to the present and their immediate problem.

"D-did they kill Mr. Sheffield?" she whispered. "Will they kill us, too?"

"I don't know about Mr. Sheffield." Dear Lord, she prayed not. He might drive her mad, but he deserved to live. She *wanted* him to live. "But I don't think they mean to kill us." Indeed, her cousin had other equally terrible plans for them. "We must try to escape, though. We shall not let villains such as these determine our fate."

Alice eyed Julia's bonds and then her own, then asked. "How?"

Julia tested the cords at her wrists, but the rope around her waist kept them pressed to the chair and the restraints did not give. "I'll have to think about it a bit."

Alice gave her a small, tentative smile. "So will I."

CHAPTER 16

Tristan had barely finished shaving when the brisk knock on his door warned him that Ravencliffe had received his missives. Maisie's minions knocked with their knuckles, Ravencliffe used his walking stick. He quickly did up the last button on his waistcoat. Now the serious search for Alice and Julia could begin.

His valet opened the door and Ravencliffe strode in without ceremony. Tristan wiped his face, then dismissed his man then took the seat opposite Ravencliffe beside the fireplace. "I'm glad you came quickly. We don't have much time to save them."

"Tell me what you know," Ravencliffe said tersely, "Leave nothing out."

At the end of Tristan's recital, Ravencliffe shook his head in frustration. "So we still don't know if it is Summerfield or someone who has access to his papers who is behind this. Nor are you able to absolve Miss Dorsey of complicity, to any reliable degree of certainty."

Tristan started to object, but Ravencliffe held his hand up to forestall him. "I know you think she has been misled and acted as unknowing accomplice, but you cannot say for sure."

"No," Tristan admitted. "I cannot prove my belief. However, in the days in which they were in my custody I observed her closely and came to believe that she truly did not act with malice. As it is, she accused me of being a false friend of Goodwin's when Alice recognized me."

Ravencliffe smiled at that. "Went for your pride, did she?" He waved his hand dismissively. "Not the first time a suspect tried to turn the tables during an investigation."

"No." Tristan bit out. "What hurt my pride was letting my guard down. They should have been with me. I should never have allowed them to remain in the house alone."

"You had no reason to believe anyone knew where they were. As you surmised, someone must have intercepted the message. My inquiry about Miss Dorsey alerted someone who acted swiftly."

"Can you get someone into Summerfield's house? We need proof if the crown has been duped for these many years by a traitorous Lord of the Realm or if someone has taken advantage of his illness."

"I have already done so. Summerfield's physician suggested a nurse be hired for his daily care after his last visit. At my request, he suggested Jane Dawes for the position."

"Excellent." Tristan knew and admired Mrs. Dawes. The daughter, then wife, of military men, she had followed the drum and learned nursing as a matter of practical course. The Foreign Office recruited her after she aided an ambushed agent, and nursed him back to health while hiding him from his attackers. Plain-faced, middle-aged and quietly efficient, she quickly became privy to untold secrets.

"I called on a childhood friend last night, and she will contact me if she hears of special offerings at any of the brothels. In the meantime, I shall make the rounds of the rooms-to-let and taverns in the area tomorrow. Gossip may reveal someone seeing a woman and child of quality in the Dials recently."

"Will you contact Lucien now you are in the city?" Ravencliffe asked.

"No. He knows I am on a mission." A flicker of guilt rose. Lucien had wanted him around for their half-sister's first Season. "Besides, my business will require visiting the more scandalous establishments of London, and you know how much he clings to respectability." Tristan knew Lucien still disliked the gossip Tristan's presence, or lack thereof, sometimes revived. "So long as I don't call at Wolverton House he can ignore any gossip that might arise should someone notice me around town."

Ravencliffe rose and took up his walking stick. "Then I shall not mention our meeting unless there is anything you wish me to tell him. We both attend Lady Ridley's garden party tomorrow."

"Only that I will see him when this mission is resolved."

JULIA AND ALICE SAT quietly for a while, but it was Alice who finally broke the silence. "Mr. Sheffield told me that people often underestimate the cleverness of little girls," she mused. "He said if I was ever in a bad place and scared, I should concentrate on what I could do and not on what I couldn't. For example, I can't use my hands, but I can use my teeth." She lifted her wrists to her mouth and began tugging on the knot that held the cords together. After a moment or two, she stopped and told Julia, "The knot is awfully tight, but I think I'll be able to get it loose."

Julia saw the gleam of hope that lit Alice's expression and had to admire her courage. Alice, too, had lost her family, had been taken from the people and places she loved, and was only a few years older than Julia had been when it happened to her, yet Alice had not turned coward. Watching the child tug at her binding while she, a grown woman, did nothing to free herself made her ashamed. And angry. And thoughtful. Courage flickered somewhere deep inside her. Tristan had told Alice that being underestimated was a tool she could use. He'd showed them several skills while playing games to keep Alice entertained.

She realized, now, that Tristan's lessons had been disguised precautions for this type of situation. Certainly he hadn't expected Alice would need his tricks while he guarded her, but a man in his position knew dangers could arise at any time and any place.

"Excellent, Alice. If my hands were not behind me, I would do the same thing." Julia glanced at the locked door and added, "Loosen them so we can release them when the time is right, but do not let Tom or Ned see how loose they are."

How long would it take for Ned to reach Renard's townhouse and return? What orders would Renard give him? Ned's claims didn't fit her view of Renard, but that flash of illusive memory of Renard's harsh words before Beatrice disappeared from her life...*How could she have forgotten that?*

Her skin prickled and she shivered to admit the unpalatable truth.

They needed to escape quickly. She assessed the night sky through the high window. Soon the streets of this neighborhood would fill with the revelries of drunken men and loose women. Once away from this room, she and Alice must find shelter as soon as they distanced themselves from the building. She had no money and she knew no one to whom they could turn for aid.

The scrape and click of the key turning in the lock gave them a moment's warning and Alice quickly dropped her hands to her lap. Julia turned her head to see Tom enter the room, a lumpy handkerchief in one hand and a mug in the other.

"Brought you a bit of supper," he said. He set the cloth and mug on the table and untied the bundle to reveal chunks of bread and cheese. "I broke them up a bit since I'll have to feed you. Ned warned me to keep you trussed up until he knows what to do with you."

"When will that be?"

"Depends on how His Lordship feels today. If it's a good day, Ned will see him tonight. If it has been a bad one, he'll be abed and Ned'll wait until morning. Bad as His Lordship's been lately, could even be another day or two."

"If he is so ill, how could he be part of this?"

"He weren't always sick," Tom said with a grunt. "And Ned takes care of everything nowadays."

Julia's stomach lurched to think of the others Ned had taken care of. How many others besides Beatrice? How many before he brought them to her on their way to ruin? She still could not quite believe Renard was part of this. "Then how do you know it isn't Ned and not Renard who is running things now?"

"His Lordship's no fool and neither is Ned. And it don't matter to me who's doin' what, so long as I get my share of the profits" He shot her a smug look. "Besides it ain't as though Ned and me ain't seen what's comin' since His Lordship had to turn the supply chain over to Goodwin. Yer cousin ain't got a lot of time left, and that's a fact."

He picked up a piece of cheese and offered it to Alice. "Here yet go, girl, eat up."

They ate in turns, Tom holding the mug of water for them to share. When they were through, he turned toward the door.

"Surely you don't expect us to stay seated in these chairs all night." Julia protested. "Can't you allow us to rest on the pallet?"

Tom glanced at the thin mattress and shrugged. "Ned didn't say nothing about keepin' you in the chairs. Don't see as how the pallet will be much softer, but I suppose you could lay down after you eat if you've a mind to."

Before he knelt to untie Alice from the chair he told her, "If you try to run or cause a fuss, I'll put you back on this chair, make no mistake."

Alice nodded in agreement, though she grinned at Julia when he turned his attention to the knots holding her feet to the chair. Julia shot her a warning look and the grin disappeared. He freed her from the chair, but left the bonds on her ankles before he lifted her up and settled her onto the mattress.

He did the same for Julia, though his hands slid with more familiarity over her while he worked. "Too bad there's such a premium on virgins," he muttered. "Else I'd get a bit of relief before Ned comes back."

He deposited her on the mattress beside Alice and stood back with his fists on his hips. "Might as well get some rest." A nasty grin widened his mouth. "I doubt you'll get much once you're sold."

He turned, exited the room with a brisk nod, then shut and locked the door.

The instant the key turned, Alice began gnawing at the cords again. Julia found it ironic that the child, not the adult, would be the one to free them from their captivity. Eventually, the cords loosened enough for Alice to free herself. As soon as she did, Julia turned her back to her and held up her own wrists. "Quick, untie me." After Alice's reminder of Tristan's lessons, Julia had realized that neither of the men who held them would expect them to know how to pick a lock with a hairpin.

Several minutes later, Julia put her eye to the key hole, praying Tom had not left it in the door. She could push it out from her side, but the clatter of a key dropping onto the plain wood floor would not go unnoticed. She almost wept with relief when she was able to look through to the front room.

Tom had draped himself over the settee and appeared to be taking his own advice to rest. If they dared wait until he was asleep they might be able to sneak out without taking that chance.

A few minutes later Julia heard a faint snoring that made her glad she'd made herself wait to see what Tom did. She reached up and pulled a pin from her hair and fashioned it into the shape Tristan had taught her. Taking a calming breath, she slipped it into the key hole and carefully manipulated it. After several seconds, a distinct click told her she'd unlocked the door.

She peered through the keyhole again to check that Tom had not stirred, then carefully opened the door. Raising her finger to her lips and then gesturing to their feet, Julia opened the door and they crept through and across the room. As soon as they reached the landing in the hall, she and Alice rushed down the stairs and into the foyer.

Rather than using the front door, Julia turned Alice to the back of the building and out to the narrow alley behind it. Outside, in the chill darkness, they found rain shower lent cover to their progress at the same time as it hindered their ability to see more than a few feet ahead. The cobbled streets gleamed with slick moisture and they had to tread carefully.

They reached the entrance to the alley and Julia peered into the street beyond. Only small patches of light penetrated the darkness in either direction, but there were more lamplights to the left, which led to the street facing the rooms where they had been held. Fighting her instinct to seek out light, she led Alice to the right, heartbeat matching the rhythm of their hurried footsteps.

CHAPTER 17

The persistent mist made Julia and Alice shiver as they felt their way along the building, away from the alley. Julia listened for tracking footsteps as they searched for a safe place to hide. At each door, Julia tried the latches, hoping to find one unlocked, but after traveling two blocks, they found no refuge. No one had crossed their path thus far, but Julia knew that females unescorted after dark were assumed to be light skirts. They could not continue to hope for an unlocked door. At the latest door, to what looked like an abandoned warehouse, Julia halted and reached for another hairpin.

The cold made her fingers clumsy. Determined to find shelter before Tom woke and discovered them gone, she worked the pin for several minutes before a faint click told her she had finally managed to unlock the door. Relieved and triumphant, she opened it and they slipped into the cavernous dark.

Inside, the walls stank of fish, rotted wood, and mold. Julia cautioned Alice to remain still and silent for several seconds while she listened for any other occupants. Tristan had told them of how orphaned children often banded together at night for safety—often breaking into abandoned buildings like this. Julia detected no movement or breathing other than their own so she took a moment to lock the door behind her, and, taking Alice's hand again, used the walls to feel her way further from the door.

When they reached the interior corner of the wall they traced their way back until Julia's foot encountered something solid. Tentatively, she took her hand from the wall to feel in front of her, trying to determine what blocked them. It took only a moment to realize it was a tightly bound bundle of hay. *Of course*, she thought, *Hay helps to keep the fish fresh until sold to the fishmongers each morning.*

Julia carefully explored and discovered several bundles lying against the wall.

"Climb onto the hay," she told Alice. "It will be warmer than the floor." She worked on one of the bundles, pulling until she loosened the hay from the ropes. At last she had enough to spread over themselves and ward off the frigid temperature of the night. They huddled together and, eventually, their shivering eased. Alice relaxed into sleep, but Julia remained awake. The situation was too much like her nightmares, the painful and frightening memories of violence and separation.

Why had Renard sent Beatrice away? Did she survive and live somewhere else? Julia shivered, the too-familiar loneliness chilled her more than the night air. Only Renard would know. Yet, if he was part of the scheme as Ned claimed, she dared not approach him to ask. But could she accept not knowing the truth now that she remembered that jumbled night when they'd arrived in England? Now that she knew Renard had lied? Tears gathered behind her lids. *Papa. Maman.* Her brothers Andre and Etienne. Gone so long, but their voices still visited her in her dreams. She blinked the tears away. She didn't know how, but if she escaped the perils that surrounded her and Alice, she would find some way to learn Beatrice's fate. To do either, she needed to formulate a plan. And she would need every bit of courage she could find.

They would have to leave the warehouse come dawn, but where could they go? Alice was the key to controlling Lord Goodwin, and the traitors gaining the information they wanted. Julia couldn't take Alice to any of Goodwin's friends. Ned and Tom would expect Julia to take her there, and that would make Alice vulnerable again.

Julia herself knew no one in London who did not also know her cousin, if they acknowledged her at all. Her disastrous behavior had made her persona-non-grata among the ton—as demonstrated by the message Tristan had received from his superior. *As confirmed by his superior's mother, Lady Ravencliffe.* Yes!

She didn't dare approach the Earl of Ravencliffe at the Foreign Office— again, her cousin would find out. But if they went to the earl's mother, Julia could contact Tristan's superior without giving away their presence to anyone connected to her cousin. Lady Ravencliffe might refuse to admit her since the countess had witnessed Julia's disgrace, but Julia could think of nothing else. She tucked Alice closer and pulled more straw over them. It shouldn't be difficult to discover where Lady Ravencliffe lived.

Despite her best effort, Julia dozed off only to wake with a start when the rattle of a wagon warned her morning had dawned. She gently shook Alice awake. "Come, Alice. We must leave before we are found."

They finger-combed their hair and brushed stay wisps of hay from their hair and clothes as much as possible. As she straightened their wrinkled clothing, Julia wondered if Ned had returned the night before or if he still might return this morning. She could not let Alice fall into their hands again.

When they were ready to leave, she knelt down and stared into Alice's eyes. "Tom and Ned may still be looking for us. If they see us or we see them, I want you to run as fast as you can and hide until they are gone. You remember how Mr. Sheffield taught you?"

Alice nodded solemnly.

"Though I pray we are not separated, do not wait for me to catch up. Find a shop and ask for direction to the Earl of Ravencliffe's residence. He is Mr. Sheffield's superior and will keep you safe. Go there as fast as you can. When you arrive, tell the butler who you are and that Mr. Sheffield sent you there for safety. I shall do the same." She hugged Alice to her and prayed nothing went wrong and that they would locate the earl's home together.

She stood and took Alice's hand. "Remember. If I let go of your hand—*run!*"

THE COLD WET OF THE day before had cleared and high billowing clouds sailed across blue skies by the time Tristan sauntered into the Gray Whale Tavern. He took a seat near the back and signaled the serving girl for a pint. Pools of lamplight eased the dark interior and the rich aroma of foreign tobaccos mixed with the sharp tang of ales and gin. The tavern's location made it a popular gathering place for both sailors and merchants, and the crowded tables meant he'd made a good choice for his investigation. Maisie's men would inform him if any word of Julia or Alice surfaced in his old neighborhood.

With Seven Dials under surveillance, Tristan hoped to rule out the docks where women often disappeared into the brothels—or illegally into ships bound for the slave markets of foreign ports. Until the tide allowed ships to sail tonight, he had time to scout the area and listen for gossip of trafficked goods. One thing his experience assured him was that gossip had no social barriers, and men in taverns were the worst of the lot.

He'd exchanged the casual clothes of a Surrey squire for the rough clothing of a dockworker again. No one paid him any attention as he surveyed the room.

Arriving home after months at sea, sailors took full advantage of the women working the dockside brothels. They also regaled each other with comparisons of the prowess and the skills of their favorites. Any new or unusual offerings would sweep through the tavern as quickly as a wave in a storm.

Jane Dawes had already sent word that Julia was not at Summerfield's townhouse. The cook, Mrs. Dawes had reported, let slip that two of the earl's footmen were missing from their posts, though she did not yet know if their absence was of any import. Tristan suspected it was. Someone had made off with Julia and Alice and he believed it was someone Julia knew. Either way, she had been rushed from the house. The question remained as to whether Summerfield knew of their actions or if someone else betrayed his name.

An hour later, he signaled the tavern maid for another pint. Sitting in a tavern waiting for some tidbit of information that might or might not come his way made him impatient and irritable. His instinct screamed at him to stride through every building along the quay until he discovered whether or not Julia and Alice were in the district. His intellect and experience told him to be patient and keep his ears alert to the gossip and conversations filling the room.

He fought his guilt for choosing to take time away from Julia and the aching awareness that plagued him whenever she came near. They would not be in the danger they were in had he kept them in sight the way he should have. Had he not allowed his personal comfort to take precedence over the child and woman in his charge, he would not have been caught off guard. In fact, Alice's chatter would have prevented him from drifting into the relaxed state that had left vulnerable to assault. Certainly Julia's presence would have kept him fully on alert.

Another hour passed before he caught the tail end of a sentence that made him adjust his seat and send a glance toward the speaker.

"–raised a ruckus, she did. Opened my door t'see what was what, but Ned shot me a look so I closed it quick. He ain't a man to interfere with."

The speaker sat with two other men at a table to Tristan's left. Rail thin with a bulbous nose and balding head, the man picked up his glass and took a swig.

"Ned's back?" This from the wiry, ginger-haired man who looked like a warehouse clerk. "He ain't brought no one to market for six months or more. Thought he'd given that up when 'is boss took sick."

"Naw. He weren't done, just set it aside for a bit." This from the third, and most muscular man of the trio. "He told me his boss had other more important fish to fry—and with better profit."

"Well, it looks like he's back to the game-pullet supply trade, and he's branched out. Had a little-un with him, too."

That made Tristan clench his fist around his glass.

"Never did like trade with little 'uns," the ginger-hair mused. "No tits or bush to raise my interest. There's more to swivin' than a poke."

That made the other two chuckle and agree.

"Speakin' of swivin'," the muscular one said. "What say we pay a visit around the corner when we're finished here? Plenty of tits and bush there."

"No time like the present," declared the bald man. They each drained their glasses and stood. "There's a buxom red-head there who knows how to give a man his money's worth."

"Hell, you fool," scoffed the ginger-hair as they wove their way past Tristan's table. "They all do."

TRISTAN ENTERED THE tall narrow building where he'd followed the bald man from the tavern, and after he left the brothel. Footsteps led him to the second floor where the sound of the door closing told Tristan the man had reached his rooms. No light showed from the windows and the building was almost silent. Someone had cooked fish earlier. And onions. The walls were thin enough he heard someone cough, but no one stirred.

The woman "who raised ruckus," surely Julia, had been on these stairs so the criminals and their captives must be on the third floor. He lit his miner's lamp, climbed to the next level, and carefully tried the first door at the top of the landing. Locked.

Time to pick locks after checking the entire floor. When he reached the second apartment, he found the door ajar. The room was empty, but footprints in the dust assured him someone had occupied it recently. His stomach lurched. They must have been moved on. To a local brothel? To a ship bound for a foreign slave market? Slavery might be illegal in England, but it was not forbidden in other lands.

He held the lamp a bit higher, and a glint beside the door revealed a woman's bent hairpin. Relief washed over him and his lips lifted into a wry smile. *Julia.* Only a pin twisted with purpose would take that shape. The one he'd shown her how to form.

Small footprints in the dust mixed with the larger ones further convinced him Julia and Alice had been held here. He carefully checked the rest of the space in the front room. There was no sign of struggle, but several lengths of rope lay on the floor. If they'd been caught, the ropes wouldn't have been left behind. They must have escaped, so where were they now? Julia knew the dangers women faced on the street at night. She would look for a place to hide until daylight, but where would they go come dawn? Her cousin's? Whoever had taken Julia had obviously been known to both her and her cousin. If her captors were employees of Summerfield, she would know better than to go there. Nor would she dare the Foreign Office. She was too clever for that. If they worked in Summerfield's home or office, as he was coming to believe, the kidnappers would easily discover where they were.

Tristan circled the block in a futile attempt to search for any clue as to which way Julia and Alice had gone. Intermittent rain-washed the street of any foot trace and there were too many darkened buildings to locate people hiding in the pitch-black night. He knew if he found sign, whoever had held them would have, too. The empty rooms convinced him Julia had succeeded in running to ground. But had she run into more trouble along the docks?

CHAPTER 18

Julia carefully scanned the crowd for their captors. Was Tom awake and looking for them? Had Ned returned? A low ground fog had risen with the passing of the rain, and she peered ahead, her heart beating quick time in her chest.

The rain from the night before hadn't lessened the rank odors from the river, nor had it washed away the grime embedded in the structures surrounding them. She checked around the corner of a narrow alley before leading Alice onto a broader thoroughfare. The wider street allowed more carriage traffic, and the rattle of delivery carts and the steady clop of horse's hooves on the cobblestones threatened to overwhelm her. She had conquered her fear of Portsmouth's streets, but London loomed larger and noisier.

The best way to hide, Mr. Sheffield had declared, was to make yourself fit in with the people around you. Julia noted that most walked swiftly as they accomplished their errands for their employers. Few dawdled, and those who did stood out from those who moved with purpose. Determination made her square her shoulders and stride down the street as though she and Alice had an appointment of import to accomplish. Swallowing her fear, Julia approached a young woman carrying a basket of fruit to ask the location of the Ravencliffe residence.

When they finally reached the address, Julia would have abandoned the quest if not for Alice. The great townhouse dominated the square with a bay window and lions atop the pillars on either side of the door. Julia might be a gentlewoman from a noble family, but it had been a long time since she had broached the exclusive environs of her theoretical peers.

Alice grasped Julia's hand a bit tighter, their bare hands nearly blue with the cold, and she remembered why she needed to take this step. The child needed a warm, safe place. Certainly, if the countess refused to acknowledge Julia, the woman would not leave Lord Goodwin's seven-year-old daughter unprotected.

Gathering her courage, Julia stepped to the door and released the knocker. She forced herself to stand straight with her hands at her sides her head held high.

The elderly butler who opened the door assessed them silently, obviously deciding if they should be sent to the servants' entrance or merely turned away without bothering the master or mistress of the house.

"Miss Julia Dorsey and Miss Alice Goodwin to see Lord or Lady Ravencliffe, if you please," Julia told him. 'It is a matter of some import."

The butler eased his stance a bit when he heard Julia's cultured speech, but he did not invite them into the foyer. "They are attending a function today. I shall give them your card if you would leave it."

Dismay washed through her. She had so depended upon Lady Ravencliffe to be home. She could not give up. They could not wander the streets until some unknown time when the earl or countess returned. Even if she did not fear being found by Ned or Tom, she and Alice were tired and hungry. If not for Alice, she would be at the end of her courage.

"I'm afraid I have no cards with me," Julia said with dignity. That made him stiffen again, and Julia said, "The child and I have been—" She stopped before revealing the details to a servant. Proper as he might appear, news spread through London through the servant connections ever faster than through the ton.

She shifted Alice to stand in front of her. "Miss Goodwin is in need of protection and a safe haven. We have no other place to go. If we may wait in a receiving room until either of them returns, I believe they will not object to finding us here."

The butler looked down his rather long nose at Alice. She returned the assessment, blue eyes wide with appeal. After a moment, he stepped back and widened the door to allow them in. "You may wait in the small parlor for their return."

As they followed him to the small receiving room, Julia's stomach rumbled loud enough to be heard all the way to the docks, and she felt the telltale heat of embarrassment wash up her neck and across her cheeks. The butler gave no sign he noticed, but soon after he left them, a young maid arrived with a pot of chocolate and a plate of scones.

During their wait, Julia assured Alice that the countess would welcome her once she knew of their presence. She answered Alice's questions about them as well as she was able. She remembered the countess had gently led Julia from the Barkley's terrace to a side room all those years ago, and closed the door in the faces of the avidly curious. Alice would be cared for properly.

But would she?

That selfish thought made her ashamed, but did not answer the question of what would become of Julia once the Foreign Office learned the truth about her cousin and took him into custody. His properties would be confiscated by the crown and Julia would need to find a way to support herself. She had no idea where to begin. Though he'd never been a particularly attentive guardian, Renard had lessened the void of family in Julia's life. Now, with her cousin's reported double betrayal and treason, the future threatened destitution. She had no one at all.

Unless Beatrice lived.

Ned said Renard sold women, had sold Beatrice. Despite her fears for Alice and worries about her own future, a tiny flame of hope burned and she vowed she would find a way to search out the truth.

The clock chimed the passing hours three times before Julia heard the butler open the door and greet Lord and Lady Ravencliffe as they returned from their afternoon out. Julia's heartbeat leapt and she clenched her hands into her skirts before smoothing the cloth again. Alice, finally warm and fed, had fallen asleep in Julia's lap.

She whispered, "Wake up, dear. They're here."

When the receiving room's door opened, they both stood. Lord Ravencliffe entered the room followed by Lady Ravencliffe. Her blond hair had a few more silver strands than Julia remembered, but her expression was as kindly as it had been when she had assisted Julia the night of the disastrous ball.

Julia curtsied. "I apologize for my unannounced arrival. I knew of no other place to go."

"Better that you had remained in Surrey," Ravencliffe said bluntly. Of similar height to Tristan, Ravencliffe had his mother's blond hair but none of her soothing manner. "Mr. Sheffield is searching the city under the impression you were abducted."

"We were." Relief surged through her. *Tristan lived.* "When the men arrived, I thought my cousin had sent his footmen to bring us to his residence." She studied the earl's face searching for some sign he believed her. "It was not until we were bound and locked into a room near the docks that I learned the truth. Bracing herself for his condemnation, she blurted, "The Earl of Summerfield is a traitor."

TRISTAN RELUCTANTLY returned to his rooms in St. James after searching in vain for Alice and Julia. When he arrived, he found a message from Ravencliffe instructing him to report to the earl's home for breakfast.

Tristan had never been invited to Ravencliffe's for breakfast in all the years he'd known the earl. He could only think of one reason why he would be now. A glimmer of hope lifted the tension he'd carried since discovering them gone. *Julia knew of Ravencliffe's role as Tristan's superior.* Had she found him?

Had it not been so late he would have chanced Raven-cliffe's ire and gone to see him immediately. He slept well, but was awake early.

Upon his arrival at the townhouse the next morning, Billings opened the door and immediately stepped back to allow him entrance. "Good morning, Mr. Sheffield. Every-one is in the breakfast room. If you will follow me?"

As soon as Tristan entered the room his gaze centered on Julia, and relief surged through him as did the usual jolt of desire. The yellow gown with the embroidered flowers had gained patches of dust that hadn't quite come clean, though he had no doubt the Ravencliffe maids had tried. He bowed to Lady Ravencliffe, then Julia and Alice. "I am glad to see you both looking so well."

"As I am to see you," Julia answered. Her cheeks flushed and her voice betrayed a huskier note than usual. "We were given to believe we would not see you again in this life."

He grinned at Julia, "I see you used your head for more than holding hair pins."

Tristan didn't notice Alice's impetuous approach until she collided with him in a joyful embrace. He looked down to see her blond head pressed against his middle, her blue eyes shining up at him. "Oh, Mr. Sheffield! I was so worried about you!"

He ruffled her hair. "The feeling was quite mutual, I as-sure you."

"If Alice will free you to move," Ravencliffe said from his place at the head of the table, "I suggest you tell John Foot-man what you would like on your plate and take a seat. After breakfast we shall adjourn to my study to discuss how best to deal with what we now know."

Alice released him and returned to her chair, but not before grinning at him in satisfaction. "Miss Dorsey is awfully good at picking locks."

Julia turned a bright red and Lady Ravencliffe laughed. "I fear," Lady Ravencliffe said with a chuckle, "that you have corrupted Alice's sense of propriety, Mr. Sheffield. She is quite proud of the skills she and Miss Dorsey gained while in your care."

They finished breakfast soon after and, when they rose to go to the study, Lady Ravencliffe took Alice to the nursery where they were to await Lady Ravencliffe's modiste. Lady Ravencliffe had insisted that both Alice and Julia must have new clothing as soon as possible, and sent word to Madam Fochet within an hour of their arrival the day before.

In the study, a room done in dark wainscoting with dark green carpet and lighter green walls, Tristan saw Julia seated in an ornate Queen Anne chair. Ravencliffe took an overstuffed chair near a brightly burning fire, and Tristan paced between them, frowning, angry, listening for clues to track down her abductors.

Julia repeated the events of her abduction.

In turn, Tristan told them his story. When he finished, he turned to Julia. "Could Ned have acted in your cousin's name to cover his own misdeeds?" Tristan asked. "He could have had access to Summerfield's papers."

"No," Julia furrowed her brow and caught her lip between her teeth before lifting her gaze to meet his. "He is completely loyal to Renard. If he had access to papers he shouldn't have, Renard likely gave them to him. Ned has been with Renard for as long as I remember," Julia said. "I never liked him much, but he was absolutely loyal to my cousin, so I ignored my feelings." She clasped her hands together and caught her lower lip in her teeth, adding, "Tom did say something that makes me think Ned does more than follow orders."

Tristan had suspected as much. "What do you know about Tom?"

She thought for a moment, then said, "Tom started working for Renard when I was ten or eleven. I never noticed him much since he was a lower footman at the townhouse. He was in and out along with Ned and never spoke to me. When he tied me up, I asked him why he went along with the abduction, he told me Renard saved him from the hangman—and paid him well."

"Mrs. Dawes says the head footman, Ned, returned but left again early the next morning after the lower footman arrived." Ravencliffe glanced over at her. "That was probably when Tom reported you and Alice had escaped, because Ned left immediately. No one at the townhouse has seen either of them since."

Tristan's brows lowered and his nostrils flared. "It is time to confront Summerfield and discover if he is as involved as Ned claims."

Julia said, "When you interview Renard I must come along. I have remembered the night my sister disappeared." She crossed, then uncrossed her arms before turning emotion-dampened eyes toward Tristan. "Renard sent Beatrice away, she was not taken by random men." She shook her head as though to deny her memory. "She screamed at me to run—and I ran—but I tripped and hit my head when I fell. The next thing I knew, I was in the carriage with Renard. I was confused and frightened... and believed him when he said she was dead. But now I don't know what to believe." Tears fell unheeded down her cheeks. "Did she really die? Did Ned tell me that to be cruel? What if what he said is true and she is still living like that? I need to know."

He hated to crush her hopes, but truth was often brutal. "After what Ned told you of your cousin's activities, it is likely true. Are you sure you want to know?"

"She is my sister!" Julia declared. "How could I not want to know?" Her ready flush blossomed though she did not back down. "If she was forced into a disreputable life it was through no fault of her own. I must know. I must find her. Even if all I find is a grave."

Her green eyes glistened with tears and Tristan had to resist the urge to gather her into his arms to console her. He recognized the need to pursue elemental answers. He'd had needful questions, too. He had needed to know who his father was though his mother had refused to name him until her death, and he understood the questions that left one isolated and incomplete.

He cherished his half-siblings and the sense of haven they gave him despite the difficult time he'd had adjusting to a life so different from his early childhood. Julia deserved a haven, too. But, if Beatrice lived, would her sister want to reestablish their relationship? There was no way to know how life had changed the girl of Julia's childhood. Life was rarely kind or fair.

Julia clutched her skirts, kneading the cloth in agitation, and her voice revealed the frustration held in check. "I need to talk to Renard myself."

A knock on the door announced the footman with word from Lady Ravencliffe asking if Miss Dorsey would be much longer as her modiste had arrived with sample gowns from her shop.

"Tell my mother Miss Dorsey will be there shortly." Ravencliffe told him before turning back to Julia. "My mother maintains that a well-dressed lady has the power to prevail in matters that demand strength of confidence. As we are clear with what must be done, I suggest you allow her to provide you with the tools you need for confronting Summerfield."

CHAPTER 19

Julia assessed herself in the mirror. Lady Ravencliffe was right. The blue and green striped muslin sample dress the modiste had altered for her immediate use made her feel confident that she could demand answers from her cousin.

The fine clothes provided during her failed season had been packed away long ago, and she'd chosen simple and practical clothes for life at the cottage. Had she been of a mind to follow fashion she could have done so, but other than a few dresses for church and trips to Portsmouth, she had paid little attention to her wardrobe. And, of course, she'd been hurried from Tristan's home with only what she'd worn that morning. The yellow dress was now quite ruined.

The maid Lady Ravencliffe had assigned to Julia dressed her hair in a new style that made her look less severe. Her maid at home, Molly, was a dear, but she was country trained and had not the skills of the young woman today who had drawn her hair into side curls that softened the thin angles of her face. She almost didn't recognize the woman who gazed back at her.

What would Beatrice look like now? If she found her, would Julia recognize her? She'd had deep brown eyes like their father and that faint dimple in her chin with a deeper one at the corner of her mouth when she smiled. Did she still get hiccups when she laughed too hard? Did she have anything to laugh about? Did she—

"Oh, you look lovely," Alice said from the doorway.

Julia turned to see that Alice also wore a new dress. Her tussle with the knots had loosened her front teeth and her tongue played across them, making them shift. Julia saw, too, that Alice wore the sides of her hair pulled back and tied with a pink ribbon in addition to the superfluous hairpins that the child had tucked into the sides. "So many pins," she teased. "Surely you know you will not be locked into a room by Lord or Lady Ravencliffe."

Though she smiled, Alice's eyes were solemn when she said, "Mr. Sheffield said one must be ready for any eventuality at any time."

"I don't suppose keeping extra pins in your hair is of much consequence, if it makes you will feel better." Julia knelt and hugged Alice, then whispered, "But now you are here you need not worry. Neither Tom nor Ned know you are here, and someone will be with you at all times until those responsible are brought to justice."

There was a light tap at the door before the upstairs maid assigned to Alice said, "Mr. Sheffield has arrived, miss." She held out her hand. "Come along, Miss Alice. Mr. Sheffield is waiting for Miss Dorsey."

Julia stood and adjusted a pin in Alice's hair that had slipped loose. "It is fine to be prepared, dear, but do not borrow troubles before time." She reached for her bonnet. "Enjoy yourself. Stay with Nan, and I shall be back soon." Julia took a deep breath, her stomach tightened and her confidence slipped as she donned her pelisse. If only courage could be donned so easily.

At the base of the stairs, Lady Ravencliffe waited with Tristan and her son. "My dear, you look ravishing." She turned to the gentlemen beside her. "Did I not tell you she would?"

"You did, indeed, Mother," Ravencliffe agreed. "You are rarely wrong about such matters."

"I know." She beamed at her son, then at Julia. "It is a gift."

Tristan stepped forward, bowed over her hand and murmured, "Current fashion suits you well, Miss Dorsey."

Once she and Lady Ravencliffe's maid took their places on the carriage seat across from him, Tristan studied Julia for several seconds before asking, "Are you sure you want to confront him yourself?"

"I do not really wish to confront him. I confess I am a terrible coward. But I have to do this." She clasped her hands together, determined to keep her nerves under control. "I need to watch his expression. I need to hear him say it. I need to know."

"When did you last see him?"

"When I reached my majority and he permitted me to move to the cottage." Tristan frowned and Julia explained. "I could not return to society. I embarrassed him greatly."

"He cut you out of his life for giving in to your fears?" Tristan's brows creased and his nostrils flared. "You were barely out of the schoolroom."

"He did not cut me out of his life," she countered. "He wrote to me regularly. He settled a quarterly allowance on me and let me make a home at the cottage. He had long assured me I would marry one day," conflicting emotions made her stop and looked out the window. "Though that was before..."

She turned to face Tristan before leaning back against the padded seat. "I am not sure how I shall face him again... particularly now that I know of his deception, but I shall."

When the carriage pulled up in front of Renard's townhouse near Cavendish Square, Julia viewed the great mansion with a profound sadness. Renard had never been a demonstrative man, but she had admired the man she thought he was. She had believed him to be a man who held his emotions close to his heart, but had never doubted those emotions or that she held a place in them.

How could Renard have ordered her sent to a brothel because she had failed to keep Alice with her at the cottage? Worse, how could he have planned such a fate for young Alice? It haunted her to think of the many young women she'd sheltered for him over the years—women Ned claimed he had sold into a life of shame as she now feared her cousin had sold her sister.

"Are you ready?" Tristan asked.

She nodded and allowed him to assist her to the street. Inside her gloves, her hands were cold as winter ice.

Renard's longtime butler showed no surprise at seeing Julia when he opened the door, though he'd not seen her since her disastrous debut. Instead, he bowed and welcomed her and Tristan, then directed a footman Julia didn't recognize to take the maid to the servant's hall to wait. After taking Tristan's hat and coat, he led them up to Renard's bed-chamber.

Each step upward flooded Julia with memories of her short time in London. Though she had lived at her cousin's country estate until leaving the schoolroom, she had taken up residence here in preparation for her Season. It had been a time of excitement and anticipation. Renard had arranged for a companion to see to her wardrobe and dancing lessons. He had acted as her partner on occasion in order to test her skills. He had spared no expense on her behalf. How could such a generous guardian be the scoundrel and traitor Ned claimed him to be?

When they reached the second floor, she caught a whiff of stale air and the taint of the sickroom. Someone had placed bowls of rose petals and spices around the hallway in an unsuccessful attempt to lessen the sour odor of illness. At the butler's knock, the door opened to reveal a slightly plump woman of middle age. She curtsied to Julia and nodded her head to Tristan.

Julia reassessed the effectiveness of the rose petals when she entered the room. The curtains had been opened wide to let in the spring sunlight but the windows remained closed, trapping the foul air.

In the years since she'd last seen him, Renard's solid frame had thinned to a brittle cage of narrow bone and flesh. His once noble features had turned dour and he lay, frail and emaciated, beneath thick quilts and propped against stacks of pillows. What was left of his brown hair had turned white and his flesh stretched over his bones like wet cloth. He looked to be nearly double his fifty years. How much of his alteration, she wondered, was the disease and how much the cost of treason?

Julia stood back until Tristan explained that the Foreign Office had reason to believe someone connected to the earl was selling secrets to the French.

"Are you aware of anyone whom you might suspect of this?" Tristan asked. "Your head footman, perhaps?"

Renard regarded him with a look of disgust. "Ned is a servant, loyal to me alone. He hasn't the imagination or connections to sell secrets."

"Are you sure?" Tristan questioned. "He recently abducted Miss Dorsey and Lord Goodwin's daughter. He told Miss Dorsey you sold secrets and women and claimed to be acting on your behalf. Is that true?"

"Did I not just say he was my man? I give him certain freedoms with the women, but he follows all my orders before implementing his own actions."

"Then you admit you have traitorously provided secret information to the French?

"I am a patriot, not a traitor." He stared at Tristan, his expression defiant and proud though his thin voice barely carried across the room. Gone was the firm baritone Julia remembered. "Nor do I suffer servants or petty clerks to take credit for my efforts." His lip curled in contempt. "Our king has lost his senses and his son is a fool, while Bonaparte is a brilliant commander whose mind is sharp and who knows how to control his country. It is my patriotic duty to help bring order to this land."

Julia stared, aghast to hear his praise for the monster who threatened the world with his greed for power. Who was this stranger? How could he have taken her into his care, educated her, fed and clothed her, even given her a home where she felt safe—yet turn his back on his heritage and the country of his birth?

Tristan cleared his throat, then asked, "Does that mean you are the one who demanded Lord Goodwin provide you with the dates and routes of troop supplies? That you ordered your man to ambush the Goodwin carriage in order to force his hand?" His voice hardened. "Do you admit you are responsible for the death of his wife and infant son, then ordered the abduction of his daughter?"

"Bunglers." Summerfield's mouth turned down. "The heir was more valuable than the girl." He shot Tristan a hard look. "Had it been the boy, Goodwin would have complied immediately."

Renard turned his head toward Julia. She flinched at the bitter anger that burned, vivid and unmistakable in his eyes. "Got away, did you? The brat, too, I suppose."

His breathing shallowed and strained wheezing filled the room. His nurse started forward, but he waved her off. "Incompetent idiots!" His hand curled into a fist before he glared back at Tristan. "And yet, you think I would trust a servant with saving England?"

He choked on another bout of coughing. When he could speak again he said, "If Ned had done his job he'd have sold the brat in Portsmouth so Goodwin would know his daughter's fate." He returned his attention to Julia. "The one you should have shared with her."

"Why?" she asked. The question rose simply and painfully to her lips.

"Why?" His voice though thin, still had the strength of conviction. "Because our country needs a leader, not a madman or lecher. Napoleon knows how to lead."

"I did not mean the treason," Julia said. "I meant why would you betray me? You saved me from the Terror. You *raised* me." She stared at him and a great yawning emptiness threatened to overwhelm her.

"Because you failed me—twice," he said bluntly. "You were to be my hostess." He raised a shaking hand, pointing at her before forming a fist and bringing it down on the bed with all the force he retained. "You were to take the role your mother should have filled, but your disgraceful exhibition ended that."

Another fit of coughing shook him and he lifted a blood stained handkerchief and wiped fresh blood from his mouth. When he recovered, he eyed her in obvious disdain. "Then you let this Foreign Office flunky," he tipped his head toward Tristan, "take the child despite my warning to keep her close. *Twice*." He wheezed. "Twice you failed me."

"What does my mother have to do with this? Julia felt the hairs on the back of her neck rise. His illness must be affecting his mind. Perhaps that explained his actions. "She died in France nearly twenty years ago."

"But she grew up in England. We were neighbors and I loved her." He stared at her. "I had everything planned. Halfway through her Season I would officially court her. We would marry in June." His mouth turned down and his voice turned bitter. "Then my cousin, your father, came for a visit and stole her from me." His eyes burned with anger. "He stole her from me and took her to France."

Julia's breath caught. This was not the man she'd known and trusted. Her stomach knotted into a twisted ball of grief.

"But once the troubles started, I knew how to get her back." Frustration colored his words and lent strength to his voice. "Life in France had become dangerous for a man of his rank and he sent word that he planned to bring Elise and their family to England. I, of course, agreed to help him." His grin made Julia shudder. "For after all, I was his cousin."

He wheezed, and Julia realized he laughed at the irony.

"I made all the arrangements and sent him word of when to meet me. I gave him explicit instructions. Elise was to be sent ahead while your father brought your belongings along a different route." Again, he paused to catch his breath. When he finally spoke, his voice took on a desperate quality. "Elise should have been with me when the crowd caught your father in the street." Lost in his memories, it was as though he talked to himself. "She would have been safe with me."

Julia's hands clenched. *Dear God.*

Renard refocused on Julia, and the chill that had enveloped her as he described his actions turned to ice. His eyes burned with fanatic glee as he described how he had destroyed her family.

"I'd planted a man in the crowd to lead them along your father's route and point him out to the crowd. But I didn't expect Elise to refuse to separate from your father." His fist pounded the mattress again. "If she had followed the plan she would not have died.

"Instead, I was stuck with his spawn." He pointed at Julia again. "I wouldn't have had to depend on *you* to take her place." His arm dropped down at his side and his voice became querulous. "*She* would not have failed me."

Julia starred at the older man in horror. Renard had planned it all. He'd directed the crowds, he'd sold her sister, he'd destroyed her life—*all their lives.* The knot in Julia's stomach grew until it filled her throat with anguish. *Papa! Maman! J'regrette!*

Another coughing fit interrupted Renard's angry tirade. Mrs. Dawes stepped forward and exchanged his saturated handkerchief with a clean one. He took it but ignored the nurse to continue. "Elise should have married *me.*" He fixed his glare on her and pounded the bed again. "You should have been *my* child."

"But what of Beatrice? Why—?"

"She was her father's whelp."

He wiped his mouth again. "She looked like him with her dark eyes and that cleft chin. The sight of her made my stomach turn."

He met her appalled gaze. "But you looked like Elise. You had her green eyes and that charming smile. It was clear you were meant to take her place in my life. You had only to grow up to be my hostess, you would mother my children. But you proved yourself to be as unfit as your sister. You had none of Elise's grace in company. After all I'd done to prepare you for life as my countess, you failed me."

Julia could only stare, stunned and incredulous, at his revelations. He felt no guilt, harbored no shame. He'd groomed her, from the age of five, to be his countess.

His countess?

She'd known he intended her to act as his hostess once she was of age, but had never once supposed he saw her as his wife. He was madder than the King.

A tremor rose deep inside, shaking loose the knot of grief and unfurling determination. "What did you do with Beatrice?" she whispered. "Is she truly dead?"

"Not by my hand," he shrugged. "Though it is probable."

Fury melted the ice that had held her still during his tirade. Her voice gained volume and strength as she demanded, "What did you do with her?"

"I had Ned sell her to a dockside brothel."

It was true. "Is she still there?"

"I know not, nor do I care. She had no part in my plans."

She stared at the man who had destroyed her family without a qualm. He had betrayed his own cousin—her father—in order to claim her mother. He felt no guilt. He harbored no shame.

Deep inside, the tremor rose, spreading from her core and through her limbs until she feared she'd crumble to the floor. But she would not allow Renard to see how his accusations and boasts tore away the last threads of her manipulated loyalties. She would not let him win again.

"I do not know you." She whispered in loathing.

She stepped closer to the bed, her posture straight and tall. "You are not the man I thought I knew. I do not wish to know your fate, nor do I wish to remain here any longer." She turned abruptly and strode across the room to the door.

Halfway there, Tristan's warm, steady hand took hers and placed on his arm. She did not look at him, fearing she would break down at the sympathy she knew she would see in his eyes. Instead, she gave her cousin one last sorrowful look. His misguided obsessions in both patriotism and love had made him a monster. She stared blindly forward as Tristan led her from the room.

CHAPTER 20

Julia's hand on his arm trembled, though her regal posture hid the conflicting emotions that must be tearing her apart. Tristan guided her away from the man who'd betrayed both country and family. He would make sure she never had to deal with Summerfield again. It pained him that Julia had defended her cousin so staunchly throughout their time together and had never doubted his honor. Her cousin's revelations had ripped away all her illusions, and Julia's chalk white features reflected exactly how devastated his revelations had left her. Yet she held on to her dignity in spite of Summerfield's caustic rant.

She was magnificent.

Now that he did not have to temper his reaction to her, Tristan admitted he admired her more than anyone he knew. From the moment he'd tackled her in the mud, she'd held her own against him and their circumstance. She bent under the forces she could not change, but did not break, even when her world crashed around her once again.

He hated the unfairness of it all, though he knew better than to expect life to be fair. Equally unfair was knowing the bitter man's title and illness would save him from the hangman.

Tristan knew Julia considered herself a coward for avoiding notice and fearing crowds, but he had seen her courage in so many ways. She had chased him to defend Alice, she had stood toe to toe with him in his demands, she had saved herself and Alice from her cousin's henchmen... He respected her strength of character.

She proved her courage again when they settled into the carriage moments later. Her green gaze focused on him, and he saw the depth of her conviction and determination. "I must find what happened to my sister. How do I go about tracing her?"

"After all this time it may prove impossible."

"True." Her brow furrowed and her mouth turned down. "But I will have tried."

"Very well." He understood the need to know the truth. It had driven him from childhood. Yet when he'd discovered the truth about his father, it had been far different than he'd supposed. He had been fortunate that the truth had been better than he'd expected. He feared Julia's truth would be worse. "Once this mission is resolved, I shall undertake the task so long as you realize the results of such a search may prove less than savory."

"I doubt the results will prove worse than the truth about my cousin," she challenged him. "Particularly as he is responsible for whatever we find." With a quick glance to her left at the maid, Julia continued, "For I shall want to be part of the search. I do not mean to leave the hunt to others."

The young maid gave no sign of listening to the unusual discussion, but Tristan knew the servant grapevine would soon be buzzing with interpretations of their less than cryptic conversation. If word spread that Julia searched the flesh markets for a sister, she would never recover her station in life, even if society accepted that she'd not been part of Summerfield's treason.

"That would be most unwise," Tristan argued, "The areas to be searched are dangerous—and far too crude for a lady of gentle upbringing.

"Had my cousin prevailed, I would have been fully exposed to it." She snapped. "Do not think to leave me at home"—she stopped abruptly. Her skin took on a green cast and she swallowed hard. Her bravado faded. "The crown will confiscate the cottage along with all of Renard's other properties. I have no home in which to remain. Nor have I any funds of my own." Her lips tightened and her voice harshened once more. "It is likely I face an equally unpalatable future, myself."

"You will not," Tristan declared. "If you have no place to go, my brother's family will provide you with one."

"Why would they do such a thing? They don't know me."

"My brother avoids scandal, it's true. But my foster mother doesn't fear it, nor would she permit anyone to be left without protection through the actions of others."

"Your foster mother may be a compassionate woman, but that doesn't mean she'll take the relative of a traitor into her home."

"She took me in," Tristan told her.

That caught her attention and she tilted her head.

"I am a bastard," he said bluntly. "To be precise, I am the late duke's bastard."

Her eyes dilated and she caught her breath.

"And it is not done to take your husband's illegitimate son into your home to raise with his legitimate children—but she did. That is how I know she will not hesitate to offer you a respectable haven."

The carriage arrived at Ravencliffe's home and Billings himself opened the door as soon as it stopped. Alarm replaced Billings' normal unflappable demeanor and his voice revealed his agitation. "There is an emergency. Lord and Lady Ravencliffe await you in the drawing room."

Julia leapt down and rushed up the stairs to the townhouse without waiting for help. Tristan caught up with her as they hurried to the upper floor. Several maids, their eyes wide with apprehension, watched them pass. The doors to the drawing room were open, in obvious anticipation of their arrival.

Lord Ravencliffe stood beside the tall windows overlooking the street when Julia and Tristan entered the room.

"Alice is missing."

Lady Ravencliffe stood with Nan, the young maid charged with the Alice's care.

Nan turned toward Julia and Tristan, her eyes red and tear-swollen. "We never left the garden." She trembled and her lips quivered. "Miss Alice was telling me about the kittens in your stable when this great hulk of a fellow dropped down from the garden wall, grabbed her, and was gone afore I could blink."

"Does that describe Ned or Tom?" Tristan asked Julia.

"Ned." she assured him. "He is taller and more solidly built than most men. Tom is shorter and leaner." And loyal as Ned was to her cousin, he was not as stupid as Renard thought.

But how did he know where to find Alice?

The answer wasn't difficult to work out. It made sense that since Ned had run errands for the earl for so many years. No one would think twice if Lord Summerfield's man asked about the lord who'd replaced the earl, or to reveal that Ravencliffe had sent his condolences.

She suspected Ned would take pleasure in proving his loyalty to Renard one more time, while lining his pockets as much as possible, then escaping London. Ned was not the misguided madman her cousin had become. He was mean-spirited and greedy.

Retaking Alice proved Ned's determination to fulfill Renard's plan. Tom had indicated Ned was prepared for when Renard succumbed to his illness, and he lost his position. Would he contact Goodwin again, or would he simply sell the child out of spite?

Julia's heart hammered in her chest. Ned had Alice and this time he would not wait politely for the deadline set by her cousin.

"He won't take Alice back to the rooms where you were captive," Tristan said. "But he was known at the Gray Whale. I'll go there again and see if anyone knows other places he frequents." He exchanged a grim look with Ravencliffe before turning back to Julia. "Do you know how Ned came to work for Summerfield? When he began working for him?"

"He was already in my cousin's employ when Renard brought me to England, though he was promoted to footman soon after I arrived. I remember, because the housemaids whispered about how grand he looked in his livery. He was not yet twenty, but was already of solid build."

"That would put him in his late thirties today," Ravencliffe said. "Is Tom of similar age?"

"He is a little older."

"What of hair and eye color, or any other features that stand out about them?"

"Ned has dark hair and eyes and regular features..." Julia shook her head, not knowing how else to describe him. "Tom has lighter hair though I never noticed his eyes." The truth hit her and she took a quick breath. "I must go with you. I am the only one who knows what they look like."

"Respectable women do not frequent taverns, Miss Sheffield... particularly at night. I shall go alone."

"We have established that my association with my sister and traitorous cousin put the opinion of my respectability in question. I shall go with you."

"You will not."

"I shall."

THE HACKNEY COACH NEARED the Gray Whale Tavern and Tristan turned to Julia. "Are you sure you are ready for this?"

"Yes." Julia's response was firm and her low voice stroked his senses as it always did.

Much as he had argued against it, Julia had prevailed in her determination to be a part of the search for Summerfield's men. As she'd pointed out, many men fit Ned and Tom's general descriptions, but only she could identify them.

Lady Ravencliffe had been aghast at the idea of Julia mingling with the patrons of a common tavern, and Tristan had been blunt in his description of the indignities she would face in the night streets of the docks. But she would not be deterred. Finally, Tristan had given in and done his best to prepare her for the task, including the procurement of a frock to help her blend in.

The hackney stopped and, with renewed concern for her fear of crowds, Tristan assisted Julia down to the streets. The pungent mix of brine, beer, and grime filled the air and all manner of refuse clung to the cobbles of the dockside street.

The Gray Whale was popular with the locals and already the crowd spilled out into the streets. The flaxen-haired girl he'd seen days before now hung on the arm of a bull of a man. His features, however, were course and irregular. *Not Ned.* Several men eyed the girl appraisingly, but a glare from the big man warned them to keep their distance.

Julia stood beside Tristan, dressed in a gown he'd found at a second-hand market. Beneath her shawl, she revealed an expanse of bosom that would make any courtesan proud, a bosom that captured his attention and added to his concern for her safety. Lady Ravencliffe's maid had arranged Julia's dark hair in a loose style that softened the sharp planes of her face and made him want to see it cascading down her back free of the pins that held it in place. *As would every other man who saw her.* He would need to stake his claim as firmly and clearly as the big man to avoid challenges from the other patrons of the tavern.

"Come along, then." He took her arm to lead her through the gauntlet of men looking for a good time. Inside, he located a space at a long table for them to sit and ordered two tankards of ale.

When the tavern girl delivered the tankards, Julia took a tentative sip, then made a face. "It is dreadfully bitter!"

"Pretend to enjoy it," he warned. "I doubt you'd like gin any better." He put his arm around her and surveyed the crowd. "See anyone you know?"

She tensed against his arm for an instant, though he'd told her they would need to appear intimate lest the patrons think her available for casual dalliance. To his surprise, she relaxed her body and leaned her head on his shoulder while her gaze darted around the room. "Not yet," she murmured into his ear. "Though I believe the man in the corner over there is the one who shut his door rather than help me."

Tristan followed her gaze and spotted the man whose conversation had given Tristan the clue where to look for Julia and Alice days before. One reason he'd chosen to return to the Gray Whale this evening was that the man had known Ned by name and reputation. Clearly, this was familiar territory for Summerfield's footman.

Julia continued to observe the room and its patrons. Her wide eyes and occasional blushes told him she had noticed the liberties taken by many of the men with the tavern maids. When one of the streetwalkers led a customer through the laughing crowd, her hand holding his member through his bulging trousers, she gave a startled gasp and buried her face in his shoulder.

Tristan brushed his lips across her forehead. "I warned you," he muttered. The clean scent of her hair rose to mask the rank odors of mutton stew, cheap candles, and tar. She didn't belong in such rough surroundings. "If it is too much, I will take you back to Ravencliffe's and search alone."

"No." She raised her head sharply. "I was merely—taken by surprise." Her cheeks burned red but her eyes had a twinkle of amusement. "I assumed you exaggerated in order to frighten me off."

"That may not be the worst you see tonight."

"So long as I see Ned or Tom, I shall not complain." She cast her gaze to where the big man sat with the blond girl on his lap and his hand possessively toying with her half-exposed breast. "Though I hope we are not driven to extremes to fit in."

For a brief, lust-slamming moment, Tristan imagined Julia's breast filling his hand. He gripped the tankard instead. "Not all men stake their claim so crudely," he managed to say. He took a healthy swig of his ale and forced himself to focus on a congealed grease spot on the table. A trickle of sweat ran down his back and he shifted on the bench to ease his discomfort. It took all his concentration to keep his other hand firmly at her waist.

She took another tentative sip from her tankard. "Now that I know what to expect it is not so bad," she mused. "The bitterness is not much different from coffee, though that is not my favorite drink, either."

She looked beyond his shoulder and set her beer down. "I see Tom."

Tristan shifted to look toward the door. "Which one?"

"The brown-haired man speaking to the blond woman at the bar."

The man in question leaned in and said something in the tavern maid's ear. His dark blue coat accommodated his broad shoulders, but hadn't the precise fit or quality of a gentleman's garment. Nor did his shoes reflect the bright shine of a man of means. But neither did he look poor. Tristan knew that look well. Tom's lean build was the type that came from a starved childhood and mean streets. Tristan rubbed the still tender spot at the base of his skull. Tom had learned the stealth trade early and well.

The woman and gestured toward the staircase beside the bar. Tom grinned, patted her on the bottom, slipped past her, and out of sight.

"I believe it might be time to explore other areas of the tavern," Tristan said. Standing, he pulled Julia up and into his arms. Nuzzling her neck, he whispered into her ear. "Forgive me, but we must give the appearance of licentious intent if we are to follow him up the stairs." He gave in to temptation, then, and kissed her.

She tensed, and her lips resisted only an instant before they softened and he coaxed her to relax against him. He traced her lips with his tongue until she accepted the invitation and met his tongue with hers. She tasted only faintly of the ale she'd sipped and far more of womanly sweetness and curious desire. *Dear God!* He'd wanted this since the moment he'd heard that seductive voice and looked into the wary depths of those green eyes. He fought to remain in control. They were on a mission.

Other than a few ribald comments, few paid any attention to them as they worked their way through the crowded tavern. Near the stairs Tristan stopped and took Julia in his arms again so he could assess their surroundings. When the bartender turned his back to put several tankards on a tray and the tavern maid dodged a patron's groping hand, Tristan grabbed Julia's wrist hand and tugged her to the next floor.

In the short corridor, he placed his ear against the door and listened for a moment, but he heard nothing. At the second it was clear someone was well into bed sport, but matters had progressed more than would be expected in the time it had taken them to follow Tom. Undoubtedly the earlier couple.

The third door yielded the sounds of someone moving about, and Tristan eased it open a crack. Inside, the man Julia identified as Tom stood beside a bed with his shirt off while he poured himself a glass of gin. Bruises darkened his flesh and his left eye had swollen shut. Signaling Julia to stay behind him, Tristan withdrew his pistol and pushed the door the rest of the way open.

Tom's grin of welcome shifted to a frown when he saw Tristan and his pistol. "What do you –?" He caught sight of Julia. "So yer back." He eyed her dress and smirked. "Always thought you had more to show than your prim get-ups hid."

"Where is Ned?" Julia adjusted her shawl, but her determination did not waver.

"Lookin' for the brat. Though if you're here I'm guessin' he found her. He swore he'd take more out of me if he didn't." He gazed between them, his battered features proof of Ned's reaction to finding Julia and Alice had escaped.

"Lord Summerfield has been arrested for treason." Tristan told him. "And now I am arresting you."

Tom eyed Tristan and released a snort of disbelief. "You think you can take me with a single pistol and a silly female too stupid to know when she's being used?" He took a swig of his gin, then suddenly swung the bottle at Tristan's head.

Tristan ducked, felt the air move past his temple.

Tom dodged around him and ran for the door.

Julia stuck her foot out and tripped him before he could reach it. He hit his head on the jamb, crumpled to the floor, unconscious.

Tristan hauled him onto the bed and pulled two lengths of cord from his coat pocket. By the time Tom regained consciousness, he was bound hand and foot.

"It seems Miss Dorsey is not as stupid as you thought." Tristan commented when he saw Tom had woken. "She escaped undetected and she directed me to you—*and* prevented you from escaping. I believe she is rather resourceful, myself." He sent Tom an amused grin. "So, perhaps you can tell us where to find Ned."

"Not me." He shook his head. "He already give me what-for fer lettin' 'em get away."

"He'll not be able to get to you where you're going."

"So ye say," Tom said with a grimace. "Ned don't give up. Even with the old lord dyin' he went back for the girl. He'll follow through. He always does."

Tristan bent down close to Tom's face and stared at him for a long moment. Finally, with a feral grin, he whispered. "I grew up in the dials. I don't give up either."

Tom sucked in a breath and his eyes went wide. He swallowed audibly and said, "If the old lordship is still breathing, and Ned has the girl, he'll see the master's orders are followed to the end. Then he'll change his name and run to ground."

"Where would that be?"

"Not in London. Too many folks would be willing to turn him in."

"Why not you?"

"If I turn him in and he gets away, he'll come back and kill me for sure. I'm for the hangman anyway, and I'll take the noose over Ned's brand of revenge any day." He shot a resentful but calculating look at Tristan. "So what's in it for me?"

"Give us Ned and I'll see that you're transported instead of hung."

"What if he's not there?"

"If we can track and arrest him from your information the offer stands," Tristan said. "If we don't find him and can't trace him, I can't guarantee anything. That will be for the courts to decide."

Tom's jaw tightened and his eyes shifted between his two captors while he weighed his choices. It was clear he feared Ned more than the quick justice of the hangman.

Finally, he said, "Ned told me he were a cabin boy on a ship the first time he met His Lordship. He ran errands for him when they got to shore, and Summerfield offered him a position as page by the time they made it back to England and his home port of Portsmouth. If he's not in London, he's probably there. His Lordship don't care where Ned does the business so long as it pays well, and female cargo can be sent from any harbor if you know the right captains. There's plenty of market for blond virgins in foreign ports. Age don't matter."

Tristan heard Julia release a stifled whimper but kept his attention on Tom. He raised an eyebrow, waiting, and Tom frowned before continuing.

"He favors The Mermaid's Tail for his lordship's business and Kate's for whoring."

Julia shifted, wrapping her arms about her waist, but made no other sound.

"Where does he take rooms?"

"He owns a gaming house in Portsmouth, he does, though he don't know I know. He don't go by Ned there, neither." Tom touched his swollen eye and frowned. "I followed him once and heard some lackey call him Mr. Newman." He released a huff of amusement. "Reckon he thought that a right funny twist since it's his new name for the new man he'll be."

No wonder Ned was loyal, Tristan admitted. From cabin boy to footman, now business man. Quite a step up. Too bad it had been through treason and trafficking.

Time for that to end.

"Name of his house?" Tristan asked tersely.

"The Pandemonium." Tom's lip lifted slightly. "Ned calls things as he sees 'em."

CHAPTER 21

Julia lay awake for a long time after she returned to Raven-cliffe House. She worried about Alice, but there was nothing more they could do until morning. Once Tom told them where they were likely to find Ned, Tristan had sent word to the earl. He, in turn, sent bow street runners to remove Tom from the tavern. It was not until she was alone in her room that Julia could take in all that she'd seen and experienced in those few short hours.

She had believed herself prepared to face Renard's treason and betrayal the day before, but she'd had no idea how bitterly vengeful his actions had been. His treason would strip her of her own financial support; their familial association would exclude her from any respectable, genteel employment in the future. Yet she needed to find a way to survive.

Her view of the world had changed vastly in the past few days, and she wondered how she would face the future. She'd heard of brothels despite her sheltered upbringing and singular life at the cottage. Her understanding, however, had been vague. The companion Renard had hired for her Season had explained little of her wifely duties other than they were expected and after the first initiation, not entirely unpleasant, and resulted in children. Brothels were where women were paid to permit men liberties without marriage. Such a life was shocking, demeaning, and scandalous.

Yet her sister might well have lived such a life from the age of twelve. And Alice—what of dear Alice? Julia still knew so little.

A bath scented with rose petals and a night shift that did not reek of stale smoke and fish had restored some of her normal sense of self. She lay in the great four-poster bed in one of the Ravencliffe's guest rooms and explored her reaction to all she'd seen and done tonight.

From the moment Tristan had assisted her into the hackney to begin their search, Julia had breathed in the faint, rich aroma of sandalwood mixed with an underlying musk and that left her with a deep yearning for something unknown. When he'd slipped his arm around her waist and pulled her to his side in the tavern, she'd been startled to realize how naturally she fit against him. She'd shocked herself when she'd pressed her face into his shoulder and inhaled the heady scent of linen and musk like a child in a bakery.

The crowd had not disturbed her as much as she'd feared. There had been an air of comradery and lack of animosity that, though unfamiliar, did not threaten. Perhaps she was gaining courage at last. True, loose women clung to their male companions in a most inappropriate manner, but no one seemed to care.

When the streetwalker led her customer from the room by his—she blushed at the memory—Julia had noticed a similar bulge in Tristan's pantaloons. A lady did not look below a man's waist, but the role Julia played tonight had not been one of a lady, and she had looked. She hated that her blushes gave away the direction of her thoughts, but she thanked her lucky stars Tristan had assumed it was the couple that had her blushing, and not her awareness of his condition.

The entire atmosphere of loose behavior and unchecked pleasure fascinated her at the same time as it repelled her. She hadn't drunk enough of the bitter ale to affect her control, but the role she played exhilarated her. She wanted to join the revelry with abandon. She wanted to know what it felt like to be free of the constraints of her childhood fears.

She'd watched that great bull of a man take that young blond girl onto his lap and caress her bosom so blatantly it was as though she could feel it herself. Her nipples had tightened at the sight and Julia had nearly swooned to think of Tristan touching her so possessively. She had craved his touch, shocked to realized she yearned to have him stake his claim as shamelessly as the man had with that girl. Yet the thought of that touch coming from the big brute's hands made her shudder.

Julia rolled to her side and wrapped her hands around her waist, determined to resist the urge to test what it would feel like to be touched so intimately. Instinct told her that doing so would only increase her desire and leave her less fulfilled than before. A vague ache radiated from her most private place sending a vibration of awareness from core to fingertips and toes.

She closed her eyes and allowed herself to focus on the one aspect of the evening she'd hugged to herself. *He kissed me.*

It didn't matter that it had been for show. He'd kissed her and the sensation of his lips against hers had grown and deepened until he'd touched his tongue to hers and set off an explosion of pleasure. Had anyone told her any man would stick his tongue into her mouth, would touch his tongue to hers, she would have found the idea disgusting. But the reality wasn't. That intimacy, the shared flavor of ale and Tristan's essence, had sent her pulse racing as her tongue tangled with his. She'd wanted more. She'd wanted the kiss to go on forever.

Nor did she believe it had been entirely for show. His breathing had been as shallow as hers when he'd broken away. Fire blazed in those brilliant blue eyes and she'd felt the growing bulge pressed against her middle. That knowledge, alone, had appeased her disappointment when he'd stopped so abruptly to lead her up the stairs.

Who knew that kisses held such power? *Everyone who had ever been kissed* came the irreverent thought. It certainly explained the severe restriction society placed on single men and women. That explosive pleasure could only lead to more explorations, which led to ruin if not sanctioned by marriage.

For the first time since she'd encountered him in the woodland downpour, she wondered if he had ever considered marrying anyone.

TRISTAN ARRIVED AT the Ravencliffe townhouse long before most inhabitants of Mayfair knew the day had begun, let alone begun to stir. Only the servants and hawkers moved about this early. Or travelers on their way to Portsmouth who needed to arrive as quickly as possible. The lifting fog raised his hopes that the day would be clear and fine.

"Miss Dorsey will be down shortly, sir," Billings told him when he opened the door and allowed him inside. He nodded, and a nearby footman who picked up a portmanteau carried it outside.

Tristan stepped past the doorway and looked up when he noticed movement at the top of the stairs. Julia descended the stairs dressed for traveling. The brown ensemble she wore, a muslin dress and darker brown spencer, reminded him of the first time he'd seen her. Now, as then, her clothing was practical and of the simplest design, but there was nothing plain or simple about the woman who reached the bottom step and greeted him with a quiet, "Good morning, Mr. Sheffield."

Lady Ravencliffe greeted Tristan with a bit more reserve than usual when she followed Julia down the stairs to the entry hall. It was clear Julia had told her of their plan to leave together for Portsmouth in search of Ned and Alice. "I cannot like your traveling with Miss Dorsey unchaperoned," she said, "But I pray you find the child quickly and before she is—" She broke off and turned to Julia. "God speed and guide you."

They reached the town of Godalming early in the evening, halfway between London and Portsmouth and a common stage stop on the road. Tristan hoped to find verification that Ned Smith had returned to Portsmouth now that his master had been charged with high treason.

"We must share a room again," he informed Julia after arranging for accommodation. "The stage arrived an hour ago and the passengers claimed all but the one I have taken."

He watched her eyes widen and that telltale flush creep up her cheeks, but she merely nodded her head. Clearly, she had reacted to their kiss the night before. Neither of them were likely to forget the desire it had kindled. He led her up the stairs to their room, set their portmanteaus on the bed, and excused himself so she could freshen up alone.

Though they had managed well enough when Julia was his prisoner, their foray into the Gray Whale together had changed everything. He told himself he'd kissed her to maintain the illusion they were a couple, he but knew he'd done so because he had wanted to from the first time he'd looked into those green eyes. He hadn't expected the immediate flash of heat that had singed his senses and stolen all thought but that he wanted her like no one he'd ever desired.

He'd behave as a gentleman, of course. He would make a pallet on the floor and hope he could manage an hour or two of sleep before they struck out on the road again.

Regardless of the fact that they traveled together without a chaperone, she was a lady. Once they rescued Alice, Julia would be able to return to society under the sponsorship of both his foster mother and Lady Ravencliffe. No one else need ever know of their scandalous travel arrangements. Now that Julia had shown she could tolerate crowds, it was not too late for her to make a respectable match and to have a home and family. One she deserved. He would not ruin a lady. And she was a lady. And he was a bastard.

Down in the public room he ordered an ale then chatted with the serving girl. She rewarded his effort with the confirmation that a man fitting Ned Smith's description had taken a room for himself and his daughter the night before. The little girl, she'd noted, had been fast asleep as it had been quite late when they arrived.

ONCE TRISTAN LEFT AND she completed her ablutions, Julia sank onto the bed and let her thoughts focus on Tristan and their accommodations. The way he held his mouth and his rigid posture told her told her more clearly than words that he had not planned their shared quarters. Instead of brother and sister, their host had taken them to be man and wife. They had not discussed such complications to their plan before they left. In fact, they'd not spoken much in the hours of travel other than of their chances of locating Alice. Until they reached the Portsmouth, there was little more they could do, and worrying accomplished nothing. Most of all, they had not spoken of the kiss they'd shared at the tavern.

She might be inexperienced, but she was smart enough to know Tristan had begun that kiss as a ruse for their trip upstairs to find Tom, but there had been no ruse in the fire it generated between them. That flame still sizzled at the edge of her consciousness, until she wondered if she would ever feel normal again. The brush of his shoulder, every bump of his thigh against hers while riding in the carriage had sent fissures of awareness through her.

Now they shared a room, as they had when she was his prisoner, and she didn't know how she felt about it. Her belly tightened in anticipation of.... what? Would this intimate setting lead to another kiss? Part of her feared the possibility. Part of her hummed with eagerness. Certainly, traveling alone with him raised a question about her reputation and virtue. She should be appalled that she wanted another kiss more than she wanted to remain chaste.

Julia turned her thoughts away from the unexpected situation. They were not at the stage stop for an assignation but as a place to rest before searching out Ned and Alice. She would focus on the possibilities of locating them and not of ruinous temptation.

Some minutes later, Julia was reaching for the door latch when a brisk knock sounded and Tristan asked, "May I come in?"

She opened the door. "I was about to come down in hopes getting of something to eat."

"Give me a quick moment to wash the dust from my face and we shall go down together. I don't recommend you going alone."

She stepped back to allow him in, then seated herself on the single chair placed next to a lamp table in the room. She turned her face to the door and tried not to think about the times she had watched beneath lowered lids when he'd changed clothing in the Surrey house. The sounds of water dripping and shifting in the bowl ceased and she imagined him using the toweling over his face—had he removed his shirt, as he had in Surrey? Heat blossomed at her core and radiated up to her cheeks at her improper wish that she could turn to see. She closed her eyes to imagine the sight. Her pulse quickened and her cheeks burned at the remembered image.

She opened her eyes when she heard him move away from the basin, and prayed he wouldn't notice her blush when he stood in front of her.

"That feels much better." He straightened his coat and offered his arm. "Shall we find our supper?"

The aromas of mutton stew, strong ale, and hearth smoke drifted up the stairs and Julia looked forward to a hot meal. Most of the tables were filled, but Tristan led her to one tucked in the corner a bit away from the other patrons, so they could converse without being overheard.

"Ned and Alice were through here last night," Tristan said after they had ordered a simple meal of stew, bread, and cheese. "They arrived late and Alice was asleep when Ned carried her in. This morning Ned had her bundled tight against the cold when they left at dawn. I suspect he dosed her with laudanum to keep her quiet."

"Then he will be in Portsmouth?"

"Once he has finished this business there is always the chance he could go to the Americas or the Indies, though Tom did not think it likely. We are just a day behind, though, and I doubt he could complete his business so quickly. He doesn't know we found Tom and he did not see me when you were taken, so he might think himself safe in Portsmouth."

Dismay cramped Julia's middle and compressed her lungs until she could barely breathe. "But what of Alice? How quickly might he act?" She blinked away the sting of tears. "Can we find her in time to save her?"

"Brothels often delay the presentation of innocents to their customers to raise their profit, but I don't know." Tristan's mouth became grim again. "We will find her though. As to Ned, few people like complete change. Tom said he uses a different name in Portsmouth, which would not require him to leave England. It is what most men needing to escape their past do." His lips lifted in a humorless smile. "It is what I would do."

Renard had changed Julia's name when they arrived in England by telling her that she was English now and her name should reflect that. So Juliette d'Orsey had become Julia Dorsey, and she'd forever turned her back on the horrors that she had witnessed. She thought of her sister. If she lived, had Beatrice changed her name as well?

She sat in silence for several minutes. Then she asked, "Do you think Ned knows what happened to Beatrice? Do you think he really was the one who sold her for Renard?" She looked up, desolation in her expression. "Will I be able to discover if she lives?

Tristan frowned. "What could you do if he did? Too much time has passed, Julia. Whatever the truth is, it will not change the past, and fruitless searching will only lead to more sorrow. That is a road you do not want to follow."

Even if she knew how to search, Julia realized it would take resources she didn't have. She caught her lower lip in her teeth then released it with a sigh. "I would not be able to pursue Beatrice even if it were not hopeless," she admitted. "I must find a way to support myself, now that I shall be without Renard's provision. Perhaps if I change my name Lady

Ravencliffe will be willing to write me a reference that will allow me to become a governess."

"I told you my family will see that you are cared for."

She shook her head and put down her spoon. "I must find a way to be independent." She picked it up again but didn't take a bite. "If I were able to find Beatrice, and she was willing, I would want to share a home with her. If she was forced into a life of shame your family would not be able to extend their patronage to us—nor would I request it of them."

Tristan put down his spoon as well. "What if she was not willing? She might be under the protection of someone who would not let her leave." His eyes reflected pity and apology when he added, "I'm sorry to speak so bluntly, but I will not lie to you. After so much time, you will be strangers. She will have changed greatly from your memories."

At twelve, Beatrice had been filled with joyful enthusiasm for life and its promise. What if she had turned into one of those women Julia had seen in the streets near the docks? Now that she was away from the novelty of what she'd witnessed at the Gray Whale, she admitted that the atmosphere had held a note of sadness under the laughter. Might Beatrice be bitter or coarse or would she resent the life Julia had lived? *Would they still like each other?*

Julia flinched to realize Tristan was right. It was as though someone squeezed and twisted her heart. Never had she considered that Beatrice might reject her. "Then she will have made a choice she did not have before," she finally admitted.

Yet after years of thinking her sister dead, the glimmer of hope that she might live had filled Julia with the need to reunite with her. She had been alone for so long, so envious an observer of those with warm family ties, it hurt to imagine a future where her sister lived, but rejected her. The idea of losing Beatrice a second time made the empty place in her heart grow larger, darker, and lonelier.

Another face, younger with blond hair and an impish grin, filled her mind and she clenched her hands. Would Alice be lost, too?

CHAPTER 22

Tristan removed a pillow from the bed, dropped it to the floor, and then pulled his cloak from the wall peg and tossed it onto the pillow.

"What are you doing?"

He looked up at the exasperation in Julia's voice. "Preparing a place to sleep. The bed is yours."

"You refused to allow me to sleep in discomfort when I was your prisoner. I see no reason you should be uncomfortable now that I am not." Her cheeks blazed in contradiction of her matter of fact declaration.

"I do." Tristan told her bluntly. "You are no longer my prisoner. And you know as well as I that we both enjoyed that kiss at the Gray Whale too much to ignore."

Her flush deepened.

"If I don't take the floor we'll share more than the bed." He saw the brief flare of desire that lit her expression before she glanced away. She licked her lips and wrapped her arms around her middle. His body stiffened in response. "As I expected us to be able to secure separate rooms, I felt it inappropriate to call attention to the fact." He faced her with his fists on his hips. She might as well see what she did to him. "But I doubt I will be any more comfortable in the bed than I will on the floor."

He could see she didn't know what to say in the face of the evidence that sharing the bed would be dangerous to her virtue and his honor. "I think it best to leave matters where they are." His body disagreed, but his conscience applauded his sacrifice when he rolled himself into his cloak and settled on the floor facing away from the bed.

"Good night, Julia."

She said nothing more before she blew out the candle. He listened to her climb into the bed and settle into place.

Tristan lay in the dark, his body aching, and cursed himself for a fool. Julia had not denied the fire their kiss had ignited. She'd been as affected as he had. Unfortunately, that didn't change the fact that Julia was a respectable woman who deserved to be treated with courtesy and honor.

He shifted on the floor, rolling to his right side now that the darkness hid the bed and the woman in it. Julia shifted, too. He could hear the rustle of the sheets. She shifted again, then a minute later, again. Listening to her movements, the slight creak of the bed slats, the little puffs of breath that escaped when she turned from side to side, only fueled his imagination and increased his discomfort. He hoped she drifted off soon.

Then, out of the darkness Julia whispered, "Have you ever visited a brothel?"

Tristan tensed. Did her question relate to Alice, or her sister—or to his obvious desire for her? "Why do you ask?"

"I know that men have... needs," she hesitated. "that cause physical discomfort—and that require relief. The women in brothels do that..." Silence stretched and Tristan knew she searched for a way to finish her thought. "And I wondered... what it is like to..."

She took a deep breath and blurted, "I want to know what such places are like—and if the women there enjoy servicing their customers." Then, faintly, she added. "And what they actually do."

Tristan swallowed a groan. Did she expect him to describe the act? Did she really want to know the pragmatic truth about the barter of a woman's body for coin? Purchased goods were used, then discarded when no longer needed. If he were honest about the conditions in most of those places she would grieve for her sister. If he preserved the illusion that brothels simply provided mutual and voluntary exchange of pleasure for coin he did her no kindness.

It served him right for losing himself in that kiss. It raised her curiosity and that was dangerous for two people traveling alone together. That damned kiss had set him aflame, yet came nowhere near satisfying what he wanted to do with her. He certainly had no intention of making himself more miserable by describing those fantasies to her.

"I know you are awake," she murmured. "I will not be shocked if ... Is that why you are a bastard? Was your mother –?"

"No."

"I am sorry," she apologized. "It is none of my business."

"She was my brother's nursemaid after his mother died."

"Oh." Julia's voice held a note of neutrality that told him she wanted to ask more, but felt she'd overstepped the boundaries of curiosity by asking about his status. He sensed the intensity of her silence. Female servants were often prey for their employers, their sons or guests. She would not ask, but he knew what she wanted to know. He had wanted to know the same thing.

"He didn't force her. Nor, it turns out, did he know about me."

"If your father didn't know about you, how –?"

"When she realized she was dying, she sent him a letter asking that he provide me with an apprenticeship –but for reasons too complicated to relate, he didn't receive the letter for more than six months. It took him several more months to find me."

More silence. The woman could say more by saying nothing than anyone he knew. He had never told anyone the details of his childhood. Indeed, he resented it when people pried, as though he were a specimen to be pitied. Life in Seven Dials had been harsh, but it was what he knew and accepted, just as Julia accepted that the Terror happened, and that she had been orphaned. But her experience had forged a strength to face whatever new situations challenged her. Though she failed to recognize her courage.

Finally, he said, "I was nine when she died of consumption." The darkness made it easier to talk about his own loss. "I was on my own for nearly a year."

She shifted again and he imagined she now faced him, though it was still too dark to see. "How did you survive?"

"I learned to pick more than locks."

"You were a pick-pocket?" Her shock made him smile.

"All the orphans in Seven Dials pick pockets."

"Oh."

Tristan shifted onto his back, stacking his hands beneath his head. "My father eventually found me, but I wanted nothing to do with him despite being taken into his household. I did everything my power to show my resentment and distrust. I knew that servants who fall pregnant are turned off without reference. I assumed that was the case for my mother despite what she told me."

"What changed your mind?"

He gave a rueful chuckle. "Do you remember when I told you about the brother's war?"

She made an affirmative sound.

"Lucien was particularly angry one day when I embarrassed him in front of his friends. He showed me the letter my mother had written and taunted me about her being linked with one of the lower footmen. Instead of humiliating me, it proved my father truly didn't know about me until then." Amusement touched his lips. "Lucian pretty much gave up baiting me after that. I never reacted the way he thought I would." The half-smile died. Except for that last time. The one they both regretted.

"It is late, Julia. Go to sleep."

AS SHE LAY IN THE DARK, Julia considered how much her life had changed since Tristan had entered it. She would never have dreamed that she would be any more scandalous than when she had made that disgraceful scene at a crowded ball.

Now she traveled with a man who was not her husband. She had kissed that man publically—and wantonly—in a common dockside tavern. That memory made her touch her lips. To be absolutely honest with herself, she wanted to kiss him again.

She had slept in the same bed with him for three nights before he allowed her a private room. Julia might still retain her virginity, but she knew she was ruined in all but actual fact. If word of this quest became public it would not matter if she retained her maidenhead or not. Nor would she ever know what it was she had supposedly experienced.

Riding beside Tristan had made her aware of all the unnamed yearnings she had ignored for too many years. The frank debauchery at the tavern and that kiss, had defined her yearning. She wanted him to kiss her again. She wanted the closeness of being held. She wanted... *she to be wanted.*

She had seen the evidence that he wanted her. More than once, though he'd tried to disguise it and she'd pretended not to notice. But she had. And now she resolved to end the farce they had maintained since the night in the tavern.

If only she knew how.

Tristan had threatened—or had it been a promise?—to truly bed her if they shared one. She had only the vaguest idea of what that meant, but since kissing was a part of it, she was willing to discover the rest.

Still, the idea of blatantly inviting him into her bed after his warning tightened her throat. The darkness of the room had emboldened Julia to ask impertinent and intrusive questions... would it make it easier to invite him to her bed? Would it make it easier to hide her disappointment if he refused again?

Julia had just begun to doze when she became aware of muffled voices on the other side of the wall from where her head rested on the pillow. A low-pitched rumble asked a question that caused a feminine giggle followed by a high squeal and another giggle. Curiosity wiped away the fog of sleep and Julia wondered what had made the woman squeal like that.

All was quiet for a space of several minutes, but soon gasps and growl-like sounds became audible. Above her pillow, something bumped against the wall and the woman's voice took on a pleading note and something bumped the wall again... and again, until the steady rhythm pounded above Julia's pillow while the woman wailed and pleaded.

Julia sat up and scrambled to the floor. "Tristan!" she whispered loudly when she reached his side. "Tristan! Do you hear that? There is a man hurting a woman in the room next door."

Tristan sat up and rubbed his hand over his face. He groaned. "He is bedding her, not hurting her."

"But she is begging him to stop, can't you hear that? It is in the tone of her voice. She is pleading with him!"

"She isn't pleading for him to stop—she's begging him to bring her to release."

Julia stopped shaking Tristan's arm and sat back on her heels. The pleading voice had shifted to a keening wail as the wall shook with increasingly rapid pounding until the male voice shouted in triumph and all sound ceased.

Julia stared at the silent wall, stunned and unnerved. For all the violence of sound and emotion, some dark place deep inside her responded with yearning as well as dread. She turned back to Tristan, her eyes wide and searching in the dim moonlit room. "That is what it is like?"

"Bed sport is something to be experienced, not listened to." He finally said. His voice had a strange huskiness, as though his words were tangled in this throat. "Definitely not listened to."

"You are sure he did not hurt her?" She whispered. "she cried out and he shouted."

"Those were cries of completion—release if you will." He gave a sigh that told her he didn't want to talk about what had happened in the next room.

"Go back to bed, Julia. With luck they will be done for the night."

Julia didn't move. "How...?"

"Don't ask," Tristan warned. "I am fighting the urge to demonstrate as it is. Now, I am pleading—go back to bed."

"What if I want you to demonstrate?" Julia held her breath. *Had she really said that*?

Dead silence greeted her. Then she heard his harsh intake of breath before his hand wrapped around the back of her neck and brought her mouth to his. His other arm came around her as he pulled her down and into a tight embrace that made her heart accelerate and her body throb with anticipation. His lips pressed, his teeth nibbled, his tongue tasted and Julia answered his demand with all the instinctual yearning of her heart.

His mouth didn't stop at her lips, but trailed down her neck to the edge of her night rail. His hands roamed up and down her back, then around to cup her breasts, and she gasped at the sharp bolt of pleasure that traveled through her. Julia's hands came up to hold his hands in, keeping them pressed tightly to her body while she gloried in Tristan's answering groan.

He buried his face against the nape of her neck—kissing, sucking lightly at the tender flesh. "Tell me to stop, Julia... Help me to stop."

Julia arched her neck to give him better access while letting go of his hands to slide hers up and around his shoulders. "I don't want you to stop."

He lifted his head and claimed her mouth again. Deeply. Wetly. Desperately. He tugged her gown low and swirled his tongue around her nipple before sucking the tip. Sharp desire arrowed deeply and Julia pressed her hips against his in instinctual response. He groaned, and his hand shifted lower to caress her thighs and that sensitive place between them.

She gasped at the pleasure of his touch. She wanted to plead for him to touch her again, to take her to that something she yearned for, but could not name. He curled his hand tightly against her and she whimpered for more.

At the sound, he pulled back, released his hold on her and rolled away, panting. Julia reached for him again but he vaulted up and strode to the far side of the room. "I'll not ruin you, Julia. Much as I want you—much as you want to know what happens between men and women."

"I am already ruined." She protested. "If I must bear the censure of society I should at least know of what I have been accused."

The moonlight revealed his rigid stance and the taut line of his frown. "You are not ruined, Julia. You are a lady. The legitimate daughter of a nobleman. I have enough sins on my conscience as it is." He clasped his hands behind his neck and took a deep breath, then another. Finally, his breathing slowed and he said, "You have had too much taken from you, I'll not take your innocence... nor will I take a chance of bringing another bastard into the world."

Julia fought to control her own breathing, but her pulse hammered wildly and she wondered if she would ever take a calm breath again. Her lips felt tender and her breasts ached to feel his hands caress them once more. She wanted him to hold her, to make her gasp, to do whatever it was that made the woman in the next room wail with such abandon. Yet his reminder of the consequences of that act shocked her out of the haze of passion.

A bastard. A *child*. She'd given up the idea of children after her disastrous season. Her lack of marriage prospects had sealed that fact in her mind. The idea of a child without marriage had never been a question. It was scandalous. *But it was possible.*

Caring for Alice had given her a glimpse of how much she had buried her desire for family... but a *bastard* child? Tristan knew better than anyone what that meant. Julia could only guess at the taunts and humiliations he had borne, but she had seen enough in the way the townsfolk treated children of unwed parentage to know how cruel people could be. It made her wonder how many mothers who arrived in a new village named themselves widows when they were not?

But to take that chance would destroy his sense of honor. He would know the truth and hate it. And if Julia had learned anything about Tristan, it was that his sense of honor was what gave him a sense of worth.

"I beg your pardon, Tristan." She hated the tremble in her voice. She rose from the floor and moved to the bed. "I did not think beyond... beyond—I understand." She lay back down and pulled the blankets high before turning to her side. "Good night."

TRISTAN STAYED AT THE far side of the room long after Julia apologized and returned to bed. His breathing slowed, but his body had not yet subsided and he still ached for release.

He should have told her she had nothing to be sorry for but he'd been unable to say more. She couldn't know how much he wanted her or how much he would despise himself if he gave in to his desire.

He had promised himself he would never be responsible for causing another child to endure the subtle snub or outright insults he had born from his earliest years. Had his father been less than a duke Tristan would not have been tolerated at any *ton* function, or most lower classes in society.

Even now, he resented his assigned place in the world. He accepted that he could do nothing more than to prove wrong those people who thought bastards had some bone deep stamp of their parents' guilt and that they were destined to be cursed and dishonorable. Respect and acceptance were little more than pipe dreams when one was illegitimate. He could do nothing but behave as a gentleman was supposed to behave... and see that he was not guilty of his father's sin of bringing another bastard into an unforgiving world.

He found the chair and sat heavily. He couldn't settle on the floor again. He rubbed his palms over his face, then flexed his fingers along his temple.

Dear, God, she tasted like heaven on earth.

SUNLIGHT FROM THE WINDOW woke Tristan where he'd finally fallen asleep slumped over the table. He stretched in a vain attempt to ease his awkward posture, then stood and checked to see if Julia still slept. Satisfied that she did, he quickly washed in the cold water from the night before then slipped out of the room and down to the public room below.

He ordered breakfast and was half-finished when she approached the table.

"I hope you were able to get some sleep."

As always, her husky voice triggered his desire and he cleared his throat before speaking. "I did."

She sat across from him. She did not meet his eyes before she poured tea into the second cup Tristan had arranged for when he ordered the pot. Her face pinked slightly when her gaze finally lifted to his then darted to the side. "I apologize for putting you into a compromising situation last night. I fear," her color deepened, "I did not think beyond... I did not think." She finally muttered. She looked at him fully then. "I shall not bother you in such a manner again."

She took his breath away. It had to be harder for her to face him than it had been for him—and he had slipped out of the room to delay this particular moment.

"No, Julia you are wrong," His lips firmed. "You will bother me every moment we are together." He took a frustrated breath and met her gaze. "I shall have to be as blunt about this as I have tried to be about the chance of finding your sister. I desire you and you desire me." Her face paled and she put down her cup but did not deny his words.

"There is nothing wrong with desire, Julia." A wry smile lifted his lips. "It is the way God insures the continuation of his creation. After all, if procreation were not pleasurable, mankind might have died out long ago." He held up a finger. "But," he said, "It is possible to experience desire and resist its pull. It is what we shall do."

Julia refreshed the tea in her cup. "Yes. That is probably best."

"It is more than best," he growled. "It is necessary."

CHAPTER 23

When Portsmouth came into view late the next afternoon, Julia asked, "Shall we go to the tavern tonight?"

They had spoken of polite matters along the way. None of the shared stories had been more than anecdotes that touched the surface of their memories. They did not delve into the events that molded them. Those were the secrets of darkness. Again, Julia felt every brush and bump that touched her as they made their way along the road. She now knew that Tristan felt them just as acutely.

"Perhaps. Once we take rooms I shall make a few inquiries around the docks." He glanced sideways at her before turning his attention back to the road. "I shall gain more information if I am alone. Rough as many of the men are, they will not speak of certain matters in the presence of a lady of quality."

"I can wear the dress I wore to the Gray Whale and pretend to be your mistress, again."

"A man may take his mistress many places he would not take his wife," He shook his head and chuckled. "But he does not take her with him when he asks about the local brothels.

She smiled. "I suppose not."

Her thoughts, when not interrupted by surges of physical awareness, centered on their conversation the night before. How blatant she had been to ask about women servicing men. She found it difficult to believe she'd been so bold. But curiosity—and the odd restlessness that had plagued her since their kiss—had driven her to speak.

Asking Tristan if his mother had worked in a brothel had gone beyond the pale... but led to an unexpected facet of the man who alternately presented blunt reality and gentle understanding.

Oddly, the darkness seemed to free Tristan of the hard-edged manner he maintained most of the time. That he had loved and revered his mother showed in the way his voice altered when he spoke of her. He'd shared a part of himself in the dark, but it was too new and private to discuss in daylight.

TRISTAN SURVEYED THE Mermaid's Tail tavern and wished he had a better idea of what Ned looked like. As things were, he needed Julia to identify the former footman, but the Portsmouth docks were every bit as rough as those in London. Seven Dials and the London docks held no secrets for him and he'd known how to keep Julia safe when they played their charade. He did not know Portsmouth and disliked exposing Julia to more night adventures, but he had no choice. They had little time to locate Alice.

His only consolation was that he'd not picked up whispers of new merchandise arriving in any of the brothels. That didn't mean Ned was not in town or that he would keep the child in his control any longer than necessary, but if offered the hope that they still had a chance of rescuing her before Ned followed through with Summerfield's plan. *If he could find them.*

He ascended the stairs and knocked on Julia's door. She opened it quickly, and Tristan could only stare at the sight she made. Obviously, she thought to be ready to spend another night at a tavern with him and had donned the dress she'd worn to the London tavern. She had even managed to procure face paint to darken her eyes and redden her lips. She had arranged her hair up in a loose arrangement, and the rich dark strands made him want to pull it down and run his hands through it.

"Don't ever open your door without asking who is there." The words came out harshly and she blinked at him in surprise. "In fact, do not ever open it unless I give the correct answer."

"The correct answer?"

"If I am alone I shall answer, 'All is well'. If I reply in any other manner, keep the door locked and do not venture beyond it under any circumstance." He surveyed the delectable, and decidedly wanton picture she presented and told her, "Change into a respectable walking dress. I have arranged for a private room and ordered dinner. I shall freshen myself and take you downstairs in half an hour."

When the serving girl left them after delivering their supper of haddock and roasted turnips, Julia asked, "Why are we not going to the tavern tonight?"

"To be frank, I doubt we will find Ned in a tavern tonight. If he is found anywhere tonight, it is most likely at a brothel. You cannot go there and I cannot recognize him until you point him out." He took a bite of his fish. He pointed to her plate, encouraging her to eat. "It has been a long day on the road and it is best to know the layout of one's location before venturing into possible danger. We shall have an early night, walk about the town in the morning, and try the tavern midday. You need not dress the part of a lightskirt. "

The next morning, before they left the inn, Julia assured Tristan her knowledge of Portsmouth was limited to the cobbler, the draper and the bank as she had never stayed in town longer than necessary. Nonetheless, when Tristan escorted Julia along High Street he kept a wary eye out for trouble. He wore the clothes of a moderately prosperous merchant and walked with a distinct limp. Julia had been alarmed for him until he explained that he needed the ruse in a town where able-bodied men were often pressed into service without warning.

Regardless of whether or not anyone recognized Julia, Tristan no longer sported the beard he'd grown during his earlier visit. That, and the fact that he was a fit man of fighting age, meant he needed to be aware of everything around them. The last thing he needed was for a press gang to sweep him along with them and leave Julia to fend for herself without protection.

When they came in sight of the tavern, Tristan warned her, "Watch for Ned, but also be aware of any strangers who take unusual interest in us." She turned questioning eyes on him and he explained, "Press gangs are known to take advantage of any lapse. I have identification papers with me, but that is no guarantee that a desperate captain would not deny their validity."

"But your limp…"

"Is not all that original as a protective deception." He grinned. "Still, it should serve as I am escorting a lady as well."

"They would act so publically?"

"They more often take men who've drunk too much and who are alone," he said. "But they have been known to slip the King's coin into a pocket or tankard of ale, then claim desertion when they *find* it in a man's possession."

"How horrible." Julia said. "What of their families?"

"If they are lucky, they may receive a letter from a foreign port in time. If not, and he dies at sea, the family may never know what happened to him."

The day was far enough advanced to find late-night carousers returning to their favorite haunts to begin their revelries again. It didn't surprise Tristan that the interior of the Mermaid's Tail resembled the Gray Whale in all but the number of tables crammed into the space and the prominence of military customers. This was, after all a tavern.

London's wharf-side businesses served more merchants and cargo ships while Portsmouth primarily served the military. The patrons here were less jovial than those in London, and the few the men drinking alone stared at nothing while they drained their tankards. War made men grim, trade made men jovially rich.

Tristan guided Julia to a table near the window so they could watch the street as well as the tavern's customers. Julia studied the men in the room, then turned her gaze on him with a slight shake of her head. "He is not here."

"It is still early. We shall wait here for an hour or so, then try some of the other taverns before dark." He signaled the barmaid and then watched the subtle undercurrents that flowed through the room.

When the barmaid deposited their tankards a few minutes later, she set Tristan's in front of him with a broad smile. "Here you are, the specialty of the house." She set Julia's tankard in front of her, then winked at Tristan before turning back to the bar.

Tristan switched tankards with Julia with a grin. "No point taking chances."

"Was she warning you, or taunting you?"

"That is hard to say until the tankard is empty." Tristan took a sip of his drink. "It is an excellent ale, though." He studied the room, but no one payed any particular attention to them.

A half-hour later Julia's hand clutched his forearm and she whispered. "He is crossing the street. He is coming to the tavern."

The man heading toward the Mermaid's Tail had the tall, well-built stature expected of footmen throughout England. Black-haired and square-jawed, Ned Smith looked like he could take care of himself in any situation. His clothes were not those of a footman, however, but of a prosperous merchant. When he entered the tavern, several of the men greeted him with deference and two men sitting at the table in the far corner of the room moved to another table. In the time it took Ned to take his seat at what was clearly known to be his favored table, the barmaid placed a tankard in front of him. The people Tristan had asked might not admit they knew Ned's name, but it was clear they knew him by reputation.

"Keep your face averted," Tristan instructed Julia. "We don't want to alert him of our presence." He shifted his chair so that he blocked Ned's view of Julia, then raised his tankard and took a drink. "I don't want to attract his attention by leaving so soon after his arrival, either. We will finish our ale, then leave."

"Leave? But—How can we...?"

"I shall return and follow him once you are safe and out of sight. We can't chance his recognizing you."

Her mouth tightened but she did not argue.

When the serving girl placed a plate of stew in front of Ned a few minutes later, Tristan stood and took Julia's arm. "Time to go."

TRISTAN RETURNED TO the Mermaid's Tail and took a seat near Ned's table. Ned was in a deep discussion with a man whose lean features had the furtive look of someone who had more to hide than to share, and Tristan noted the way his eyes scanned the room with vigilance. Tristan met his dark gaze briefly, crooked a slight smile of acknowledgement and let his eyes go blank as he looked beyond the pair to the room in general, then lifted his tankard to drink deeply. The man looked back to Ned and continued his conversation.

They kept their voices low and though he strove to listen, Tristan was unable to hear more than a few words, but they were enough. The child broker would arrange an auction before the end of the week. After a few minutes, the broker rose and left. Tristan glanced sideways and saw that Ned watched his departure with a satisfied smile. Ned soon paid his shot and wove his way through the tables and out the door. Tristan waited a few seconds, then followed.

The late afternoon sun lit the exterior walls of the shops that lined High Street and the chilled sea air whipped the riggings of the ships along the quay. Tristan shaded his eyes against the sudden brightness and spotted Ned just before he turned the corner and set off along a narrow alleyway. Walking swiftly, he trailed his quarry through several turnings until Ned entered a gaming hell nestled between a brothel and a tobacconist shop.

Tristan followed him in. The interior was not yet crowded, though a few dedicated gamesters played with quiet intensity at several tables. Lackeys circulated the room delivering wine and brandy while attractive women dealt cards and encouraged their customers to continue playing. Ned was nowhere in sight, though Tristan caught sight of a door closing at the far end of the room.

"May I direct you to a table, Sir?"

Tristan focused on the slender woman who smiled at him. He recognized the assessing calculation in her blue eyes and played along. "Perhaps... unless you'd like to direct me somewhere more private?"

She gave a throaty laugh and tapped his wrist with her fan. "You mistake your location, sir. This is a gaming house only. For privacy you must try Kate's next door."

"My pardon," he bowed slightly. "I did not mean to offend my hostess. Are you the proprietor as well?"

"Oh, no. That would be Mr. Newman." She glanced in the direction of the now closed door then back at him. "So how may I direct you?"

A small commotion at the back of the room attracted their attention when Ned stormed back through the door and across to the woman beside Tristan. Her eyes widened when he demanded, "Have you seen my niece?"

"No, sir."

He shot a glance around the room and at the patrons who had looked up when he spoke His brow lowered when he turned back to the wary man who'd followed him. His voice little more than a hiss, he said, "I told you she would try to run away. Find her and bring her back."

He turned to Tristan, "My pardon for interrupting, sir." The smile he offered was tight and his eyes glittered with fury. "Should you see a small blond girl wandering about I beg you would inform my staff. She is a willful child who has yet to accept she has been orphaned." He inclined his head and excused himself before he gestured to a liveried waiter who followed as he left the building.

Tristan met the gaze of the woman beside him and murmured, "Mr. Newman, I presume?" Summerfield had indicated he allowed Ned freedom beyond his duties, but Tristan doubted the earl knew Ned owned a gaming house under an assumed name.

She smiled and nodded. "The poor child refuses to accept the truth and imagines that Mr. Newman is some great lord's footman named Ned who abducted her from her family." She shook her head. "I have worked for Mr. Newman for nearly three years, sir. His name is Edward, not Ned, and I assure you he is no more a kidnapping footman than you or I. He is a respectable businessman who runs an honest gaming establishment." She gestured to the tables where the gaming had resumed. "I hope you are still of a mind to play?"

Alice was here—or had been. Tristan made himself smile and let her direct him to a table at the back of the room. *Perhaps she is still here, but hiding.* Though play had resumed and all looked normal, he caught sight of several men inspecting alcoves and slipping in and out various doorways.

He took his seat at the table then thanked her and added, "I hope Mr. Newman's niece comes to no harm."

After half an hour's play Tristan rose from the table lighter in the pocket and convinced that Alice was no longer in the gaming house. Quiet as Ned's staff had tried to be, it was clear they had thoroughly searched everywhere and not found her. He'd known she was a clever child, but he could not but wonder how she had escaped so completely. He stood and excused himself. She might be clever, but she was too young to be aware of the rougher streets of this port town and might well have leapt from the kettle into the fire.

As he surveyed the street, he noted the warren of alleys and shadowed recesses that formed a maze of possibilities for a child to hide. He'd shown Alice how to blend into shadows and told her of the tricks that had helped him evade angry shopkeepers when he was her age. She had listened with delight while Julia had frowned and protested against his revelations. But Alice's disappearance was proof that Alice remembered and applied the lessons well.

CHAPTER 24

Julia stood at the window of her room and watched the busy streets for Tristan to return. Was Alice already at some brothel? Tristan was sure there would be some whispers that would give warning before the child was ruined, but could he be sure? What if, instead of selling her in Portsmouth where people might recognize Lord Goodwin's child, Ned sent her to a foreign market? As brief as her time in London had been, Julia had heard of such things. Waiting passively while Tristan followed Ned made her impatient at being so useless.

The afternoon had nearly faded into dusk when a furtive movement on the far side of the street caught her notice. Sunlight highlighted a blond head before it slipped into the shadow beside a candle shop and her breath caught. Alice? *Of course not.* She'd observed many blond-haired people in the hours since Tristan had returned her to the inn.

She watched the shadow for several minutes, but saw no further movement and wondered if her imagination had played tricks on her. When whomever she'd seen did not return to the street, she decided there must be a narrow passage between the shops. Still, the movement had been secretive and unobtrusive. Had she not been looking at that spot at the time she would never have seen it. Certainly, no one on the street below had paid it any attention. Curiosity and frustration ate at her.

She knew better than to go into the streets without proper escort, particularly as evening neared, but that odd sense of something important weighed on her. Tristan had spoken of the street children who roved in and out of the alleyways in search of pockets to pick and food to pilfer. It must have been one of them. But something in the way the figure moved had struck her. *What if— ?* She scrutinized the shadow again. Gathering her courage, she donned her pelisse, hat, and gloves and went downstairs.

A narrow break did, indeed, exist between the chandler shop and the coffee house beside it. She peered down its length and saw a patch of light at the far end where another alley crossed at the back of the buildings. Whomever she had seen was gone. Calling herself foolish for imagining things that she only hoped to see, Julia turned back toward the inn and froze. Ned strode down the street, his every movement revealing anger. She ducked between the buildings and watched him enter and leave several shops as though looking for something... or someone?

Excitement mixed with alarm and her pulse leapt as she stepped further back into the narrow passage and out of sight. If Ned saw her he would know he'd been traced to Portsmouth and Alice would be in more immediate danger than she already was. Julia swallowed to ease her dry throat, then slipped away from the street to the patch of light at the far end of the passage.

The opening was barely wide enough for her to pass, and she tried not to think about whatever it was that slickened the cobbles under her half boots. When she reached the end, the late sunlight had faded and the passage ended into a shadow-darkened alley wide enough for supply wagons to make deliveries. Refuse lined the back walls of the buildings and several small creatures scurried away when she stepped into the open space. She wrinkled her nose when the rank odors of rot, mold, and human waste mingled with the scents of candle tallow and coffee.

She saw no one, but the movement she'd seen from her window had come from the right of her position, so she turned left. She had traveled halfway down the alley before the feeling that she was being watched made her stop and look over her shoulder. Nothing.

She passed another shop's back door, then spied another narrow break in the wall leading further away from the main street. She peered around the corner before taking a chance and following her intuition. Halfway down that passage she turned into another until she was not sure where she was or if she could find her way back. Yet, the further away from the main street she went, the less chance she had of running into Ned... as did whomever she'd seen from the inn window.

The gloom made it difficult to see, and the twilight would soon turn to nightfall. It was foolish beyond measure for her to have allowed her imagination to lead her through the labyrinth of paths and alleyways. She should return to the inn.

Light flared up ahead when someone lit a candle and Julia's heart jumped into her throat when the warm glow exposed a blond head that ducked down as soon as it was revealed.

"Alice?" Julia hurried forward.

The blond head reappeared and a disbelieving voice quavered, "Miss Dorsey?"

Alice leapt up and ran to throw her arms around Julia's waist. "Oh, I am so glad it is you! I thought you were that woman Ned said would take me away."

They stood in the faint island of light clinging to each other, and trembling with relief. Julia held Alice tight and whispered. "I am so glad I found you." After a moment, Julia loosened her hold and knelt to inspect Alice. "Are you alright? Did anyone hurt you?"

Alice shook her head, "No, but Ned made me drink something that made me sleepy. When I woke up I had an awful headache and was very thirsty. He told me he'd make me drink more of it if I didn't do what he said." She looked beyond Julia and asked, "Where is Mr. Sheffield?"

"He is looking for you, too." Julia straightened and held out her hand. "We'll go to the inn so you can tell us how you got away."

Julia took Alice's hand and they hurried back the way she'd come, weaving their way through the labyrinth of passageways in the increasing gloom. After several turns Julia stopped and looked around. Surely they should have reached the main street by now? So intent had she been in watching for Alice's blond head, she'd lost count of the turns she'd made. Now nothing looked familiar. How could it when she'd not noted landmarks?

"Are we lost?" Alice asked.

"I am not sure," Julia listened for the rattle of carriages and voices of people along the more heavily traveled street.

There. She turned to her right. "I think we need to go this way." She hurried forward again, anxious to reach the safety of the inn.

Beyond the next alley crossing, she glimpsed the narrow passage leading to High Street. She stepped toward it but collided with the man who turned the corner. A heavy hand clamped onto Julia's arm to prevent her from falling, then tightened when she looked at the man who held it.

"Well what have we got here?"

Ned.

He grinned, then grabbed Alice with his other hand. "Two for the price of one?" He gripped Julia's arm tighter when she tried to pull away. "Make that the price of two. Gent's pay well for grown virgins, too." He raised his voice to a shout. "Eh, Bill! Come give me a hand. I found her but she's not alone!"

The man who answered Ned's summons was lean, deeply weather-tanned and did not hesitate to follow Ned's instructions to secure Julia's arms behind her.

Alice tried to pull her hand from Ned's grip, but he held on until the man called Bill had Julia. Then he yanked Alice up and pinned her arms at her sides so she could not fight him. "We'll take them in the back way," he directed as he strode in the opposite direction of the busy street beyond the narrow passage.

Two blocks later, they turned into another alley and Ned unlocked a door before hustling them up a narrow stairway and into a private office. The man called Bill pushed Julia into a chair, then took a guard stance blocking the door. Ned sat, still holding Alice with one arm while he opened a desk draw and pulled out a green bottle. "I told you not to try any tricks," he told Alice. "You can sleep until Charlie's woman comes for you." He pulled the cork from the bottle with his teeth and pressed the bottle against Alice's mouth. Alice tried to turn away, but he held her tight and tipped the bottle until she was forced to swallow. "That will keep you quiet," he muttered when the cork was back in the bottle.

He turned his attention to Julia and frowned. "How did you know where to look for her? You aren't smart enough to chase me down." He swore and pinned her with a look. "It must have been that agent. Tom said he'd taken care of him, but I should have checked him myself."

Julia stared at him, her mouth tight, and willed herself not to show fear. Alice's eyes drooped and closed. How much had he given her?

Ned looked down at Alice, gave a grunt of satisfaction, and stood. "Here," he held Alice toward Bill. "Take her back to the room and stay with her—in the room, not outside the door. If she wakes before time, give her another dose."

He handed Bill the bottle and Alice, then turned back to Julia. "If you traced me back to Portsmouth you must have found Tom. The fool thinks I don't know he followed me here after I opened this place. He has no conscience, but no brain, either." He returned to his chair. "Now, the question is, how long will it be before the king's man realizes I have both of you?"

TRISTAN DID A QUICK search of the area around the gaming house. No one had seen a blond child in the vicinity, but that didn't mean she had not passed by. She was a clever child who had taken to his hiding games with rare talent. She would not giggle and give herself away now. As soon as he reassured Julia that Alice was out of immediate danger, he would do a more thorough search. He could only hope he found her before Ned.

He reached Julia's room, knocked, then frowned when Julia did not answer. He raised his voice and used the code phrase again to let her know it was safe to open her door, but she still did not answer. Alarm flared, and he tested the knob. It gave easily. He eased it open and realized the room was empty. Nothing looked out of place... except for Julia. Where was she? He hadn't seen her in the public rooms and she knew better than to leave the inn lest Ned see her and know his secret was out. So where was she?

He descended the stairs, to question the staff.

The serving girl thought she'd seen the lady leave the inn an hour or more earlier, but she had not left a message for him. Nor had she asked for directions to any shops.

He left the inn and strode up the street, looking for her. *Devil blast and take it! Why would she*—he stopped abruptly, then apologized to the couple who nearly bumped into him. Could she have seen Alice from her window? He did not doubt Julia would have gone after her if she had. But if that was the case, why hadn't they returned to the inn?

Ned had gone searching, too. Had she seen him instead of Alice and followed him in hopes of finding her? She, too, had shown talent for remaining unseen, but that didn't mean she had succeeded in following Ned undetected. He crossed the street. His best chance of finding either Alice, or Julia if she followed Ned, was to return to the gaming house. This time, however, he would enter from the back and explore the private areas behind the public rooms.

"SO YOU'VE FOUND A NEW protector," Ned said with an assessing look. "You are cleverer than I thought."

"I am not particularly clever," Julia told him quietly. "I believed what my cousin told me. He had saved me, after all, and raised me. I thought him a good man." Her heart grew heavy and she acknowledged the truth. "I was wrong."

Ned smirked at that. "Depends on who's side you're on. His lordship has been extraordinarily good to me." He waved his hand to indicate the comfortable room. "He gave me opportunity and didn't interfere so long as I did his bidding."

"Like selling girls and women into disrepute?"

Ned grinned. "Not until you and your sister arrived. When his lordship saw the profit to be made selling her maidenhead, he decided to *assist* other families fleeing France... or girls fleeing arranged marriages... any female silly enough to choose flight over fate. My share bought this." He gestured to the room at large again. "I guess I owe your sister my thanks, too, since she started it all."

Julia closed her eyes, unable to look at the man who saw her sister as nothing more than an object from which to make profit. "Cousin Renard told me she'd died. I'd like to know her true fate."

He burst into laughter. "Are you still frettin' about that whore? His lips twisted into a malicious grin. "She disappeared long ago. I never kept track of them once I'd been paid. The earl split the money with me, fair and square."

"I think you do know." Julia met his gaze with disgust. "You are too cunning not to have realized there was some reason Renard kept me but not Beatrice. I believe you followed his instructions to get rid of her, but as lacking in conscience as you have confessed yourself to be, you would also have made sure you knew where she was if the earl ever changed his mind... or if you ever needed insurance against being dismissed."

"So what if I did... but only for a while." He glared at her. "After a couple of months I had enough insurance I didn't need to keep track of her. She was just one of half a dozen females he'd sold off by then. A whore is a whore after all."

Julia winced at his callus words. Beatrice had been a girl. Just a girl. Too young. Too vulnerable. The ember of anger that had burned since Renard had revealed the ugly truth kindled into flame. *Ned knew.* She was sure of it. "I believe you would try to keep track of her, anyway." She bared her teeth in a grim imitation of his cocky assurance. "Insurance is insurance after all."

Ned said nothing for a moment. Finally, he grunted and nodded his head. "No reason for you not to know. You'll soon be away from England and in no position to point fingers for the law." He leaned back in his chair and crossed his legs. "I took her to Aphrodite's Scademy. From what I heard later, dear little Trixie left the house about a year later under the protection of a ship's captain from Poole. By then, his Lordship had explained as how he kept you because you looked like her mother and never mentioned the older girl again, so I didn't bother finding out the captain's name."

"Her name was Beatrice, not Trixie" Julia challenged him. "You are lying."

"Names get changed," Ned told her with a shrug. "for any number of reasons. There was another girl there called Beatrice. Aphrodite changed your sister's name." He gave a huff of amusement. "Changed her own name, for that matter. She retired as Mrs. Arbuckle and lives in Portchester."

Julia blinked and tried to swallow, but her throat had tightened with the realization that a name changed once could be changed again... and again. How could she trace the fate of someone whose name she did not even know? This Aphrodite, or Mrs. Arbuckle might recall something that could tell Julia more. But after so many years?

"Now suppose you tell me about your new protector? Have you lost value while you traveled with him, I wonder?" Ned studied her closely and Julia felt her cheeks heat though her forearms chilled and goose flesh rose at the calculation in his expression. He rose and pulled on a cord against the wall. "I'll have Kate check you over. Best be prepared if you need to fake a maidenhead."

Julia's heated cheeks chilled.

Fake a maidenhead?

CHAPTER 25

Tristan pulled a set of narrow tools from a kit in his coat pocket and selected one. One more glance around the alley, then a few deft turns and the door lock released. Before he eased the door open, he picked up a broken wheel spoke from the ground and gripped it firmly. Inside, he checked the narrow corridor at ground level before mounting the stairway that rose to his right. He hesitated at the first landing long enough to verify none of the gaming staff saw him, then climbed another level. Finished woodwork on the floor and along the corridor told him this floor likely held private gaming rooms and possibly office space. Ned had claimed Alice as his orphaned niece so the floor above was probably his residence. With Alice gone, he'd start with the office.

He took a step forward, then retreated when he heard footsteps ascending from the street level. He pressed back out of immediate sight as a statuesque woman of lush proportion and artificially red hair reached the landing and walked to the end of the hall where she gave a two short brisk knocks, then entered.

He waited and watched. Moments later the door opened and alarm sent a wave of shock crashing into his chest when Julia was led to the stairs by the titian-haired woman. Julia's hands were bound behind her back and the woman had tight hold on Julia's arm, but she appeared unhurt.

"Don't fight me or make a fuss and it'll be over and no harm done," the woman said as they mounted the stairs. "No need to be shy. It's just business." Her voice drifted down the stairwell. "You'll get used to it."

Tristan gritted his teeth and fought the instinct to race up the stairs after them. A door opened halfway down the hall and a footman exited one of the private rooms, a tray of empty glasses in his hands. He turned away from the stairs, and pressed a lever against the wall. A panel slid open and he set the tray inside, closed the panel, then tugged a cord hanging from the wall. When he returned to the room he'd left, Tristan slipped silently up the stairs.

As he suspected, the top landing ended at a door with no corridors leading either left or right. Another deft application of his lock picks and he was inside Ned's private lair. Clearly influenced by his master's town house, the receiving room was formal, spacious, and impressive. He ignored the drawing room and followed the sound of voices to the left, Julia's voice held protest, the woman's voice undeterred. Julia's voice protested again, just as he reached the closed door. When he heard a hand striking flesh and Julia's cry of pain, he shoved the door open.

The red-haired woman spun around and her surprise gave way to shock as he lunged forward to pull her away from Julia whose wrist had been secured to a narrow bed post. He clapped one hand over her mouth and the other around her middle, locking her arms.

He looked over at Julia. A cord hung from the other wrist, but wasn't yet tied to the opposite post. A handprint reddened her cheek. "Are you alright?"

"Yes."

He glanced around the room and saw two more cords on a small table beside the bed. "Do not call out, madam," he threatened, "I grew up in the stews of London and will not hesitate to knock you out." He uncovered her mouth, reached for the cords, and tied her hands behind her, then secured her to a wooden chair.

"Alice is here," Julia told him while he dealt with his prisoner. "Ned drugged her. She is being guarded somewhere on this floor."

Tristan eyed the redhead. "Where?"

The woman glared at him. "How should I know?"

He narrowed his eyes and leaned forward to whisper in her ear. "Where?"

Her eyes widened at the menace in his whisper. "Second room across the hall," she muttered. "Two taps on the door and he'll open it."

"Stay here," he told Julia. "Make sure she doesn't get loose." He lifted the woman's skirt and tore a strip from the bottom that he tied around her mouth, then handed Julia the wooden spoke he'd dropped when he lunged at the redhead. "If she tries anything, hit her on the head with this. As hard as you can."

Julia took the spoke and moved to stand close enough to act as instructed. "Do not worry." She touched the mark on her cheek. "I will do anything necessary. Now go get Alice so we can get her away from here."

Tristan quickly located the room and rapped the door with two sharp taps.

The door opened and Tristan rammed his fist forward before the man on the other side could react. A second blow ended any opposition and Tristan stepped past the unconscious guard and scooped a sleeping Alice from the bed.

"Time to go," He stopped only long enough for Julia to join him, then guided her quietly down the stairs and out into the night. "Keep your hand on my shoulder," he warned Julia as they made their way back to the inn. "It is easy to lose your footing in the dark."

Once he had Julia and Alice back at the inn, Tristan left for the Portsmouth military headquarters. He didn't want to wait until morning lest Ned go into hiding again. With Ned in custody, Julia and Alice would be safe.

Once he returned, and Alice recovered from the drug's effects, she told them how she had slipped out of the room when her guard was distracted by one of the women who dealt cards. "I was going to hide until morning, then go to the building where Papa goes when he comes to Portsmouth every month. I was going to sneak in and hide there until he came again. But Miss Dorsey came down the alley and we found each other." She scowled. "Then Ned caught us."

"You need not worry about Ned," Tristan assured her, "He has been taken into custody. He will no longer be a danger to you or to the country."

After Julia settled Alice for the night, she told Tristan what Ned had revealed about her sister. "Do you need to return to London immediately after we deliver Alice to her father?" She asked. "I know the chance of locating my sister is unlikely, but I should like to go to Portsea." She leaned forward and clasped her hands together in her lap. "It is not a great distance from the Goodwin estates, and Ned said the woman who owned the brothel lives there."

Tristan recognized her need to know more. He had been driven by the same need. His mother had sworn his father was a good man who'd not known Tristan existed. The questions had plagued him from the time one of his friends had first asked him, "Who's your da?"

"We'll go." He nodded. "You deserve to know the truth."

JULIA TRIED TO LISTEN to Alice's happy chatter while they traveled that afternoon, but her mind never strayed far from Ned's admissions. Could the answer to her questions be as near as the town of Portsea? Would the former brothel owner remember her sister? Did she dare hope that Beatrice had been the girl called Trixie?

They rounded a turn in the road and Alice went quiet and clasped Julia's hand. Her tongue worried her loose front teeth and her lips trembled. Startled by her sudden change in mood, Julia noted several damaged shrubs and broken tree limbs and realized this must be where the accident had occurred.

"You will see your Papa soon." She whispered. "You are safe."

"I know." Alice nodded, then added, "But I miss Mama."

Julia wished they could have taken a route that had not reawakened the child's pain.

But as they left the scene of the accident and drew nearer to home, Alice recovered enough to hope cook would make her favorite cream cakes to go with supper.

The manor came into sight and, when they pulled abreast of the house, the door opened and Lord Goodwin hurried down the steps.

"Papa!" Alice jumped down from the carriage as soon as it stopped and leapt into her father's arms, laughing and crying at the same time.

Lord Goodwin clasped her tightly kissing her cheek and whispering endearments while tears rolled down his face. Giving her a fierce hug, he eventually lowered her back to the ground.

"Thank you, Mr. Sheffield. I am forever in your debt."

"I am glad we were able to recover your daughter." Tristan said as they shook hands. "But you should know that it was Miss Dorsey who delivered her to safety."

Goodwin gave him a startled look, then bowed and invited them in for refreshments when Tristan introduced her.

In the drawing room, Lord Goodwin settled Alice beside him before thanking them again.

"Miss Dorsey is Summerfield's cousin." Tristan told him. "And has been as betrayed by his actions as much as you and Alice."

"I was told I was protecting her from kidnappers," she explained. "I did not know it was my cousin who threatened her."

Tristan's comment had referred to Julia's childhood loss, but the quick glace she sent him kept him from correcting the reference. Further explanation served no purpose.

"You have my absolute gratitude." Goodwin said. "If ever I can do you a service in return, you need only ask."

Julia hesitated, clearly embarrassed "My cousin revealed information about a missing relative and I hope to confirm whether or not it is true, but once I return, I shall be in need of a letter of recommendation in order to gain employment."

Goodwin returned her gaze and she saw dawning understanding of her position. "I do not know the degree of your dependence upon your cousin or of your other relative." He cleared his throat. "But if the loss of Summerfield's protection puts you in need of a respectable post, Alice will need a companion and governess. The position is yours should you need it."

"Thank you, Lord Goodwin." Julia curtsied. "Though I do not know how long I will be gone. Nor do I know what I may find."

Tristan appreciated Goodwin's grasp of Julia's difficulty. Still, genteel as such a position would be, it was a drop in rank that pained him for her. She deserved a family of her own and a place in society.

"The offer stands at any time, now or in the future, Miss Dorsey."

"Oh, Miss Dorsey," Alice begged. "I should like that above all things."

Goodwin turned to Tristan. "I shall resign my post at the king's convenience. The Foreign Office need only inform me when my replacement has been selected." He lay his hand on Alice's fair hair. "As I told you before, I suggest he be a single gentleman."

Lord Goodwin insisted they stay for dinner and the night. As they journeyed away from the Goodwin estate the next morning Julia asked, "Do you think this Mrs. Arbuckle will be of any help?"

"I wish I could say yes," Tristan admitted, "But I cannot begin to guess."

"A FRENCH GIRL NAMED Beatrice seventeen years ago?" The woman who had called herself Aphrodite chuckled and sat back in her chair. "Dearie, must have had a dozen or more girls with that name over the years. Back then, there were lots of French girls, too. Once, I had three at the same time. Changed their names right away, though. Can't have a gent ask for Beatrice and send him the wrong girl."

The former madam had greeted them with all the charm of a woman used to playing hostess when her housekeeper led them into the drawing room. The curves of her once lush figure had softened into aged flesh and her hair had been augmented with dye, but it was clear she had once been a beauty.

"My sister was just twelve years old... and spoke English." Julia clarified.

"Twelve or thirteen is not uncommon, neither, my dear. I was thirteen myself." Her forehead creased in thought. "Spoke English, you say? Several of the French girls spoke English." Let me think..."

She poured herself a fresh cup of tea and added a generous portion of gin to the cup before taking a sip. "Seventeen-ninety-three... so many emigres," she mused. "Ahhh, that *was* the year of the three Beatrices. And two of them could speak English from the start." She tapped her finger against her chin while she reflected aloud. "Beatrice, Trixie, and Queenie. That's what we called them."

"Do you recall what happened to them?" Tristan asked.

She shot him an amused glance. "What happens to any girl in a brothel, of course."

Julia hated that the telltale flush of that crept across her cheeks. She met the older woman's eyes and strove for a matter-of-fact tone. "We are hoping you can tell us where each of them went."

"The one who kept the name Beatrice died of the pox." Mrs. Arbuckle said as she took another sip of her tea. "Queenie never learned her place—which is why we called her that—and one of her customers beat her pretty bad. Trixie said a customer found her and took her away." She added a spoon full of sugar to her tea and gave it a brisk stir. "Bad as Trixie said Queenie was, I'd be surprised if she lived. I never saw her again." She put down the cup with a clink and a frown. "The next week Trixie went to Poole with a merchant ship's captain who took a fancy to her." She shrugged. "Girls come and go all the time. Some come back, most find themselves on the street. Didn't know when they had it good."

Julia leaned forward. "Do you recall the captain's name?"

"He was Irish," I remember that. "Had a head of red hair you could see half a league away and smile to charm the birds from the trees." She pursed her lips. "Doyle... Dougal—no, *Donnelly* That's right. Captain Donnelly."

"Thank you," Julia said as she stood. "We have taken enough of your time and will be on our way." She curtsied to the former madam who looked both surprised and gratified at Julia's sign of respect.

"I hope Trixie is indeed your sister, Miss Dorsey." Mrs. Arbuckle said as she walked with them to the door. "I must warn you, though, that society will not recognize you if she is. Families do not to acknowledge young women caught alone with a gentleman in a sitting room, let alone a woman who has been in the trade."

"I have no other family," Julia said before Tristan led her to the carriage. "And I do not take part in society. I'll not deny her."

"Before you ask, the answer is yes," Tristan said Julia as he assisted her into the carriage. "I'll take you to Poole. But we still don't know if the girl Mrs. Arbuckle remembers is your sister," he said as he flicked the reins, "So try not to become too hopeful."

Julia nodded her head to show him she understood, but excitement bubbled through her. They had a name. They had a place. Surely they would succeed.

TRISTAN GLANCED TO the woman at his side as they were served their supper. Despite her agreement not to expect success, he could feel Julia's anticipation. Her eyes sparkled and she had smiled the whole way back to the inn. He hoped she wouldn't build fairy castles of happy endings. He hoped this wasn't a wild goose chase.

"Do you think the captain married her?" Julia asked him during dinner.

Tristan's food suddenly lost its appeal. So much for hope. He chewed his bite of food slowly and searched for a way to answer that didn't sound as though Julia's sister had no worth. "It is unlikely that he could keep her past secret from his shipmates." He avoided her gaze by spearing another piece of meat. "Some of them might have even..." He hesitated.

"Used her services?" Julia finished his sentence softly. "I understand."

He looked up at her, then. "I'm sorry, but if she remains with him, she will be his mistress, not his wife."

"If she remains," Julia's face paled and her the sparkle left her eyes.

"Ship's captains are at sea for months, even years, at a time. She might have found a protector on land while he was gone, or he might have tired of her and replaced her with someone else."

She put her fork down and pushed her plate away. Her eyes shimmered with unshed tears and her lip trembled. "And she still might not be *my* Beatrice."

Tristan said nothing and the silence lay like a shroud over them both.

"I believe I shall retire early." She stood, walked to the door, and then turned back to him. "Thank you for your honesty."

Once she was gone, Tristan took a deep swallow of ale and cursed. Honesty made him feel like an ogre. Since learning that the woman known as Trixie might be her sister, Julia had almost glowed with joy. But instead of letting her enjoy her moment of hope, Tristan had caused her to leave the room dejected and fighting tears. He and his honesty had a lot to answer for... and it left him feeling disillusioned as well.

Before leaving the next morning, Tristan checked with the authorities at the naval yard and learned that a merchant captain named Donnelly still operated from Poole. He noted the difference in Julia's silence this morning and hoped by all that was holy that the woman known as Trixie *was* Julia's sister. He also hoped she still lived in Poole with her captain and had not been taken elsewhere by a new protector. With luck, the journey would end with the sisters reunited and in harmony. Luck however, rarely arrived when needed.

He knew Julia had come to the same conclusion when she broke her silence by asking, "What Mrs. Arbuckle said about the Beatrice who was beaten," She twisted her gloved fingers in the folds of her woolen pelisse. "Does that happen often?"

He wished more than ever he had never told her he would not lie or sugarcoat the truth. "Not always, but more often than it should. Some men drink too much and take their physical release further than bedding." And some men, he refrained from saying, believed a woman purchased for her body gave tactic permission for it to be used in any way the buyer chose... including fists and knives. He might tell her the truth, but he didn't need to cause her additional distress by exposing it all.

She rode in silence again for perhaps a mile before she commented, "I find it odd that I can speak of such things with you. These are not topics I would ever have expected to share with a man other than a husband—If, indeed I spoke of such things at all—but I must know more about my sister's possible experience if I'm to form a connection with her. I don't wish to tax her with questions that might seem to be malicious curiosity, yet I can't begin to comprehend what it would be like to be freely touched by strangers."

Dear God. Tristan gritted his teeth and fought the urges her words sent charging through him. He dreamed of touching her freely. Passionately. Though she had little to say as they traveled, simply listening to her voice when she commented about a cottage or pastureland sent waves of fire through him. Once this quest was over, he would ask for a mission along the borderlands. Something as far from the woman at his side as possible.

THEY ARRIVED AT POOLE by late afternoon. Today Julia had been more talkative than usual, and Tristan suspected she chattered in an effort to distract her thoughts from what they might find. Her odd mix of vulnerability and determination made traveling with her fraught with tension. He had assured her that they could resist their desire for each other, but he had his own doubts about that. She was too willing to see herself as ruined, and he was too conscious of how glorious it had been to plunder her mouth and explore her body.

They secured a meal and two rooms at the Ewe and Ram before Tristan escorted Julia along High Street. A pretty town, Poole's wide quay and long, sandy beach had a different atmosphere than Portsmouth. This was a merchant, rather than military, port. Its citizens focused on the trade triangle of Dorset wool, Newfoundland fish, and Mediter-

ranean olive oils. Red brick and limestone buildings dominated, and people bustled about with a sense of purpose.

After asking directions from a passing errand boy, they located the building where merchants and ship owners gathered to do business.

Inside they found a counter set up at the far end of the room with two clerks in attendance while several men stood in small clusters, chatting quietly.

Tristan led her to an empty chair near the door. "Wait here while I make inquiries."

CHAPTER 26

Julia sat in the chair Tristan indicated and waited impatiently while he strode to the counter and spoke to both clerks. The first shook his head when Tristan spoke to him, but the second one nodded in the affirmative.

Tristan shook hands with the second clerk, nodded to the first and crossed the room to where she sat. "Captain Donnelly is out of port at the moment, but he keeps rooms at the edge of town."

"Alone?" Her eyes darted to the two men nearby, then back to Tristan. She stood and walked to the door and outside before turning back for his answer. "Did they say if—"

"I thought it better to locate his residence first." He took her arm and led her away from the building. "Do you mind walking? After so many days in the carriage, I would like a bit of exercise, but if you prefer—"

"Walking would suit me as well."

By asking in various shops and stopping an occasional man or woman on the street, they arrived at a tall, narrow limestone residence where they had been assured the red-headed captain lived when not at sea.

"The stoop has been swept the door knocker is in place," Tristan noted. "So someone connected to him is in residence." He rapped the knocker and waited.

Lavender plants grew in large ceramic pots on either side of the door, their scent wrapping Julia in warm memories of her mother's love. Though a common enough plant in both France and England, it raised her hopes to find it planted on the doorstep.

The dark haired woman in her middle thirties who opened the door studied them with gray eyes, however, not brown. Julia felt the sudden sting of disappointed tears and blinked rapidly lest they well over. The woman studied them curiously as she waited for Tristan to state their business.

"We are looking for Captain Donnelly's home," Tristan said with a slight bow. "Have we the honor of speaking with Mrs. Donnelly?"

"I am Mrs. Piers, his housekeeper," the woman responded. Though it was quite faint, her words revealed a hint of a French accent. "Captain Donnelly is not married." She held out her hand. "Nor is he home at the moment. If you will leave your card, I shall see that he receives it when he returns."

. "We are hoping he can help us find a woman of French origins known by the name of Beatrice, Trixie or Queenie," Tristan said with a charming smile, "It is difficult to explain. May we come inside?"

Mrs. Piers' eyes widened, then narrowed. "That is an odd collection of names. They sound rather disreputable," she said coolly. "Captain Donnelly is a respectable gentleman. Why would you think he would know such a person?"

Julia feared the housekeeper would refuse them entry when her posture stiffened and she looked beyond them to the street and anyone passing by.

"We were told The Captain assisted her several years ago," Tristan told her. "It is a matter of family connections."

In the end, she stepped back and led them to a small receiving room on the ground floor. They seated themselves, but she remained standing.

"We were told he rescued a young girl from unhappy circumstances." Julia said. "I'm looking for my sister. We were separated many years ago."

The housekeeper looked at her with more interest than she had since answering their knock. "When?"

"She disappeared from Portsmouth in ninety-three." Julia watched the woman's face as she added, "I was told she had died, but I recently discovered that to be a lie." She hesitated. "Pardon me if I overstep—and I mean no disrespect, but might *you* have known her?"

Mrs. Piers paled, and Julia felt sure she knew something. She chose her words carefully. "Our confusion arises in that there were three women of the same name at the establishment, so were called different names to distinguish them. She raised her hands in a gesture of bewilderment. "We know not which might be my sister."

Julia hesitated to be too specific on the chance Mrs. Piers did not suspect what type of employment was involved. "We were told one of them was badly injured, and that the captain removed her from... her situation."

Mrs. Piers said nothing for a moment. Finally, she asked. "Who told you this tale?"

"Their former employer." Julia said. Again, she tread tentatively through the maze of pitfalls her story held for polite conversation. "Who is known as Mrs. Arbuckle." Julia waited to see if her supposition had born fruit.

Several seconds passed before Mrs. Piers responded.

"Very well." she said. She took a seat opposite theirs and let out a sigh that revealed her resignation. "You obviously know I once worked in a Portsmouth brothel." She directed a challenging look at each of them. "I was abducted from the ship that brought me and my companion to England."

She frowned at the memory. "I was fifteen and my family had arranged for me to attend a finishing school. My companion became quite ill during the trip and died. One of the crew offered to arrange transport to the school, but I was taken to Aphrodite's Academy for an education of a far different sort than my family envisioned."

"When I arrived, another Beatrice already worked there so Aphrodite decided to call me Trixie." Her mouth twisted in distaste. "A whore's name." She quickly looked up at Julia. "I beg your pardon, but if you have come this far, you must accept the ugly truths that come with such circumstances."

Julia nodded and was grateful she had not blushed at the blunt speech.

Mrs. Piers smoothed her dress over her knees, then continued. "The first Beatrice was a year older than me, but had already worked there for two or three years. Then, a day or so later, a much younger girl was brought in. Perhaps your sister? Dark hair and eyes with a faint cleft in her chin?

"Yes." Julia nodded. "That sounds like her."

"When the girl told Aphrodite her name was Beatrice, and announced she was related to an English earl before demanding to be taken to his home, Aphrodite laughed and dubbed her Queenie."

"That certainly sounds like her. Even if she had not mentioned the earl, Beatrice always made her wishes known. She would not have bowed meekly to her fate."

Mrs. Piers stood and went to stand by the window, her back to them. "A week later, they stripped us down to tissue-thin chemises, painted our faces, and auctioned each of us off in front of a crowd of cheering, leering men."

She stared out the window for a full minute or two before she said, "Men who bid for the privilege of taking a girl's maidenhead do so for one of two reasons. They wish to avoid disease or they wish to exert power."

She turned back to them. "I was fortunate. The man who bought me wished to avoid disease. Other than the obvious, he did not hurt me. The man who bought Queenie liked power."

Julia riveted her attention on Mrs. Piers, clenching her hands in her lap and dreading what came next, but determined to listen.

"We had been there a year when he came back to the house and asked for her again. He wanted to *see what skills she'd gained and if she had learned her place* while he was away." She shook her head and wrapped her arms around her middle. "The captain—my client that night—found her in the hallway where she'd crawled before passing out." Mrs. Piers' eyes flashed with unforgotten fury. "That beast had left her, beaten and bleeding without anyone knowing."

She met Julia's shocked gaze and announced, "The captain scooped her up and took her to real surgeon, not the drunken sots who tended us for favors. The surgeon kept her at his clinic until she was recovered." She smiled faintly. "The captain came back to the Academy a week later and offered me a position as his housekeeper."

"Do you know where she went after she recovered?"

She took her seat again. "The captain told me she remained as a helper with the surgeon for a time, then married one of their patients and moved away."

Julia could barely contain her excitement. "What is the doctor's name? Is he still in the area? Better, yet, do you know who she married?"

"The surgeon was a Mr. Meyer, but I don't know if he is still operating his clinic. He was in his middle years at the time, and it has been many years since the captain dealt with him. Nor do I know her married name. I'm sorry for your sake that I can't help you further."

"You've helped a great deal and I thank you for sharing your story and hers," Julia said as she stood. "I wish the captain was here so I could thank him as well. It is clear Beatrice wouldn't have survived if not for him."

Julia's mind whirled from what Mrs. Piers had revealed and she barely noticed their surroundings when they left the captain's house. They had traveled halfway down the block before Julia asked, "Do you think Mrs. Piers is more than the captain's housekeeper?" Julia had seen the soft light that came into Mrs. Piers' eyes whenever she mentioned the captain and suspected she was.

"What do you think?" Tristan had remained in the background during their visit, but Julia knew he'd missed none of the nuances in the housekeeper's story. Considering his childhood experiences, he understood far more than she did.

"I believe she loves him." Julia said. She walked further, then said, "I hope he loves her."

CHAPTER 27

As Mrs. Piers told her tale, the changing emotions passing over Julia's features made Tristan wish she had been spared the details of what had happened before the two women had been rescued. The story the housekeeper told was a common one, with a most uncommon ending. That both women escaped and found respectable lives—or in the case of Mrs. Piers the *appearance* of respectability—was miraculous.

When they returned to the inn, he told Julia, "I can see you're anxious to return to Portsmouth. If we rise very early, and travel long, we may be able to reach Portsmouth by nightfall."

Traveling to Portsmouth in a single day would be grueling, and he admitted he was not sure it was possible except on horseback, but he didn't want to take the chance of sharing a room again. Unlike most of the hamlets and villages along the way, Portsmouth had several inns where they'd be able to find separate rooms if they arrived late. Fortunately, the full moon would suffice to guide them if necessary.

The sooner they arrived and secured separate rooms, the sooner he could distance himself from the temptation Julia presented. Time spent in her company played holy havoc on his good intentions and he thanked heaven he had resisted her the night her curiosity almost overcame his scruples. He wasn't sure if he could resist a second time.

They left in the pre-dawn as soon as the innkeeper loaded the two food baskets that they requested the night before. Julia never lingered in the morning, a trait he'd come to appreciate about her. She had not complained when he'd named the time of their departure, nor had she needed to be roused. When he knocked on her door, she had opened it, valise in hand. Though it was late in May, their early morning breath clouded in the crisp air and made Julia's cheeks and nose bright pink.

Each time they changed horses once the afternoon had passed, Tristan considered asking about rooms but decided to continue on with the hope of reaching the port city by dark. The grueling trip became a test of endurance for both body and will. Along the way their conversation had ebbed and flowed, picking up topics when they changed the horses or encountered some view that inspired comment, then faded into companionable silence as the hours plodded by and the constant motion, bumps and jostling of the road wore them down.

They arrived in Portsmouth long after twilight faded to dark. When they pulled into the coaching yard where they had stayed before, both were exhausted and too stiff to do more than climb the stairs to their rooms before crawling into their respective beds.

Tristan awoke far more refreshed than he expected the next morning. The hour was not particularly early, but neither was it late, so he didn't knock on Julia's door. He went downstairs where he soon tucked into a hearty breakfast.

He'd finished and ordered a fresh pot of tea when Julia joined him an hour later.

"I hope you slept well and are feeling refreshed," he said as she took a seat opposite him.

"I did and I am," she replied with a wide smile. "And I am now ferociously famished for I was too tired to eat last night."

He signaled to the serving girl and, moments later, she delivered Julia's meal. "I thought we would ask around the merchant district to see if Mr. Meyer still operates his clinic. Mrs. Piers indicated that he was not the usual incompetent gin drinker who treats the women in such places. Since the captain knew of him, he should be well known among the merchants. Hopefully, we'll locate him quickly."

As soon as Julia finished her meal and retrieved her reticule and pelisse, they started out for the shops along High Street. It didn't take them long to learn that Mr. Meyer still maintained a clinic near the almshouse at the edge of town.

Mr. Meyer, when he was able to break away from his patients, proved to be a friendly, if harried, man of perhaps sixty years of age. His short, sparse frame, balding pate, and long, narrow nose gave him a gnome-like appearance.

When they explained their mission, his face blossomed into a wide smile of pleasure. "Of course I remember her. She was with us for nearly a year before she married Squire Groves." His smile faded and he shook his head. "She was in a very bad way when the captain brought her here." His brown eyes darted to Tristan as though gaging how much detail to disclose about her condition.

"Miss Dorsey knows where her sister worked and has an idea of how difficult her life became," Tristan assured him. "As a child she and her sister witnessed the horrors of the Terror. You may speak freely."

The surgeon's gaze returned to Julia and his expression reflected his sympathy. "You are the little sister she called for in her nightmares. She feared you had been sold as well."

"I believed her dead." Julia said.

"She nearly was." He gestured toward a door to the left. May I suggest we use my office so we can speak privately? I shall have my assistant bring us a pot of tea."

He lead the way to a cramped room that held a narrow table, three straight-backed chairs and a glass fronted cabinet filled with instruments, books, and miscellaneous items most likely stored there for lack of any other place for them. Once they were seated and the tea pot in place on the table, Mr. Meyer returned to his story. "When the captain brought Beatrice to me, several of her ribs were broken as were her arm, her nose, and clavicle. Her entire body showed damage of one type or another."

He stopped and looked at each of them in turn. "Suffice it to say the man did not spare her any pain or... indignity. I've never seen anyone treated with such brutality since, and I've seen a great deal."

So had Tristan. Tristan knew the kind of marks men left on women they cut. Such men always cut faces first. Some carved initials, as though branding them like cattle. "I assume he left scars?"

The surgeon sighed. "Yes."

"Are they disfiguring or simply noticeable?"

Mr. Meyer's lips thinned. "They are not grotesque, but some are more than simply noticeable. Had he pressed a bit harder with his knife at her neck, she would not have survived long enough to receive aid."

Julia's face had paled and her fingers clenched her skirts when Mr. Meyer described her sister's injuries. "You said Beatrice married a squire," she released the cloth and smoothed the crushed fabric across her knees. Her voice had the strained quality of someone attempting to remain calm though choked with emotion. "Do they live nearby?"

"His lands are near the village of Boarhunt where he raises sheep."

"Boarhunt?" Julia straightened in her seat. "That is only two hours from my home." She grimaced and added. "My *former* home."

"What can you tell us about the Squire?" Tristan asked.

"As you might suppose, he is much older than Beatrice." His voice softened. "She was so very young." He leaned back in his chair and rested his folded hands across his middle. "Though he was a relatively young man in his early thirties at the time. He was involved in an accident when in town, which is how he came into my clinic and they met."

A brief knock sounded at the door before it opened and his assistant leaned in to say, "I am sorry to interrupt, Mr. Meyer, but we've an emergency case and need your help."

Tristan stood. "We have taken enough of your time, Mr. Meyer. Thank you for your help. We shall leave for Boarhunt as soon as we are able."

Julia stood and curtsied to him and echoed his sentiments. "You cannot know how grateful I am for your care of my sister in her time of need. Thank you."

JULIA MOUNTED THE INN stairs in a daze of mixed emotions. Beatrice was alive. Despite all that happened to her, despite all that polite society declared, Beatrice was a respectable *wife*. Julia's pulse leapt with excitement before reality intruded. Julia's fantasies of living together with her sister no longer fit. Julia might be an unwelcome reminder all the trauma of France as well as the way she was thrust into the life that she'd endured. What if her sister wanted no reminders of any sort from her past? What if...? Too many formless questions swirled now that she neared the end of her search.

Overwhelmed by the turn of events, when Tristan suggested they wait until morning to begin the final leg of their journey, she felt as though a great load had been lifted from her shoulders. She needed to absorb it all. She shifted her gaze to the silent man beside her in the carriage and realized she wanted another day in Tristan's company. Once she reunited with her sister, he would leave and they would have no reason to meet again. That probability weighed her down more than she expected, and left her feeling empty.

She wasn't ready for him to go. She had become used to his companionship. She liked his droll sense of humor and penchant for telling her stories that made her laugh. He made her feel safe when walking the boisterous streets along the dock. He sent licks of heat through her body when he looked at her. He made her feel alive.

CHAPTER 28

Their first glimpse of Boarhunt came into view by early afternoon. A church of flint and rubble construction stood apart from the whitewashed, thatched homes scattered through the village. A hill rose to the north and Julia suspected the view from the top provided a breathtaking vista of the broad, green pastures.

The familiar scent of wild grasses and spring flowers replaced the brine of the port towns. Across various meadows, flocks of sheep clustered together and the bleating of lambs mixed with birdsong. When they reached the central square of Boarhunt, they found it to be little more than a crossroad with its Saxon styled church at the end of the square.

In addition to the church, Boarhunt housed a small public house and a blacksmith shop. Julia recognized signs of a farmer's marketplace beside the town square. Tristan directed the carriage to the church and Julia waited while the vicar gave him directions to the squire's home.

As they left the village green Julia said, "If she is agreeable, I should like to stay for a few days while we get to know one another again."

Tristan nodded his agreement, but made no additional comment. On the drive to Boarhunt Tristan had regaled her with tales of his first days in the country and the shock of silence and open spaces. He talked about how he'd lain awake most nights listening to the strange lack of carriages, watchman cries of *All's well*, and other city sounds he knew so well.

He laughed when he told her that the call of an owl had sent him from his bed in the middle of the night, sure that someone had spoken outside his window. He swore the chirp of crickets had threatened his sanity and admitted snakes gave him the willies—though he would deny it if she ever told anyone.

She knew he tried to distract her from her thoughts, which swung from giddy anticipation to the terror of rejection. Her life had changed so much in such a short time and his stories let her know she wasn't the only one who had ever faced upheaval. She recognized his attempt to take her mind off her uncertainties and loved him all the more for—*loved?* Dear Lord, *no*. She *appreciated* his efforts.

She turned her gaze to him in alarm. He attracted her, yes. They had both admitted that. But lust was not love. Nor was gratitude. She was *grateful* for his willingness to assist her in her quest. She *respected* him though she suspected he did not expect people to see him as deserving respect. She could not *love* him. He would be leaving as soon as she was settled. No. She simply enjoyed his company and appreciated his thoughtfulness.

They rounded a curve in the dirt track and Julia saw a modest country home on a rise. Of a modern style, it nevertheless was nearer in size to a manor house, and its warm brick façade gave it a welcoming appearance. Her mouth dried and she clenched her hands together.

Soon.

As they drew nearer, Julia saw activity off to the left and saw two small girls playing tag while two older boys tossed a ball back and forth. *Children.* Why had she not imagined Beatrice might have children? Were these her nephews and nieces?

When the children noticed the carriage they stopped their play and stood watching to see who they were. The oldest boy went into the house, and by the time they reached the front portico a man of about fifty, with graying temples edging his brown hair, stepped out and onto the stair. Julia's throat constricted and she took a deep breath before allowing Tristan to assist her down from the carriage.

Slightly shorter than Tristan, he had the sturdy, muscled build of a man who'd grown up engaged in vigorous activity. Deep blue eyes studied them as they approached the stair, curiosity rather than caution lent question to his features.

"We beg your forgiveness for arriving without warning or introduction," Tristan said. "But are you Squire Groves?"

"Yes, I am." His eyebrow lifted in inquiry. "How may I help you?"

The squire visibly started when Tristan introduced Julia.

"Actually, we wish to speak with you and your wife about a private matter." Tristan explained, then added, "May we come inside?

The squire invited them in and led them to a receiving room on the ground floor. No lingering aroma of tea or perfume lent the atmosphere of recent company. The polished neatness and scent of lavender and beeswax revealed it as a room seldom used. As they took their seats, he requested that the maid bring them tea after informing his wife of their arrival.

Their presence drew the children to the entrance hall until their father told them to go back to their games. The open curiosity of his greeting had shifted into wary civility as he asked them about the weather during their travels.

Julia found it difficult not to fidget while they waited. Her mind blanked while her heart thudded and her hands felt cold inside her gloves. Tristan apparently sensed her state of mind and engaged the squire in the polite conversation about weather and road conditions.

Light footsteps announced the squire's wife as she came through the door. "Mrs. Otis said you wished to see me?" The woman's dark eyes widened at the sight of company. "Oh, we have guests—" She broke off when Julia stood and turned to her, then gasped. All color leached from her face and her hands sought the support of a nearby chair as she whispered, "*Maman?*"

Julia took in the high cheek bones, the faint cleft in the woman's chin and the widow's peak defining her dark hairline and knew she'd found her sister. Two narrow scars ran diagonally down each side of her face from temple to the edge of her nose. Another ran across her throat in what looked to be a full circle of her neck. Time had faded what must have been bright red cuts to thin pale lines. White as her face now was, the lines still showed starkly.

Beatrice blinked and focused on Julia again. Her face remained pale, and she clutched the top of the chair with whitened knuckles. Faintly, as though still unsure, she asked, "*Juliette?*"

"Yes. Oh Beatrice, I was told you died that night." Julia stepped forward, arms outstretched, her eyes stinging with tears of joy. "Renard lied to me. I didn't know until recently what he'd done."

If anything, Beatrice's face blanched even more. "You know–?"

Squire Groves moved quickly to Beatrice's side, releasing her grip on the chair and guiding her to sit in it instead. Julia let her arms drop back down and wrapped them around her waist, dismayed that she had further shocked her sister.

The squire knelt in front of his wife and looked into her eyes, sending her some unspoken message before rising to address them again. "Obviously, you are well informed, yet you have come anyway," he said quietly.

He stepped to the door and checked the entry hall before closing the door firmly. "Our children know nothing of the past events, only that their mother was attacked by a knife wielding villain when she was very young. We should like to keep it that way."

"Of course." Julia murmured. "I didn't wish to alarm you. Only to see you. To..." She trailed off. "I didn't know when we began what circumstances you might be in... or if you still lived." Heat burned her throat and cheeks. "I thought we might find a way to be together again if you did."

Tristan made eye contact with the squire, "Their cousin, the Earl of Summerfield, has been charged with treason and is dying of consumption. You need not fear he will play a role in either of their lives again."

Groves looked at Julia, then away. It was clear he wanted to ask if Julia had been sold as well, but hesitated.

"I wasn't sold." Julia told him. She looked back to her sister. "Renard saw our mother in me, as did you, and kept me with the idea of making me his hostess when I was of age." She then explained the events that had led to her discovery of all he had done and planned. "So you see, I didn't know what to expect. I am heartily glad that you were able to escape and find someone who most obviously cares for you."

As her story played out, the color began to return to her sister's face and the dazed shock faded from her eyes. By the end, tears had gathered there also, and a faint smile softened her lips. She rose and crossed to Julia and they embraced. "Oh, Juliette, I missed you so. I am so glad you are unharmed."

She released Julia and curtsied to Tristan. "And thank you, sir, for assisting her. I am glad she found a champion willing to take on so improbable a quest."

Beatrice seated herself again. Her poise returned and she poured tea while Groves offered Tristan a glass of brandy. When the basics of their current lives had been exchanged, Beatrice asked her husband to call the children in to meet their long lost aunt.

They clattered into the room, then stopped and stared when their mother explained who their visitors were. The eldest boy studied Julia intently when his mother explained that she and Julia had become separated in the chaos of their arrival in England.

"I am Charles Andre... named for my father and Mama's father," he announced as bowed politely in introduction when his mother finished. "Mama says I am like my grandfather in many ways, though I favor my father in looks."

Indeed he did, with his light brown hair, blue eyes, and his father's sturdy build.

"I am Stephen." The other boy, showing equally sturdy promise, announced as he bowed before her. "I shall be nine next month."

"I am pleased to meet you." Julia told him solemnly. *Stephen. The English form of Etienne, their brother's name.* He too, had light brown hair, though of a more chestnut shade. His eyes were the same as her sister's dark brown.

The girls each curtsied and Julia gave them a tremulous smile as she returned the favor. They announced themselves as Elise, aged six, and Juliette, aged four. Their dark brown curls and blue eyes betrayed the combined coloring of their parents. Julia felt as stunned as Beatrice must have felt when she saw Julia.

Not only had she found her sister Beatrice... but she had a brother-in-law. She had nephews and nieces. *She had family.*

TRISTAN WOULD HAVE preferred to take a room above the public house rather than infringe on Julia and Beatrice's reunion, but Groves insisted that he stay.

"I suspect we shall both be ignored for a while," he said with a chuckle as they sat in his study that afternoon. "They have much to resolve. We can get to know one another, in the meantime. I know you felt obliged to assist Beatrice's sister after the way her cousin used her, but I suspect you will have a continuing role in her life now that they are together."

"That will not be possible," Tristan watched through the window where Elise and Julia had coaxed her into their game of tag.

"Why not?" Groves gave him a sharp look. "You have been in constant company with her for weeks. I do not judge, as shown by my own marriage, but the temptations of the road and the realities of social norm are still in play. She has been raised as a genteel lady. I do not think it honorable for you to abandon her."

"Tempted though I might have been to pursue my attraction, I have never lost sight of the fact that Julia should be able to return to society. Only a select few know of this trip and, though she may have lacked a chaperone, she has been accorded all the respect within my power."

Well, nearly all. He should have slept on the floor outside her room rather than beside the bed. He should never have kissed her or spoken of his desire for her.

"The Countess of Ravencliffe, who is one of the few who know of this journey, and the Duchess of Wolverton, my foster mother, would both sponsor her." He continued. "But that is all the more reason I shall distance myself."

He walked over to the window and took a sip of his brandy before explaining, "Lest you think my refusal less than honorable, you should know I am the natural son of the sixth Duke of Wolverton. I am accepted within my family's near circle of friends, but am merely tolerated by the rest of the *ton* because of my family's influence. I am not an acceptable match for a lady of quality."

"Beatrice would not be thought an acceptable bride for any man according to that gage." Groves mused. "Yet I find her quite acceptable." He grinned suddenly and added, "In fact I find her to be nearly perfect in every way."

Tristan picked up on the proviso in his statement. "Only *nearly* perfect?"

"She has a tendency to argue when she disagrees with me." Groves chuckled.

"Then you will be twice cursed when Julia is near. She argues as well."

Groves joined him at the window and watched Julia and Beatrice laugh as they chased the girls about the yard.

"You will be leaving soon, then, I suppose." He didn't look at Tristan when he added, "Julia will be welcome here for as long as she wishes to stay. If she decides to accept the patronage of the ladies you mentioned, I shall see she has a maid and postilion riders to take her there."

Tristan nodded.

Hours later, when everyone had said goodnight and gone to bed, Tristan knocked on Julia's door. "I came to say good-bye," he said when she opened it. "I am leaving for London early in the morning."

"So soon?" Julia's face paled. "I thought you might stay another day. We have traveled so many miles, I would think you would want to rest a day or so."

"You should spend your time getting to know Beatrice again," he told her. "Groves is a good sort and has assured me you are welcome to make your home with them if you choose. I belong in London."

They stood in silence for an awkward moment.

"I shall send you word of what happens with your cousin and your cottage. Ravencliffe promised he will petition the king, who may allow you to retain your home. Your cousin's treachery should not cost you any more than it already has."

Julia's eyes widened and Tristan saw he had startled her. "Do you think he might?"

"I sincerely hope so. You deserve to be happy and free to choose where to live." He reached out and traced her cheek with his finger, then leaned forward to kiss her forehead. He did not trust himself to kiss her other than in the briefest way. "I shall be gone before daylight." Then, before she could say another word, he returned to his room.

He left Boarhunt before the sun was more than a glimmer on the horizon.

CHAPTER 29

It took him three days to reach his rooms in St. James Street. The day after leaving Boarhunt, the rains came again and the roads turned into a quagmire that forced him to rest his backside in a tiny village whose name he forgot as soon as he took to the road again. The local pub had two rooms to let, each barely large enough for the narrow cots they contained. He tossed and turned most of the night, waking often, only to remember that he traveled alone.

Only two other times had he had so disliked being alone with his own thoughts. The first was after his mother died and he'd realized he was completely on his own. Grieving and angry, he'd found his way to the townhouse in Mayfair where the sixth Duke of Wolverton lived. He'd stared in confusion at the home of the man who had given him life, but whom he believed had not bothered to answer his mother's plea on his behalf.

The second had been when he ran away from that same Mayfair home three years later. His father brought him home again, sick with an illness from which Tristan had recovered but his father, who caught the fever from him, had not.

Why did he feel like that forlorn ten-year-old boy? No one had died this time. Nor did he suffer the guilt of that re-

269

bellious thirteen year old. He felt something equally empty though. His mood was not helped by the low dark clouds and weeping weather that had kept him sitting, alone and brooding, in an anonymous public house.

He missed Julia. He had come to enjoy her quiet conversation and dry sense of humor. She was well read and an intelligent companion. She was good company. He missed listening to her low, seductive voice and seeing the sparkle of excitement every time they found a new clue to her sister's whereabouts. Yes, he'd desired her. And, yes, he had kissed her. But he'd not betrayed his honor by going further. At least, not *much* further.

Damn, but he'd wanted to.

Still, that was all it was. *Desire.* Hours spent in the company of a woman whose voice raised his pulse and whose proximity made his body ache did not mean she would not fade from his thoughts soon enough. Once he finished tying up the loose ends of his mission, he would think of her no more. *Or at least not often.*

Julia preferred the country and quiet. He felt most comfortable in the city with its familiar racket of people and action. Even if an association with him would not lower her in the eyes of the *ton*, they would not suit.

A day later, he opened the door to his apartments and sighed. It was not yet soon enough, and he still missed her.

He'd sent warning to his man, Reilly, that he would be home soon and hoped the message arrived before he did. He needed a bath and fresh clothes that did not bear the stains of travel. He needed a good meal and a night's sleep in his own bed. And he needed to put Julia out his mind. Reilly met him at the door and Tristan soon succeeded in all but the last.

Shortly after breakfast the next morning, he received a reply to the message he'd sent his Ravencliffe before going to bed. Ravencliffe suggested they meet at White's so Tristan could fill him in on his journey and learn where things stood with Summerfield, who still clung to life.

He spent the rest of the morning dealing with various correspondence and invitations that had arrived in his absence. He might not have a large circle of friends, but it was large enough that he did not lack for an active social life. Finally, he sent a note to his brother but did no more than inform him of his return and to explain that he still had business to attend to before paying his family a visit.

He found Ravencliffe at a table tucked in a corner of the dining room as far from the other tables as possible. When Tristan joined him, he signaled the waiter that they were ready to be served, then settled back against his chair.

"So you found the sister. Amazing." He shook his head. "I was sure you were doomed to failure."

By the time Tristan finished telling Ravencliffe how they had finally tracked Beatrice down, Ravencliffe had an amused smile. "My mother will be pleased to learn that the sisters are happily reunited and safe. She has been most impatient for word."

"You may assure her that Groves seems a good sort who is devoted to his wife, and that he has promised Julia a home for as long as she desires." He leaned slightly forward. "Speaking of which, what of the cottage? Were you able to present the petition for her?"

"I was told the king will take it under advisement. I believe he may look favorably on the petition since Goodwin's wife was a great favorite of the queen's." He frowned. "Though the king's illness causes him to deal with such matters irregularly." He took a bite of his roast duck, then said. "This morning I informed the council that you had returned and promised that I would forward your report by the end of the week."

They finished their meal and Tristan returned to his rooms while Ravencliffe went home to dress for a betrothal ball.

In the intervening days, Tristan wrote his report with the details Ned had revealed in his bid for clemency. He also made a point of being present when Tom was loaded onto a ship bound for the penal colony. He did not visit Ned, who had been transferred to Newgate.

He replaced his boots and visited his tailor, but avoided his usual company of friends. The masculine banter they shared did not suit his mood at the moment. He also discovered he did not find the noise of London as comfortable as he had before. The streets seemed more crowded than usual, even for the peak of the season. He found the crowds irritated rather than invigorating him as they had in the past.

Visiting his brother and sisters did not appeal, either. Ravencliffe had informed him that the Longborough sisters had taken up residence at Wolverton House when a family emergency left them without chaperones for the Season. As friends of his half-sister Anne, Her Grace had insisted they stay with her for the remainder of the Season. Tristan had absolutely no desire to become entangled with a gaggle of giggling debutants.

In the weeks he'd spent traveling with Julia he had become more comfortable with open spaces and the slow pace of life away from the city. For the first time in his life, he did not feel the constant need to watch his back or concern himself with hiding in the shadows.

During their travel, Julia had surprised him one afternoon by imitating different birdcalls, and from that time on, he paid closer attention to the different songs they sang. Because of her, he'd become accustomed to frogs croaking in the distance at night and found amusement, rather than annoyance, in the chatter of scolding squirrels. He missed her voice.

He missed *her*.

When the second week passed, he received word from Mrs. Dawes that the Earl of Summerfield had succumbed, at last, to his consumption. He was believed to be the sole remaining male of his family, but solicitors had been assigned to search for any distant relatives who might stand to inherit the title. It still remained to be seen if the king would confiscate the properties that went with it.

He wrote the news to Julia in care of Squire Groves and told her Summerfield would be laid to rest in the family crypt without fanfare. She need not pay respects to the man who deserved none. He made a point of emphasizing that point. She was not to wear black for a man whose soul was black enough.

"AUNT JULIA! COME SEE the new puppies! Aren't they the most cunning and sweetest things you have ever seen?" Juliette, the youngest of her nieces grabbed her hand and tugged her into the far stall of the stable.

Julia adored her nieces and nephews. Juliette, who had been told she was named for her aunt, had taken a particular fancy to her. Every day brought a new flower to see, a new accomplishment to share, and a new interest to explore.

Elise had their grandmother's gentle sweetness and steady, calm outlook. The boys reminded her of her brothers in more than their names. The eldest was more serious, the younger more rambunctious.

She knew all was not perfect. Her sister was not the same fearless, saucy girl Julia remembered. She couldn't be after the horrors she had endured. No matter how cheerful and positive she appeared on the surface, her past had left more evidence than her marred face and neck. Those thoughts, too, sometimes made Julia's eyes sting.

Her sister's husband Charles was cheerful, kind, and loved her sister with a devotion that warmed her heart. Conversely, she felt further estranged from her sister than ever. Her sister's husband and the children accepted her without question or reserve, yet they were not *her* husband or *her* children.

How very selfish I must be to envy my sister.

But Julia did envy Beatrice the happy, busy life she now led. Her sister had borne far more than Julia could imagine. She deserved her loving husband and children. She deserved the laughter that rang through the house as the children charged up and down the stairs. She deserved all the good Julia could imagine for her.

But was it selfish to want a husband and family of her own? She had told herself she was content with her spinster's life. She told herself she'd be satisfied to embroider and garden. After her public display of panic during her Season she'd accepted that she would remain alone, and she blamed no one but herself for her foolishness.

But Beatrice's family revived the almost forgotten sense of belonging that glowed like a beacon in her memory and awakened the yearnings she had forced into dormancy. She'd supposed them buried them forever. Until Tristan kissed her. Until she had looked at her nephews and nieces and imagined dark haired sons and daughters with crystal blue eyes and devilish grins.

The heavy rains that fell the day after he left had seemed like sympathetic tears for their parting. In fact, the uneven spring weather, first cloudy, then sunny, then rain or fog seemed to reflect the ups and downs of her emotions. Did he think of her at all?

He'd not lingered once they found Beatrice. Had she imagined more than desire in their attraction to each other? She must have. How else could he have left so quickly? He'd kissed her forehead and not her lips when he said goodbye. She was a fool. And she missed him terribly.

When she received Tristan's letter informing her of Renard's death and the lack of funeral ceremony she knew better than to pin her hopes on returning to the cottage. In point of fact, she didn't know if that was what she wanted after all. She was no longer the fearful girl she had been at seventeen. The idea of returning to the cottage felt a bit like giving up on life.

It was time to think of the future. One that didn't tie itself to the past. Her cousin, his actions and the evil he'd done were past. Her brief time of sharing her days with a man of humor, intelligence, and honor were past. He had acknowledged his attraction to her, but made it clear it went no further than the normal inclinations of nature–something to be controlled among respectable people.

She was silly to have imagined more. Had it been more, he would not have left at the earliest hour of the earliest day he could after delivering her to her sister.

Much as she enjoyed being with Beatrice, there were many years they could not talk about. That, too, was past. They would move forward with stories that developed in the future. They would remain in contact and visit each other often. But Julia knew she would not be able to make a permanent home with her sister. It hurt too much and she did not care to wallow in self-pity.

So, just two weeks after reuniting with her sister, Julia wrote to Lord Goodwin accepting his offer as Alice's governess.

CHAPTER 30

Tristan had been about to end his self-imposed isolation by spending an hour or two at Jackson's boxing establishment when the morning post brought a letter of summons to the palace at St. James. He stared at the letter in stunned silence, rereading the official language of the summons several times before its meaning sank in. He was to attend the king's levee to be raised to the rank of baron for his service to the crown in by exposing Summerfield's treason and restoring Alice to her father.

A baron? Him? A title faded the stain of illegitimacy in the minds of most of the *ton*. He read the summons again. Yes. He was to report to the clerk at St. James before Wednesday to provide the proper information that would be on the patent of title.

A Peer. *Dear Lord.* He grinned for the first time since he'd left Julia.

He was to be a lord of the realm.

When Tristan reported to St. James the next day, it was still with a sense of disbelief.

"What name shall I enter as your title m'lord?" The clerk looked up from the paperwork, pen in hand. "It is your choice."

His mind whirled at the thought. Nothing had prepared him for a choice. No longer Mr. Sheffield the bastard, but Lord...*who?* He stared, his mind blank. Then it hit him. Unable to give Tristan his name, his father had given him family... and *property*. "I should like to take the name of the land my father willed me," he finally said. "I shall be Hartford of Surrey."

The only thing missing in his day was Julia.

Ravencliffe met him at the palace on the day of the King's Levee. "You should pay a visit to your family once your business is finished." Ravencliffe said. "In addition to your news, there are family matters that they would like to share with you."

"Has Anne accepted an offer, then?"

"Not that I know of." Ravencliffe replied, "But you should visit them, nonetheless." Tristan suspected Ravencliffe recognized his reluctance to socialize, and had been told by his family that he had not called on them since his return.

At precisely three o'clock he and Ravencliffe were admitted to the receiving room. The king did not look well, but neither did he look as mentally unfit as Summerfield had declared. Fifty years on the throne must surely take its toll. Everyone knew Princess Amelia, the youngest of the king's daughters, was gravely ill, which must be a terrible strain on a man as devoted to his children as he was. Regardless of rumor, however, today the king appeared competent and alert so far as Tristan could see.

When it was time to present the king's honors, the clerk unrolled the patent of title, and read, "*In honor of his service for Us Our heirs and successors We do appoint give and grant unto Tristan Sheffield the said name state degree style dignity title and honor of Baron Hartford of Surrey to have and to hold unto him and the heirs male of his body lawfully begotten and to be begotten..."*

As the clerk finished reading the rest of the patent of title, Tristan darted a glance in the king's direction to find the man smiling at him benevolently. Still not quite able to absorb the reality of it all, he bowed and thanked the king.

"The queen was greatly saddened at the loss of Lady Goodwin and her son. We are happy to provide her daughter's rescuer appropriate reward for his service." The king told him. "Of course, it is Our expectation that you will continue to serve the Foreign Office."

Tristan bowed again. "Of course, Your Highness. It is my pleasure to serve Your Majesty in any way you please."

The king leaned forward and announced, "We understand a Miss Dorsey assisted you in the child's rescue. It would also please Us if you were to fetch Miss Dorsey to London so the queen might show thanks to her as well. She informs me Lady Goodwin was a favorite and will be missed at court."

His lips twitched before he settled back again. "As the daughter of a nobleman, though he was French, she is to be escorted with every courtesy and comfort."

Tristan's pulse jumped. How much had Ravencliffe revealed to the monarch of their unorthodox search? "I shall be honored, Your Majesty."

"It is time you found yourself a wife, young man. Fill your nursery and show the ton your father made no mistake in acknowledging you." Tristan blanched to hear the king speak publically about the scandal. The king raised his finger, waggling it back and forth in admonishment. "Oh, yes, I have not forgotten the stir Wolverton created when he took you into his home. You have your late father's looks and courage, though you bear a different name."

Descendants. He had never allowed himself to think in those terms. His father had willed him property and a generous annual income, but could not provide him with rank or the respect legitimacy provided. Too baseborn to be matched with a female of quality, but too lofty to be trusted by the lower classes—he'd never allowed himself to imagine a family of his own.

Once the news spread, all but the highest sticklers would ignore his origins other than that he was the younger son of a duke who the king considered worthy of a title of his own. The idea left him lightheaded, as though he'd run a mile uphill without pause. He'd believed himself resolved to his place in life, but he acknowledged, now, that he craved the acceptance of his brother's peers for his own sake. *Breathe.* A grin split his face. *Lord Hartford.*

This changed everything.

Dared he hope?

Julia plagued his dreams each night. Their kisses had left them both panting with need, but how much of her response had to do with their intimate proximity while they traveled? The night at the Gray Whale had opened Julia's eyes to the earthier side of life and stirred her instincts. How much of her response had been the natural awakening of womanhood and how much had been an attraction to him personally?

Yet he had seen her face when introduced to her nieces and nephews. He had seen her interactions with Alice. She should be married and have children of her own. An image of Julia, great with child–his child–formed and his throat clogged with unfamiliar emotion.

Would she wish to marry?

Would she wish to marry *him*?

As they mounted their horses to leave the palace, Ravencliffe said, "If you are to fetch Miss Dorsey to London, I should tell you that she sent word she accepted Goodwin's offer and is now acting as Alice's governess."

"Why didn't you tell me this before?" Tristan demanded.

Why did she inform Ravencliffe and not him? Why had she left her sister's home after all the effort they'd made to find her?

"Was there a problem with her sister or the squire? He assured me she was welcome to make her home with them."

"Miss Dorsey didn't say. She merely informed me of her change of location so I would know where to contact her once the petition was resolved. As to why I didn't mention it, the letter arrived just before I was called away. Then, when you turned in your report you indicated that you considered Miss Dorsey safely situated, and you said you were ready for any new assignments the crown chose to give you, so I didn't think it mattered." He gave Tristan a shrewd look. "Apparently, I was wrong."

CHAPTER 31

The schoolroom door opened and the housekeeper told Julia, "Mr. Goodwin requests you join him in the drawing room, Miss Dorsey. There is a gentleman to see you."

Julia's spirits lifted in excitement as she set aside the lesson she was preparing and crossed the room. *Tristan.* She could think of no one else who might visit her here.

Squire Groves wouldn't come without Beatrice, and Lord Ravencliffe had no reason to come at all, though she'd sent him word that she had accepted the position as Alice's governess. Until matters were settled, her whereabouts were of concern to the crown. Perhaps Lord Ravencliffe had told Tristan where she was. She stepped to the mirror on the wall, smoothed her hair, and brushed her skirts until they lay neat and smooth. Her fingers trembled on the bannister as she descended the stairs.

"Ah, here is Miss Dorsey." Lord Goodwin said when she walked through the door.

The gentleman who rose from the wing-backed chair to face her was not Tristan and Julia's bright smile faltered. This man barely came eye level with her, and his broad waistcoat should have been let out half a stone-weight ago. His dark eyes sparkled with humor, though, and he bowed to her with proper respect. She guessed him to be in his early forties.

"May I present Mr. Malcom, Miss Dorsey? He has come regarding some irregularities that arose during the crown's investigation into Summerfield's affairs. If you wish to deal with him privately I shall leave the door open and be available across the hall."

Julia didn't know what to make of such a situation. Irregularities? Did that mean the crown deemed her part of her cousin's schemes after all? Yet Mr. Malcom didn't give the appearance of someone delivering stern judgement. She looked between the two men who seemed to await her decision, but she could not think. She could not breathe.

"I believe I would like you to stay, Lord Goodwin. I cannot think how my cousin's affairs could involve me. He acted as my guardian when I was a child, to be sure, and he provided me with a place to live and funds to support myself, but I knew nothing of his actual dealings." Stomach quaking, she took the nearest seat.

"I fear you misunderstand me, Miss Dorsey." Mr. Malcom quickly corrected. "It is not you who are to blame for the situation, I fear it is I, or rather my firm, that was unaware of the circumstances." He pulled out a handkerchief and passed it over his brow.

"You see, until his recent passing, I was unaware that your cousin had not fulfilled his duties as your guardian and informed you of a bequest left to you from your maternal grandmother. When you came of age, he assured us that you had requested he continue to supervise your income. As you had taken up residence in the property involved, we accepted his claim without verifying your wishes in person. It is an oversight for which we are truly apologetic."

"What bequest? When?"

"Your maternal grandmother passed away shortly after your rescue from France. Hearing of your survival, she had amended her will. When Lord Summerfield learned of her death, he contacted our firm in your name as your nearest male relative. Since you were but a child, he was granted the control of the bequest."

"Then the cottage is mine? I do not need the king's permission to live there?"

"It was your petition that raised the question of your inheritance." Mr. Malcom explained. "As soon as we realized you had no knowledge of the situation I took it upon myself to correct the matter."

He reached down to a leather portfolio and brought out a sheaf of papers. "I have brought you the deed to the property and statements showing the investments made with the principle and your quarterly portion of the funds."

An hour later, Mr. Malcom took his leave and Julia excused herself to go to her room. She needed time to absorb the news that she had an independent living. Then she had to decide what to do about it.

"MISS DORSEY, I DID it!" Alice called from the tree branch she had climbed as part of what she claimed was her training to remain fit and agile. Mr. Sheffield, she had assured both Julia and her father, had explained that climbing trees, running swiftly across open pastures and learning to swim were all activities that kept one prepared to deal with emergencies. She regularly picked the locks of the various rooms in the house and had discovered a book on tying knots that she practiced with as much diligence as she did with her embroidery.

Her experience at the hands of her captors and the success of their escape because of the lessons Tristan had taught them had left her with the determination to be prepared for any future disasters. She spoke of him daily. *Did she remember when Tristan said this* or *did that*? They were memories Julia cherished, but also ones she preferred to forget.

He had his life and she had hers. It did no good to dwell on their time together. It had been an anomaly of chance orchestrated by the evil actions of men and war. Tristan had not contacted her since leaving Boarhunt other than to inform her of Renard's death.

Of course, it would not be proper for him to correspond with her. A gentleman did not write personal letters to an unmarried lady unless they were betrothed. Nor could she write him to tell him that she had taken the position of Alice's governess. Contacting Lord Ravencliffe had been business. Telling Tristan where she could now be found, was not.

It was a silly rule. Why shouldn't men and women exchange letters simply because they had not promised to marry? If anything, it seemed to her, such exchanges would be an excellent way to learn of one another's manner of thinking. To understand the heart of the one writing of events and aspirations.

Perhaps she would write Tristan despite the rules. She could explain her reasons for becoming a governess. She could tell Tristan how much he had influenced Alice and that she did not see herself as helpless against villains but as someone who could outsmart them. She could tell him about the cottage... though he would know that by now. She could tell him–

She could *not* tell him she missed him. She could not tell him that she wished he had been a less honorable man the night she'd heard the couple in the next room. She could not tell him *anything*. She must remember that he had acted out of duty to the crown and for no other reason. She would never forget him, but she must bury her foolish dreams and build a new future. One in which Tristan Sheffield had no part.

"Oh, Miss Dorsey! I can see much farther from up here. There is a postilion traveling on the main road and I can see the vicar driving his gig back to the vicarage. Who do you think he was visiting?"

"I would not know, nor is it any of our business." Julia told her with a smile. "I do know you should you come down and wash your face and hands then change into a clean frock. It is time for your pianoforte lessons."

Alice had changed and was carefully picking out the notes for a new piece of music Julia had set her to, when Connors entered the room and announced, "Lord Harford of Surrey to see you Miss."

Lord Harford? She knew no one by that name. *Of Surrey?* The house where she'd been held with Alice was in Surrey. Had Tristan asked someone to deliver a message from him? She took a deep breath and willed nerves to calm. She would not allow herself to be disappointed a second time.

"I shall be down in a moment, Connors."

When the footman opened the door to the drawing room five minutes later, Julia's heart leapt in her throat when Tristan rose to greet her. Her pulse fluttered and jumped. *He came.* An empty corner of her heart filled with joy.

A quick glance around the room revealed no one other than Lord Goodwin. Where was the mysterious Lord Harford?

She curtsied and fought to keep her voice steady. "Mr. Sheffield, how good it is to see you again, if a bit of a surprise. Connors said my visitor was a Lord Harford." She caught a whiff of the sandalwood and leather she associated with him, and her heart hammered with the awareness of how he affected her senses. She raised her eyes, locking onto his steady gaze.

His eyes crinkled and a ruddy flush mottled his chiseled features. "His majesty considered the quiet conclusion of Summerfield's treason and the safe return of Lord Goodwin's daughter worthy of a recognition." He glanced to Lord Goodwin, then back to her. "Though most would consider knighthood more than enough, he chose to make me Baron Hartford as a curtesy to my late father's memory."

"How wonderful for you! Congratulations, my lord." That corner of joy in her heart swelled. *He wanted to tell me in person.* "It is an honor well deserved." She met his gaze and grinned in delight when his ruddy flush deepened. He was not used to praise, and his embarrassment charmed her.

"Thank you, Miss Dorsey." Tristan straightened, then said, "His majesty also sends you greetings. He has asked me to escort you to London so the queen may further express her thanks for your role in keeping Alice safe."

Julia felt her smile falter. *Is that why he came?* Sent by the king's command and not of his own volition? Disappointment froze her giddy excitement.

"A coach awaits us outside. To lend appropriate chaperonage, I took the liberty of borrowing my sister's maid to attend you. My man, Reilly, also travels with us."

Irritation jostled with bewilderment as she looked between her former champion and her employer. The king's command, though, gave her no choice. "I don't know what to say. Lord Goodwin, I beg your pardon for this imposition, but a royal request–"

"Of course you will go. One does not refuse the king. Particularly when he wishes to show his appreciation. In fact, the maid has been sent to your rooms and is packing as we speak."

"But my position, and Alice..."

"Will be held for you should you decide to return. I have known since Mr. Malcom delivered your legal papers that you were likely to change your mind about remaining a governess."

CHAPTER 32

Julia sat across from Tristan in the carriage after they left the Goodwin estate and wondered how different their conversation would be if they were alone. She wanted to ask him if the monarch's request had been his only reason for coming. He addressed her so formally. Was she truly nothing more than a duty in his mission for the crown? Had she been wrong to think he cared more deeply than physical desire?

Certainly, she didn't feel she could speak to him about private matters with his sister's maid sitting beside her, let alone with Tristan's valet sitting across from them. Julia had become so comfortable with speaking frankly to Tristan as they traveled, but it would be bold, and perhaps desperate, to ask if he had missed her, no matter if they were alone or not. She cast about her mind for safe, normal conversation.

"Won't you tell me about your audience with the king? How very pleased you must be, Lord Hartford."

His eyes glinted, but his response held the same formal civility he'd shown since his arrival. "And greatly surprised as well." He glanced the maid who stared placidly, and carefully, at the passing landscape and his expression sobered. "When we change horses, perhaps you might like to walk about a bit."

"I believe I would." Julia noted that Reilly, the valet, also had his head turned carefully toward the passing scene. "The weather is certainly fine enough to make such exercise most welcome."

Had he missed her company as she had missed his?

Perhaps his title made him feel self-conscious. His rise to a peerage must seem strange. Yet it gratified. So many little things he'd shared as humorous episodes of competition with his half-brother had revealed his need for recognition as his brother's equal.

Tristan's father had accepted him into his legitimate family but society did not. She recognized that he loved his family yet hated his place in it. She felt much the same about her cousin—thankful he had provided shelter and education but horrified by why he had done so.

They stopped at a village an hour later, and Tristan assisted her from the carriage after instructing Reilly to arrange for a light meal before they took to the road again. He led her away from the stable yard toward a copse of trees where a narrow footpath traced its way to a stream at the back of the inn. The maid followed as was proper, but at a distance to allow them privacy of conversation.

"Tell me what you have avoided saying in front of the servants," Julia said when they reached the stream. "I am not used to dealing with you so formally." His lips twitched, but the tension around his mouth and eyes revealed concern that alarmed her.

"I believe the king is aware of our lack of chaperone in our travels," he told her. "He was particular in his instructions that you were to come into the city properly escorted and with every honor. That might have been his way of showing London that you were not to be reviled because of Summerfield's treason, but he followed those instructions with... *advice*... to me—" He broke off and seemed at a loss to continue.

Julia's nerves tightened until her skin chilled. Welcome advice did not make a strong man falter and look away. "What did he advise?" she prompted. "He would not have raised your rank if he found you wanting."

"He told me I should marry and fill my nursery to carry on my new title." He continued to avoid eye contact while he explained, "I believe he was telling me to do the honorable thing... and marry you."

Julia's breath hitched and shockwaves of dismay made her reach for the support of a nearby tree. He hadn't come for *her*, he came for *honor*. No wonder he'd remained distant. If he didn't marry her he would lose honor in the eyes of the king, his family, and himself. Tristan was truly a man of honor. Julia had recognized that in him even when he had thought her an enemy and suspected her of being someone's traitorous mistress. Failing his honor would ruin his already limited sense of worth.

He shot her a quick glance as though gauging her reaction, but quickly looked away again. *He is so embarrassed he can't even face me.*

But what of her? Was she to be an *honorable choice*, saved from ruin that was not really ruin? *Ruin he had refused to allow even when she had begged for it.* Was she now to accept marriage as the price of expediency in travel? To be acknowledged as a fulfilled obligation? It would be expected, but would it be right?

Where was the honor in that for *her*? Kings thought nothing of marrying for political union, but she wanted a love union. Did the king think she had no pride? She pulled in a breath with effort, and strove to find words to save them both.

"I am honored that he would think me in need of such protection, but I believe we shall all be best served if I decline your offer." She straightened away from the tree and turned back to the path and the inn. "His efforts in bringing me to the city with proper escort will be quite enough to protect my reputation, particularly as I shall return to a life of quiet and privacy."

"Julia, wait!" Tristan's voice held a note of panic as he reached out and stayed her with a hand on her shoulder. "I handled that badly." He moved to stand before her, but now it was she who kept her eyes cast down. "The king didn't say more than that I should marry." Tristan cupped her jaw to raise her face and she finally met his gaze. "But I immediately thought of you when he said that." His gaze didn't falter and Julia's throat dried at the sincerity she read in his eyes. "That is what I meant to tell you." He stroked a finger along her cheek. "I have missed you."

She looked up at him then. "I missed you, too. But it may well be that we simply became used to each other's company, just as we were used to being alone before. Now that you have title to go along with your land you can court any woman you choose. You will become used to her as well."

"I don't believe that."

A glimmer of hope flared, but she dared not trust her heart, though it was clear he regretted speaking so bluntly earlier.

"I choose *you*, Julia. I am not interested in some child recently emerged from the schoolroom. Nor do I want to marry anyone who would not have deemed me worthy of consideration before the king's blessing. I've long had an income with which to support a wife had I been willing to make an offer and she to accept it. Yet I did not know any woman who could overlook my place in the world and not despise the position she would hold if I did."

He stroked her cheek with the back of his fingers and she recognized honesty in the direct intensity of his gaze. "You behaved no differently toward me after you knew of my bastardy than before. You didn't despise me for my lack of rank—merely for my treatment of you." He gave her a crooked smile. "Though I think you grew to like me better after I untied you."

That made her smile.

"I thought so." He slipped his arms from her shoulders and folded them around her. "I would have preferred it if the king had not prodded me in the direction he believed I should go. It is a choice I'd have made on my own. But others might comment on it and I felt you should know what he said."

Was it wishful thinking that she believed the warmth in his gaze? The events of the last month made her doubt her ability to recognize the truth. Yet Tristan had not lied to protect her feelings before, why would he do so now? Her heart beat faster.

She didn't resist when he gathered her closer and brushed his lips against her ear. Heat bloomed where his lips touched and spread outward and down to her most intimate core. Dear heavens. He'd barely made contact with her ear—her *ear*—and the yearning, hollow need threatened to overwhelm her as it had at the inn. Desire again. Was it enough?

"Marry me, Julia," he whispered. "Not because the king thinks it is a good idea, but because you do... and I do."

Flutters raced down her spine. She trusted Tristan. Dared she trust herself? She leaned back. "Why is it a good idea? Because we desire each other?" she whispered. "Even I know desire fades. Marriage is for life."

"But there is more than desire, Julia. There is friendship, and love." He kissed her briefly, lightly, as though to show her he would not use passion to make his point. "I confess I was half in love with you after you insisted I tie you back in the chair rather than share my bed, and I admired the way you stood toe to toe with me to protect Alice." His eyes met hers, steady and direct. "I toppled the rest of the way when you defied Summerfield's malicious attack by walking out undefeated." He stopped and hugged her close and dropped another kiss on the top of her head. "You humble me with your courage."

"I am not courageous," she protested.

"Oh but you are, my sweet." Tristan assured her. "You have faced your fears—and that takes true courage. What is more, you are kind." He kissed her again. "You are loyal." His hands cradled her face and he looked into her eyes, "You are everything I could ask for in a wife. But above all, I love you.

Deeply. Passionately. Eternally. So tell me you will marry me." His eyes glinted and there was more than desire heating his gaze. There was tenderness. And devotion. "You won't be alone anymore. We can be our own family, where we both belong."

Julia closed her eyes. The warmth of his words filled her with hope. This is what she had craved all her life. Someone to love who loved her for herself. Someone who understood the sense of standing on the outside of life while yearning to have a place in it. How could she let pride keep her from taking what she knew she wanted more than anything? She might be a coward, but never a fool.

"Yes, Tristan." She nodded and smiled up at him. "I'll marry you." She reached up to stroke his face. "Not because the king says so, but because I love you, too."

"Thank heaven," he breathed before he kissed her fiercely.

Passion flared and flutters of anticipation raced from her heart to her core. *Thank heaven, indeed.*

He finally broke away to trail lighter kisses along her jaw until his lips touched her earlobe again, and his breath brushed lightly along its edge. Julia gave a moan of pleasure. She felt his lips broaden into a smile against her neck. "Are you still curious about bed sport?"

She gasped and he chuckled. He nuzzled the tender spot at the base of her neck. "I promise I'll satisfy your questions... and you," he whispered.

The End

If you enjoyed Chasing Scandal
I'd love for you to post a review for others to find.
You can email me at leslieknowlesauthor@aol.com
or visit my website at
www.leslievknowles.com

Continue reading for a sample from **Scandalizing the Duke**

Chapter 1

Charlotte Longborough looked out at the nearly dry Mayfair street below her bedchamber window and grinned. *Finally*. It had been so disappointing to see nothing of London other than the soggy view from the carriage window when she and her sisters arrived in the city. She'd not even ventured to Hyde Park, though it lay just two blocks from their aunt and uncle's door. But now, sunlight dawned, a page had turned, and the adventure of her Season beckoned. Flutters filled her stomach and took flight into her throat.

She tugged the window up and took a deep breath. Charlotte loved the freshness of the air after rain. She loved that there were broad green havens like the park in the middle of the city. But most of all, she loved that Aunt Poppy had agreed to sponsor Charlotte's Season and had insisted Elizabeth, enjoy a second one. Aunt Poppy had even allowed Sarah to come, though she was too young to take part in the Season itself.

An unwelcome thought intruded, and she caught her lip between her teeth. Until she arrived in London, it hadn't bothered her to know she was the least interesting of her sisters, but Elizabeth hadn't had a single offer last year. If her beautiful and talented sister hadn't received any offers, how could Charlotte, with her mouse brown hair and ordinary features, hope for one?

Charlotte dearly wanted a family of her own. She wanted a husband who adored her as much as Papa had loved Mama, and babes of her own to hold and care for. Yet, if she did receive an offer, it wouldn't seem right if she married before Elizabeth. Charlotte crossed her fingers, then wondered if it were sacrilegious to do so while she prayed both she and Elizabeth would succeed in making respectable matches by summer.

A soft whuffle, and a tongue that dampened her fingers, made her look away from the view. Amber brown eyes gazed at her with worshipful expression. "What do you say, Harry," she said as she scratched behind the ears of the half-grown beast who leaned against her leg. Even seated, the dog's head reached her waist. "Would you'd like a walk in the park as much as I would?"

She laughed when he barked as though he understood, tail wagging wildly. He'd been a pathetic collection of matted fur and bone when she saved him from an abusive drunkard at an inn along the way to London, and his appearance had only slightly improved with a bath.

After she rescued Harry, Elizabeth had warned her that such impulsive actions could jeopardize her standing as a well-behaved young lady, and that it didn't take much to become the brunt of society gossip. Had that happened to Elizabeth? Surely not. Charlotte was the impulsive member of the family, not Elizabeth.

Charlotte went down to breakfast where she found Elizabeth and Sarah enjoying hot chocolate, eggs and toast with their aunt and uncle. Since they'd come to London, Elizabeth dressed her hair in a softer style than she wore at home, and Charlotte envied her the rich sable color that made Charlotte's own light brown hair look non-descript and boring. Sarah's hair was darker than hers too, and had a glint that was not quite auburn, but made the deep brown glow with life even when confined to her schoolroom braids. Envy aside, she was glad they were here with her.

She seated herself, accepted a cup of chocolate from the footman, then turned to her Aunt. "Now that the sun is shining at last, may we walk to the park this morning? Poor Harry needs exercise even more than I."

"Oh, yes, please," Elizabeth and Sarah added together.

"Enjoy yourselves," Aunt Poppy agreed with a nod, "But don't linger too long. I, too, look forward to an outing. I thought we might go shopping later."

As soon as they finished breakfast, Charlotte, Elizabeth, and Sarah set out for the park with Harry, their maids, and a trailing footman. The clear sky and light breeze refreshed and lightened their spirits after days of damp gloom.

Once there, Harry made erratic progress as he alternately pulled ahead, then stopped to smell odd places on the park's gravel path. His sudden surges and stops made Charlotte wonder if she should relinquish the lead for the large exuberant creature to the footman until Harry received proper training. At the moment, however, she preferred to keep him on the move. Since it wasn't the fashionable hour to stroll, there were few in the park, though Charlotte saw some nursemaids supervising their charges on the far side.

A gentleman on a distinctive gray gelding trotted by along the row and Charlotte admired the horse's spirited gait. She glanced at the rider when he passed them and her step faltered. Though she couldn't see his face properly, cold dread washed over her, as though the waters of the fast-flowing river back home pulled her under, robbing her of breath. Gooseflesh rose on her arms and she watched his progress with all the horror of her childhood fears until he reached the far end of the park.

Harry jerked against the lead pulling her back to the present. Her sisters had paused for her to catch up and Charlotte took a calming breath before she rejoined them. She struggled to dismiss her reaction to the stranger on the horse. *Surely, she was mistaken.* But the chill of unease remained. *What if she wasn't?*

"There are no people over by the trees, so it might be best if we walked in that direction," Elizabeth said as she scratched behind Harry's ears. He showed his appreciation with a personal sniff in the natural manner of dogs and she gave a startled gasp before carefully shifting his nose to a more genteel location. "Harry is a dear, but he has still to learn his manners."

Sarah giggled and Charlotte gave the lead a sharp tug.

Her disquiet eased when she looked at her younger sister, whose dreams often revealed joys and upsets to come. If actual danger threatened, Sarah would surely be the first to know, and warn her.

Charlotte turned to speak to Elizabeth but Harry suddenly gave a delighted woof and nearly pulled her off her feet when he took off toward the trees. She fought to hang onto the dog's lead and to keep her balance while he hauled her across the grass. She yanked back on the leather lead. "Harry," she cried. "Stay!"

Charlotte tugged to no avail and fought to remain upright while Harry pulled her to where he barked and leapt against a large oak. The abrupt lack of tension in the lead and a protruding rock combined to pitch her forward just before three horsemen thundered out of the trees directly in front of her. She fell to the ground with an unladylike grunt, let go of the lead, and landed in a puddle of mud.

Harry gave another sharp bark.

A man's voice cursed, "Bloody Hell!"

Charlotte ducked her head and the horse's hoof missed her by inches. The damp earth beneath her cheek vibrated when the horse stamped about in a confusion of barking dog, cursing male and the distant cries of her sisters above her head. Instinctively, she froze in place lest she put a limb in the way of anyone or thing that might land on it. The commotion seemed to last forever before a snuffling muzzle at her cheek followed by a tentative wet puppy lick let her know that the danger had passed.

"Oh, Harry," she muttered. "You silly beast. What were you chasing?" Charlotte opened her eyes and focused on a pair of booted feet before a gloved hand reached down to offer her assistance.

"Are you hurt, Miss?"

A man knelt beside her. His baritone voice touched something deep inside, made her nerves spark, and her breath hitch. A peculiar warmth blossomed through her when she looked into vivid blue eyes. Her pulse galloped and her voice trembled when she answered, "I don't believe so."

Charlotte blinked and looked away to the gloved hand he held toward her, and accepted his assistance to stand. She took a deep breath and caught the faint scent of sandalwood and leather mixed with freshly crushed grass and damp mulch. She raised her gaze to observe his squared jaw, clamped mouth and lowered brows before noting that his eyes met hers only briefly before they glanced at her mouth then lowered to her bodice.

A flicker of something—a darkening focus—made Charlotte glance down. The warmth of her awareness turned into the fire of humiliation.

Grass stained her bodice in the most embarrassing locations and mud covered her blue walking dress. Her embarrassment doubled when she saw her rescuer's pantaloons were also splattered with muck.

"I beg your pardon for putting you into more danger than your circumstances had already thrown you." He glanced at Harry, who sat nearby with his tongue lolling.

"It is I who should apologize," Charlotte protested. "Harry is new to the lead, and I should have given him over to a footman to control until he has learned not to give chase without command."

"Dash it all," a new voice made Charlotte look to her right where a sandy-haired man in buckskins and a bottle green riding jacket settled his horse and dismounted. His bronzed skin marked him as a dedicated sportsman. "Tell me you've not maimed the lady."

Elizabeth and Sarah caught up to her, eyes wide and faces pale. "Charlotte, are you hurt?"

"Only my dignity," Charlotte assured them.

Charlotte glanced around to see who else had witnessed her embarrassing downfall and found herself observed by another blond gentleman, the third rider of the group. He also dismounted, doffed his hat and announced, "Any lady who can cause Wolverton to nearly lose his seat must be made known to us. Pray allow us to make acquaintance with these ladies, Your Grace."

Wolverton? *As in the Duke of Wolverton?* Charlotte nearly groaned aloud. She'd made a point of reviewing her aunt's copy of Debrett's Peerage to learn whom she might meet during the Season, and the Duke was at the top of the list of unmarried gentlemen she'd assembled.

The duke surveyed her and her sisters, before his lips firmed and his expression shuttered. "I have not had the privilege myself, so you must curb your curiosity, Ravencliffe." He gave Charlotte a stiffly correct bow and told her, "I am sorry to have intruded on your day. As you are unhurt, I shall take my leave. Should we meet again I hope it will be under more favorable conditions." He remounted his horse as did the other two gentlemen. "Lead the way, Norcross," he told the sportsman. All three gentlemen doffed their hats before guiding their horses out of the park at a much more sedate pace.

Charlotte had known it was silly to include gentlemen above her station in her notations, but she had. Along with the duke, Lords Ravencliffe and Norcross would be stricken from her list as soon as she arrived home. First impressions counted, and all three gentlemen would forever associate her with mud and chaos.

THE HUM OF CONVERSATION in the upper room of White's Gentleman's Club should have relaxed Lucien Caldwell, Duke of Wolverton, where he leaned back in his club's leather chair with a frown over his unsettling day. He'd nearly trampled a young woman with his horse this morning. Even if the woman hadn't been pulled into his path by her unruly dog, he'd ignored the ordinance against racing in the park. He never acted impulsively, but he'd challenged his friends and taken off with uncharacteristic disregard for the reason the ordinance existed. He knew better. But for some reason he'd given in to the sudden urge to ignore propriety and ride wild and free.

He studied his half-brother, Tristan, who had just added another conflicting layer of relief and irritation to his disquiet. No longer the skinny gutter-rat of a boy their father scandalized society with by bringing him into their home, Tristan remained lean, but now appeared as respectable as Lucien or any other gentleman in the club. Of course, most of the members would never consider a bastard respectable.

He contemplated the single finger of brandy remaining in his glass before telling Tristan, "Anne will be devastated if you miss her come out."

"She will be exposed to ridicule and whispers if I take part in her Season."

Lucien's jaw tightened. The flash of relief he'd experienced when Tristan announced he would be gone during his sister's Season irritated him. It also irritated him that the old scandal still threatened his peace of mind after all this time. The scandalous outrage had never been that the late duke had fathered the boy, but that he'd insisted Tristan be raised with his legitimate offspring.

For Lucien, who had been twelve to Tristan's ten years, it had been a blow that left him angry and resentful for longer than he cared to remember, and had resulted in consequences that had impacted them all. Familiar guilt tightened his chest and clogged his throat. At least that aspect of their relationship had been resolved.

Tristan gestured toward the wood-paneled room where a host of gentlemen conversed over wines and spirts. "If anyone here disapproves of my presence and gives me the cut direct, it doesn't hurt Anne's feelings, or her chances for a good match." He sipped at his own glass and met Lucien's gaze, "But if I take an active part in her come-out, the gossips will have a field day reviving the scandal. Anne will be faced with snide remarks and simpering sympathy." He paused, his eyes reflecting sardonic amusement. "And she won't be able to challenge them to fisticuffs the way we did."

Lucien's knuckles whitened around the glass. He recalled all too well the sudden silences in conversation when he passed his schoolmates, and the embarrassed suspicion that their laughter was aimed at him. He'd learned to disguise his humiliation behind a wall of civil reserve, and when he gained the title, he had vowed he would never allow the family to be gossip fodder again. He defied the gabble-mongers by living a pristine life.

Tristan's eyes didn't waver. "If I'm not available, the waters of society will remain smooth and untroubled."

The footman returned and Lucien considered Tristan's argument while the man replaced Lucien's empty glass with a fresh one. The heady scent of aged brandy rose when he swirled the amber liquid.

"You do realize that if you're not at Anne's ball it will draw more attention to the past than if you are. Any lack of family unity after all these years would send a message of discord and create a new scandal at a time when it would affect Anne's future the most." He sipped his brandy and glared at Tristan. "We need no scandals of any kind—real or inferred—to interfere with Anne's Season."

The footman moved on to another patron and Lucien sat forward to argue his point. "The rest of the *ton* might remain calm, but when Anne realizes what you've done and why you've done it, those waters will become very choppy and your boat-full of good intentions will be sunk in a sea of outrage and disappointment. She isn't brainless."

Tristan shifted in his chair. "There is that."

"So you'll at least attend her come-out ball."

Tristan avoided Lucien's gaze when he stood to leave, his expression pensive. "I'll think about it."

Lucien ceased his argument. Tristan would do what he wanted to do—or not—as he always did. Lucien only hoped Anne would accept Tristan's decision as well. As it was, Anne showed a decided disregard for the traditions of rank and the strictures of polite society. She accepted Tristan without question and scorned those who didn't. Though Lucien was proud of her independence, her spirited attitude made him shudder at the social dangers it presented. In her support of their illegitimate brother, he worried she might encourage friends or suitors who were truly unsuitable.

Lucien's thoughts were interrupted when Norcross arrived, took the seat Tristan had vacated, and released a deep sigh. "My mother has decided that she is quite ready for grandchildren and has begun visiting all the families who have marriageable daughters." He shuddered dramatically. "I suspect she is making a list of ladies who strike her as potential daughters-in-law." Tall, athletic, and a viscount since childhood, Norcross had been the target of marriage-minded females long before he reached his majority.

"Fortunately, a list of candidates is not a marriage contract," Lucien assured him. "Nor are you obliged to confine your eventual choice to a list made by your mother. Certainly, my stepmother knows I would never countenance the presumption of anyone else making such a choice for me." The image of a blushing face with large gray eyes suddenly filled his mental vision. He blinked and took a quick sip of his brandy to banish it. His eyes narrowed and he declared, "She also knows I decided long ago that I'll not marry until both Anne and Rowena are launched. I don't need to start a new family until I've seen to the one I already have."

As his youngest sister, Rowena, was only thirteen, he had at least five years grace before he succumbed to the duty of his title and took a wife. His gut clenched when a sudden realization hit him. The crop of ladies he would be considering at that time were currently little girls who still played with dolls.

Dear God.

The concept made him slightly nauseous.

No.

When the time came, he would find a spinster—or a widow.

Want to read more? Here is a link to buy it from your favorite source:

UBL: https://books2read.com/u/m0wLGJ[1]

---

1. https://books2read.com/u/m0wLGJ

Don't miss out!

Visit the website below and you can sign up to receive emails whenever Leslie V. Knowles publishes a new book. There's no charge and no obligation.

https://books2read.com/r/B-A-BEDN-NVENB

BOOKS2READ

Connecting independent readers to independent writers.

Also by Leslie V. Knowles

The Wolverton World
Chasing Scandal
Scandalizing the Duke

Watch for more at https://www.leslievknowles.com/.

About the Author

I live in Southern California with my husband where we raised our two children. Our daughter has a cake decorating business, is married, and the mother of three grown sons. Our son is an aerospace engineer who made watching The Big Bang Theory seem oddly familiar.

When I'm not writing I enjoy photography, painting, and of course, reading. Together, my husband and I explore the question, "I wonder where that road goes?"

Read more at https://www.leslievknowles.com.